THE DARK VALLEY

Also by Valerio Varesi in English translation

RIVER OF SHADOWS (2010)

Valerio Varesi

THE DARK VALLEY

Translated from the Italian by
Joseph Farrell

MACLEHOSE PRESS
QUERCUS · LONDON

First published in the Italian language as *Le ombre di Montelupo*
by Edizioni Frassinelli
First published in Great Britain in 2012 by

MacLehose Press
an imprint of Quercus
55 Baker Street
South Block, 7TH Floor
London W1U 8EW

A CIP catalogue reference for this book is
available from the British Library.

ISBN (HB) 978 1 906694 33 3
ISBN (TPB) 978 1 906694 34 0

1 3 5 7 9 8 6 4 2

Designed and typeset in Caslon
Printed and bound in England by Clays Ltd, St Ives plc

For my father, Aldo
— known as Fabio —
who taught me the names of trees

TRANSLATOR'S NOTE

There are various different police forces in Italy: the CARABINIERI, led locally by the maresciallo, are a military unit belonging to the Ministry of Defence; the POLIZIA are a state police force answerable to the Ministry of the Interior, the GUARDIA DI FINANZA are charged with dealing with financial crime and answerable to the Ministry of Finance. The VIGILI report to the local authorities of cities and the larger towns, and are translated here as the "municipal police".

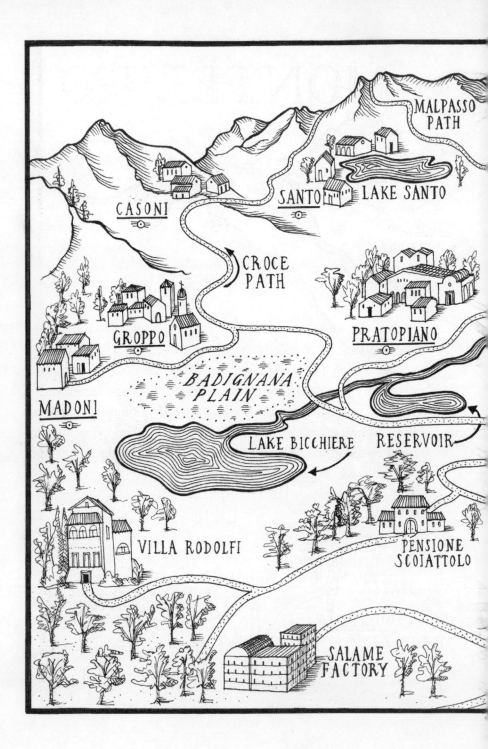

MONTELUPO

CAMPO
GRANDE

BOLDARA
ROAD

MACCHIAFERRO
STREAM

VILLA DEL GREPPO

PIAZZA

BAR OLMO

MONTELUPO

BAR RIVARA

I

The posters were first seen in the village on the feast of San Martino. They said that Paride Rodolfi had not disappeared, that he was alive and in good health. The last one had been stuck up shortly before Commissario Soneri arrived. He could see, as he stood reading it, that the glue was still wet. Something about the wording, with its suggestion of disputes and mysteries, troubled him, and that was even before he heard the rumours that the Rodolfis were in deep trouble, rumours in part prompted by envy and restrained only by the dull respect accorded a family which owned a huge villa on the coast and an enormous salame factory in the village. The name Rodolfi brought back to Soneri the once-familiar trademark featuring a chubby, moustachioed pork-butcher standing alongside a plump pig. The image, which had haunted his imagination since boyhood, appeared on the coloured, oval labels attached to the hams hanging from hooks in grocers' shops which smelt of lard. This memory had nothing in common with the ambiguity of the newly issued posters which, even if they appeared to convey good news, could not entirely conceal the impression that something was awry.

A curiosity he found irksome began to niggle at him. He looked up at the ring of surrounding mountains, cut in half by low, mouse-coloured clouds, and his imagination transformed those jagged peaks sticking into the underside of the clouds into a well-used set of dentures. Further down, the chestnut woods were losing their leaves and becoming moist with the heavy dew that would keep them damp until the first frost. The thought of that humidity cheered him, since it would promote the growth of the mushrooms – the very reason he had returned to the valley he had known since boyhood. He hoped to acquaint himself again with the guttural dialect of the mountain people, and with the pleasure of walking with only himself for company. This summer in the city, passed perspiring in a heat he detested, had been particularly oppressive. Autumn had brought a change of police chief, with the round of new regulations, circulars and directives which such changes invariably involve, and all this had left him thoroughly out of sorts. In spite of the years spent in the questura, he felt his exasperation grow day by day. For that reason Angela, his partner, had more or less ordered him to get away. Rather than spend two weeks on the Costa Azzurra, he had decided to go foraging for mushrooms.

Having seized the opportunity to escape from the mists of Parma, he now found himself in a valley in the Apennines where the faint winter sun hardly ever arrived.

"It's true," he had said. "I need a bit of peace, I can't stand any more of this office politicking."

"Go anywhere you like," she had said. "I won't be able to go with you just at the moment. I am up to my neck in work."

So he was able to leave without any sense of guilt, but as soon as he set foot in the village he found it in the grip of a feverish turmoil. There was a chorus of malevolent whispers beneath the tranquil surface, like a cold sweat soaking an immobile body.

There was a poster on the notice board at the Comune in the piazza. Soneri read the words carefully as he lit his cigar: "We are happy to reassure the community that Paride Rodolfi is in excellent health and is perfectly capable of meeting all obligations. We are grateful to everyone for the good wishes they have expressed."

He tried to keep his mind on mushrooms and on the fallen trunks of beech trees which would provide the perfect environment for their growth. He could not wait for the sky to lighten a little to allow him to climb into the hills and pick a mature cep. He wanted to get away from it all and lose himself in the woods.

He didn't give another thought to the posters until Maini, the boyhood friend with whom he had remained most closely in touch, reminded him about them.

"You couldn't have come at a better time. We really need a commissario here," he said.

"I want nothing to do with any kind of police work," Soneri said.

They were sitting in the *Rivara* bar, looking down at the piazza lined with stalls for the Sunday morning market, but the continual murmur which arose from them seemed to carry with it an underlying sense of disquiet.

"What brings you here in November?" Maini said.

"You know I'm a great one for mushrooms," the commissario said, gesturing vaguely towards the mist-covered mountains.

"You've chosen a bad year. The summer was too dry and they got burned before they could ripen."

"They always say that." Soneri shrugged. "It's either too dry or too wet or there's some disease. You're not going to put me off."

Maini laughed, looked over at the tables where the older men and women were seated, and changed the subject: "What do you make of these posters?"

"It looks to me like somebody's idea of a joke. This is the local feast day, isn't it?"

At that moment Volpi, the gamekeeper, and Delrio, the municipal policeman, turned up. They each gave a nod and sat down beside them.

"The fact is no-one's seen Rodolfi around," Maini said.

"Someone did, yesterday evening," Volpi said. "There was a car like his parked in front of the pharmacy."

"Who said so?"

"They were talking about it this morning" was the vague reply.

"About a week ago he left word he was leaving," Delrio said. "A business trip, or so his secretary, Biavardi's daughter, heard him say."

"And yet on Friday that team of hunters from the Case Bottini recognised his dog wandering about Costa Pelata," Volpi said.

"Maybe there was somebody else there," Delrio said.

"He might have had a row with his wife." Maini laughed. "It's hardly a secret there's no love lost between them nowadays, and every so often he takes off to spend time in the woods in the company of the wild boar."

"And there's someone firing a gun during the night," Volpi said. "Some shots were heard up there. They seemed to come from a double-barrelled Franchi."

"There's plenty of gunfire, and no way of telling who's doing the shooting. They're always single shots, apparently fired by someone lying in wait for something," Delrio said.

"These mountains are overrun with poachers. You'd need a whole army to catch them all," the gamekeeper said.

"If they're quick on their feet, nobody could ever catch them. Not even the Germans managed it with the partisans," Maini said. "Anyway, are you sure they're poachers?"

That sentence was left hanging in the air. Soneri, who had been listening with a gathering sense of unease, became aware of the rising volume of noise in the bar, and found the stench created by the stale smoke and the dampness uncomfortable. After a few seconds, Volpi raised a hand and let it fall heavily on the table, a gesture the commissario recognised as sign language. The others understood too and smiled, allowing Maini to say, "It seems that recently Rodolfi was not exactly…" and he moved his hands so that the palms were facing upwards. "A nervous breakdown?"

"Exactly, anyone who goes round putting up posters…"

Rivara, the bar owner, came over with the Malvasia, put down the glasses and opened the bottle. Every movement of his big, calloused hands was calm and precise, but then, quite suddenly, he said: "They saw him this morning."

"Where?" Maini said.

"In his own house," Rivara replied, jerking his chin in the direction of the mountains. "He was moving around the courtyard, but he seemed to be in pain."

"Who saw him?" Volpi asked.

"Mendogni. He passed by in his tractor on his way to Campogrande."

"Is there anyone to back him up?" Soneri said.

"I'm more worried about the gunfire," Delrio said. "At any hour of the day or night, and after the closure of the boar-hunting season…maybe there's something going on."

"Let the carabinieri know," the commissario said.

"They know already. And they can hear it for themselves," Delrio said.

They raised their glasses in a toast.

"I imagine you've all been out already," Soneri said, referring to the mushrooms.

"There's not much to find. It's a matter of luck this year," Volpi said.

The clouds were higher now in the sky, allowing the men

to make out the Passo del Duca with its dark stretches of pine trees.

"I'm half inclined to go up there this afternoon," the commissario said.

Volpi looked at him with a grimace of disapproval. "It gets dark by four o'clock. You'd be better going in the morning and getting back by lunch time."

There was a kind of concern in his voice, but Soneri paid no heed. Volpi continued: "Mushrooms develop in the night air. You'll find them first thing in the morning, or not at all."

"I still say that if he'd wanted to let everybody know nothing had happened, all he had to do was take a trip into the village. What's the point of posters?" Delrio said. The question was evidently preying on his mind.

"And when did he ever come to town?" Volpi said. "The only one who ever came to the piazza was his father, when he was doing deals to buy pigs. But he was born nearby."

"Didn't Rivara say a while ago that Mendogni saw him in the courtyard?" Maini asked.

Delrio looked at him, puzzled: "People are always seeing things that don't exist. The road to Campogrande is quite a distance from the villa."

"His Mercedes was parked in front of the pharmacy yesterday evening"

"It could have been his wife. She seems to get through a great many medicines," Delrio said.

Soneri made every effort to concentrate on something else, especially the paths in the woods. Meantime, while the cloudy sky closed off every beam of sunlight on the mountains, he watched the stall-holders in the piazza begin to shut down their stalls. One of them, wearing heavy boots, came into the bar to get out of the cold.

"You leaving already?" Rivara asked.

"What's the point of staying on? Nobody's buying. I don't know what's wrong."

"It's the feast of San Martino," the barman said.

The man did not seem convinced. "It's not San Martino that's on their minds. Their heads are full of this Rodolfi business. Any idea what's going on?"

"It seems he disappeared, then turned up again. And today they went round sticking up posters to tell people he's safe and sound."

"I saw them. It's a funny business," the stall-holder said, swallowing his *grappa* in one gulp.

Delrio turned to the others: "You see? Even someone who's not from here understands immediately that there's something not right."

"The commissario came here for just that reason," Rivara said, nodding in the direction of Soneri.

The stall-holder turned to look at him in disbelief. "Is it really that bad?"

"It might be," Volpi said.

"Who knows how it will all end?" Delrio said.

"Look, I'm only here for the mushrooms," Soneri said. The stall-holder grinned, paid and went out.

It was not altogether true. As he rose to his feet and watched the people moving out of the piazza, he realised that the story did intrigue him, but this unlooked-for interest irritated him, somewhat as would the symptoms of a cold.

"Are we going to see you tonight for some *torta fritta?*" Maini asked.

Soneri looked up at the sky, which was growing darker by the minute, before replying: "I think so."

"It's a pretty futile hope," Maini said discouragingly, referring to the weather. "There's going to be no change today."

The commissario stretched out his arms, took his leave

and walked over to the *Scoiattolo*, the *pensione* where he had booked a room. As he went in, the scent of *tortelli* with chestnut filling, served with mushroom sauce, re-awoke childhood memories of long-forgotten dishes and flavours not found in the undistinguished eating places his work too often obliged him to frequent.

Sante Righelli, the proprietor, greeted him with a reserve typical of mountain men, a gruffness easily mistaken for discourtesy. Soneri looked him up and down and was struck by how much he resembled the pork-butcher on the Rodolfi label.

"You're out of luck with the weather," Sante said.

"It's November," the commissario said. "The damp weather will bring out the mushrooms."

Sante shook his head. "I don't think you're going to be lucky there either."

"We'll see how it goes, but at least I'll get a rest."

Sante showed him into the room where several diners where already seated. He stopped in the doorway.

"I really hope that you do get a rest," he said in a low voice, but there was some doubt in his tone.

"Do you think I won't sleep at night?"

"No, no," Sante said, "I'm sure you'll sleep just fine. The problem is that there's a lot of unrest in the village."

"I know. Those posters…"

"Let's hope that's all there is to it," Sante said, with a doleful expression.

The unfinished sentences he had heard seemed to hint at something deeper, but Soneri had resolved not to let himself get involved. He turned his attention to the owner's wife, Ida, a large lady, dripping with perspiration, who emerged from the kitchen. She was a real woman of the mountains, with the wide hips which had the indestructible appearance of a peasant dwelling.

"No man could resist those scents surrounding you," the commissario complimented her.

"If only!" the woman replied. "Those days are long gone!" She threw a disappointed glance in the direction of her husband, who said nothing.

"The quickest way to a man's heart is ... how does it go?"

"It's the only way. And it works. They come here in droves, some even turning off the main road, people on their travels, lorry drivers who go up and down the motorway. I've admirers everywhere," she laughed.

"And today is the feast day."

"Every day is a feast day now. They get the same menu on Mondays as on Sundays. It's other things that are changing."

"At table, I prefer the tried and tested," Soneri said, warding off the question he saw coming and moving to a free seat.

"So you don't want the menu then?" Sante said.

"I'll leave it to the chef."

It was not a mistake to give Ida free rein. A first course of *tortelli* with three types of filling – chestnuts, potatoes and herbs – was followed by a main course of assorted rabbit, boar and goat meats with a little polenta on the side, and finally by *crema di zabaione*, all washed down by a blood-red Bonarda. When the meal was over, the substantial helpings, the wine and the rising chatter in the restaurant left the commissario so drowsy that his mobile had to ring several times before he heard it.

"So you've arrived?" It was Angela. And on a poor line, which meant her voice had a kind of quiver.

"I can't hear you very well," he said, moving outside.

"You're at the *Scoiattolo*?"

"Yes."

"I might have known."

"What do you expect? I feel at home here. I know the owners."

He heard a sigh at the other end. "Just think how many better places there must be that you've never been to."

"And why should I change if I'm comfortable where I am?"

"One of these days I'm going to come and check up on you," she said in a good-humoured way. "Is there something up? You don't seem quite yourself."

"No, no, it's not what you think," Soneri mumbled, but his denial did not carry conviction. "It's just that everybody here is talking about a man who's supposed to have disappeared and then turned up again. Nobody has any idea what's going on, so there's no end of rumours and counter-rumours. They know what I do for a living, and they're all keen to get me involved."

"Isn't it you that's getting curious?"

"Well, maybe a little. I want to talk about mushrooms, but everyone I meet is determined to raise this other subject," the commissario said.

"Who has disappeared? Someone important?"

"Paride Rodolfi, the salame and *prosciutto* manufacturer."

"Good heavens! So he *is* important. I know the lawyer who looks after the company's affairs, and I can well believe everybody's talking about it. Everybody there has some connection with the Rodolfis. They either work for him, or they're suppliers."

"I know, but the fact is…" the commissario's voice trailed off because he had suddenly lost his train of thought. He realised he had no idea why this business seemed so odd to him.

"Tell me," Angela said.

Soneri outlined the facts, chiefly to clarify them to himself. "Some posters have been put up to say that Rodolfi is alive and in good health, but no-one had ever said he was dead in the first place. They all assumed he'd gone off somewhere."

"Whenever someone disappears, there's always a suspicion

that they might be dead," was Angela's tentative explanation.

"Certainly, but even after these posters have gone up, no-one's still really sure whether he's alive or not. One or two people claim to have seen him, but nobody will swear to it."

"Good God, Commissario," Angela murmured, "I've never heard you so confused. I hope it's only because of the heavy meal you've just had. Go for a walk and clear your head and then try to get some rest."

"I have the feeling that they all know more than they're letting on, but since I don't have any facts to go on, I'm getting steadily more puzzled myself. I'm not thinking clearly."

"Do you want my advice? Steer clear of the whole thing. Go for a walk in your mountains and let them look for Rodolfi by themselves – if he really is lost."

At half past two, the village was still sleeping off its *brodo di carne*. Soneri went up to his room, put on his wellington boots and slipped out without letting Sante see him go. Just this once, being familiar with the woods and feeling totally at home among them, he was happy to follow Angela's advice. He took the road to Montelupo intending to climb for a couple of kilometres and then turn into the beech groves. He felt the need to stretch his legs and clear his lungs, so he set off at a relaxed pace, turning back from time to time to watch the village grow smaller behind him. He raised his eyes to the hills only when he reached the reservoir, where there was a small, familiar fountain. The mist was not so much higher above him, no more than ten minutes' walk away. At Boldara, the point where the road ends, the first wisps began to float around him, and from there on he walked into and out of the swirling greyness of mist and low cloud carried on the wind. Only when he took the path through the beech woods did everything close in on him. The trees and brush all around him, the thick mist pressing down from above and the black earth beneath his feet made him shudder. He was uneasy as he made his way along a tunnel of trees which grew darker with every step. He had the sense that he was not alone. Birdsong and the squeals of hedgehogs alternated with the sound of a large animal not far distant in the woods. The mist and the breeze carried the sounds deceptively in all directions.

He had walked quite a distance before he began to feel warm. His heart was beating wildly and he was gasping for breath. Were his cigars presenting their bill? He looked down at his boots encrusted with mud and understood. At every step, he was carrying what looked like a kilo of earth. He scraped the boots clean on moss-covered roots. In less than an hour, he reckoned, it would be dark. He went on a little way, but stopped when he heard the sound of breaking branches. It might be a wild boar, he thought, and for a moment he feared it might charge him, but the beast, without emerging onto the path, could be heard racing down a gulley which cut across the slope to seek shelter in the thickets.

As he was setting off again, a shot rang out. Its echo swelled across the valley like thunder. The bullet passed no more than ten metres ahead of him, allowing him to hear its whistle and the crack of the branches it struck. Instinctively, he crouched on the wet forest floor, waiting for a second shot which did not come. He stayed in that position for a few moments, wondering if the shot was aimed at the boar or at him, and deciding that thinking about it was going to get him nowhere. Twenty minutes later, he came out onto the road, and even before emerging from the mist he heard the band striking up on the piazza below.

2

According to tradition, on the feast of San Martino things were taken from houses as a joke and left somewhere in the village where they could be rediscovered. All the various objects which had been spirited away the night before were piled up in a quiet lane behind the church. There were farm implements, bicycles, hats, cars and even a pony, which was feeding quietly from a nosebag. A man was cursing as he attempted to pull an old scooter out of a tangle of rubbish, but just as he had succeeded and was about to move off, the town band turned up and the street was closed off.

Soneri waited until the majorettes and bandsmen, decked out in uniforms, hats and sequins, had passed by. He could not understand why the sound of drums and trumpets in all their solemnity always made him laugh, but as he was thinking this over, Maini emerged from the disorderly crowd shuffling along behind the band, took him by the arm and led him into the body of the procession.

"So you've had a go, eh!" he exclaimed, glancing down at Soneri's mud-covered boots. He had forgotten to change but no-one in the village would notice.

"I went to stretch my legs and get a breath of fresh air," Soneri said.

"How far did you get?"

"Up past Boldara, towards Montelupo."

"You've got guts," Maini said.

"Is there someone from around here who goes shooting in the mountains?" the commissario asked, abruptly.

The din from the band gave Maini an excuse for taking his time. "Did you hear anything?" he asked.

Soneri nodded, without turning to face him.

"Where?"

"I have just told you where."

"But do you know where the shot came from?"

"I only know it wasn't more than ten metres away when it went whistling past. There must have been a boar in the gulley, judging by the noise coming from there."

"These mountains have become very dangerous. I don't know what's been going on recently."

"There've always been poachers in these parts," the commissario said without much conviction.

"During the day? With this mist, in a hunting reserve?" Maini's tone was incredulous.

"In the mist you can do anything you want. It gives you cover."

"True enough, even for a murder. Nobody can see you."

Soneri felt a tremor run up his spine, but he said nothing. They were back on the piazza after walking around some of the streets where old women at the windows looked down at the band. A big stall was serving *torta fritta* and salame to a crowd gathered hungrily around it. On the other side of the piazza, some volunteers from the tourist office were roasting chestnuts. Delrio, clearly displeased, came up to join them. He was wearing full uniform.

"Don't tell me that you've got to work today as well," Maini said.

Delrio shrugged. "More problems."

"What's up?"

"One of those damned things…" he said, waving his hands

vaguely in the air. "It's beyond my understanding…"

"There are many things like that," Soneri said.

Delrio gave him a quick look, as though he wanted to enlist his help. "Last night was very peculiar, even for San Martino's," was all he said by way of explanation. He was referring to the custom of flitting, or stealing things as a practical joke.

"The young nowadays carry off things we would never have touched," Maini said.

"It's the first time anyone has ever taken a coffin," Delrio said. "The thing is that nobody noticed, because it was covered by the Ghirardis' marquee. It was only when the pony started tugging at the canvas that the coffin came to light."

"Where have you put it?" the commissario asked him.

"Where do you think? In the graveyard chapel."

"Is there an undertaker near here?"

"The nearest one is about twenty kilometres away," Maini replied.

"No-one has ever stolen a coffin," Delrio said again. "The people in this village are all cheerful and good-natured."

This time it was Soneri's turn to shrug.

"Nobody's going to tell me all this was dreamed up on the spur of the moment last night," Maini said.

The smoke from the roasting chestnuts mixed with the smoke from the fried food. They were passing in front of the stalls where people were queuing up to buy *polenta* and *vin brulé*, when the band re-formed and struck up another number.

"See that? People having good-natured fun," the commissario said.

Delrio glowered, supposing Soneri was laughing at him. He moved off in the direction of the band just as the lights went on, in response, it seemed, to how far down the mist had come.

"He's a worried man," Maini said, indicating Delrio, as he was swallowed up by the crowd. "In fact, in spite of appearances, everyone in the village is a bit worried."

"I know. It's because of the Rodolfi case," Soneri said.

"Everyone's livelihood depends on them, and in spite of all their faults…" His voice stuttered to an embarrassed halt.

"Have you heard anyone criticising them?" the commissario asked.

"No, no – apart from the usual chatter. You hear rumours here and there…some bits of their business…But there's so much jealousy around here. Anyway, who knows how much they're worth? They can toss their money about…"

"Yes, they can toss it up in the air, or add yeast to make it rise like *torta fritta*," the commissario said, as he gazed at the squares of batter swelling up on contact with the hot oil in the pan. Maini was watching too and smiled, but then turned serious once again. "But the coffin…what do you think about that?"

"I think an empty coffin is always waiting for someone to fill it."

Maini looked down and changed the subject. "If you're planning to go up there tomorrow morning, you're as well setting off at first light. These are the shortest days of the year."

"And the mushrooms are well hidden, unless you know precisely where to go looking for them," Soneri said.

"In the woods, nothing's that precise. You have to search about, like when you're looking for a place to pee."

Soneri stared at him for few moments, noticing the frown on his face. He had been in the village only a few hours and already the tension in the air had got to him. Now that he was plunged into that stressful atmosphere, heavy with unanswered questions, his hopes for a carefree break were already vanishing. Perhaps Angela had been right when she said that worries live inside us, not outside, because we can never be wholly impregnable. And he knew he was too impressionable.

Fortunately he was distracted by the priest at the head of the procession, cutting his way through the crowd milling about in the piazza. His only followers were elderly ladies, while the altar boys around him had the look of young men who had just been served with their call-up papers.

"More like a funeral," was the acid observation of Volpi, who had just come over from the roasted-chestnut stall.

"At least you won't find the priest changing his home," said an ancient at Soneri's shoulder, repeating an old joke, trotted out each year, about flitting from one house to another on San Martino.

No sooner had the procession moved on than the mayor appeared alongside the commissario. "Good to see you back. You'll be here for…" he started to say, but could not get the words out.

Soneri noted the embarrassment on the man's face, so reassured him. "I'm only here to pick mushrooms."

The mayor smiled. "Well, you know, with all these mysteries…"

"I'll steer clear of mysteries for at least ten days."

"Someone's been putting about rumours, whispers, gossip. It's a set-up. Let me assure you that nothing has happened. A minor mishap which has been blown up into a big story."

"You're all great fans of the Rodolfis, but you worry too much," Soneri said, with a touch of irony.

The mayor studied him warily, to make sure he was taking him seriously enough. "It was a mistake to put up those posters. It's not the first time he's gone missing."

"Couldn't agree more. Going round sticking up posters is…" Soneri said.

"Yes. It was an odd thing to do, and it only heightens suspicion. They should have left well enough alone."

"It would be better still if he were to appear in public," the commissario suggested.

"Certainly, certainly, but he never was particularly sociable. You can understand it, a busy man like him…"

"What do you plan to do? Maybe you should just try to calm things down."

"And what do you think I'm doing? I'm getting out and about as much as I can. I speak to anybody and everybody, but these mountain folk are so distrustful. You should know that, shouldn't you?"

"It seems someone saw Rodolfi this morning, or last night."

"That was Mendogni, but now he's not so sure. He saw a man who might have been Paride Rodolfi, but he couldn't swear to it."

Soneri stretched out his arms. "Send for the carabinieri!"

"On what grounds? Because a man has failed to return home? I'll get charged with wasting police time."

"Talking about wasting police time," the commissario said, looking over at the piazza where Mendogni, surrounded by a crowd of people anxious for news, had made an appearance.

The mayor went over to question him, speaking over those who were already talking. He dragged Soneri with him to witness what looked like a public interrogation.

"They tell me you're not certain whether it was him or not."

"When I first saw him, I was almost certain," Mendogni mumbled, annoyed at having to repeat his story yet again. "But if you ask me if I am a hundred per cent certain, I'd have to say no. Do you know the path that leads to Campogrande? It's not that close to the Greppo villa."

"Who else could it have been?" someone asked.

"How should I know?" Mendogni said. "There are so many folk coming and going to that house. You see big cars driving up and there's no way of being sure who's inside."

The mayor was growing increasingly agitated because Mendogni's words, far from calming people down, were making them more suspicious. Another voice cut in. "Biavardi's daughter says he's still not come back, and that it's a whole week since they had any news."

"They must have had some reason for putting up all those posters," someone else said.

Soneri listened in silence to the hubbub, with images previously seen a thousand times chasing each other around in his head. In the early stages of an investigation, everything was always so confused and contradictory, and that did not mean that the outlook was necessarily any clearer at the end. He had no wish for this to become "his" case, so he took advantage of a lull in the exchanges to move away. He was determined to remain an onlooker.

The darkness, made more impenetrable by the mist rolling down from the hills, had in the meantime enveloped the village. He walked towards Rivara's *osteria* with the intention of ordering a glass of Malvasia, but when he saw how crowded the place was, he walked on towards the old district. As he passed in front of the *Olmo* bar, he looked in and was reassured by the atmosphere of mid-week calm which reigned there. This was the bar frequented by the village elders, and it seemed to have grown old with them.

He went in and leaned on the bar to light his cigar. At the table directly in front of him, four men were silently engrossed in a game of *briscola*.

"Fireworks tonight," one of the men said. The others shrugged without raising their eyes from the cards.

"Who do you think the coffin's for?" one asked.

"As long as it's not for us."

Soneri was struck by the stoic indifference of the card-players, but he felt himself being observed. He turned round and recognised Magnani, the owner.

"If you're here, it means something really has gone badly wrong," were his words of greeting.

"You're wide of the mark this time. The only investigations I'm doing are in the undergrowth," Soneri said.

"In that case you're going to have your work cut out," Magnani warned him, as he filled two glasses of white wine without waiting to be asked. He raised his glass. "Here's to your good health and to the investigation."

"To my health, then. I'll take nothing to do with any investigation."

Magnani stretched out his hands, palms open. "I meant your investigations into the state of the mushrooms."

"What can you tell me?"

"I've never taken much interest in them. They tell me that this year the outlook is grim after the dry summer we've had. You could search higher up in the hills, where it's always a bit cooler. Assuming there are any left, that is."

"They've picked the lot already?"

Magnani made another eloquent gesture with his hands. "There are some who are up there every day."

"They're not afraid of the gunfire?"

Magnani stared hard at Soneri, and in that one moment a complete understanding was established between the two. "It's a big, high mountain and there's space for everybody."

"Where do you go for the licence?"

"The usual place, the Comune," Magnani said before adding: "You're looking well. You haven't changed a bit."

"Nothing has changed here either," Soneri replied, looking around the bar with its dated furniture and the wallpaper peeling where the chairs had rubbed against it.

"That's not true. Everyone here's growing old. After a while, the years begin to take their toll."

"You're an institution."

"So is the cathedral. And we're about the same age."

The four men continued their game, interrupting the silence only for brief comments on the hands they were dealt.

"The one advantage age gives you is that you can stand back and look at what's happening without getting too upset. And I'm really keen to see how it's all going to end," Magnani said.

"Do you mean here in the village?"

"That's exactly what I mean."

"Do you believe there is something behind this disappearance?"

"I think somebody is cheating, and that this little game is likely to end badly," Magnani said, looking at the cards which were piling up in the centre of the table. "I have the impression we're sitting on a powder keg."

Soneri listened to the old man's words and remembered how confused he had been when he had tried to explain to Angela what was going on. He was just as confused now, but every time he tried to seek explanations, everyone became evasive, so it was no surprise when Magnani said, "There's so much going on…it's not easy for someone who doesn't live here."

The door opened, letting in a gust of wind and rain. An elderly man, slightly out of breath, stood in the doorway and, raising his walking stick in front of him, announced, "Now Palmiro's gone missing as well."

The four men around the table let their cards drop and turned round quickly. The elder Rodolfi was evidently much more popular than his son.

"What is this? Some sort of plague?" Magnani muttered.

"He went out this afternoon for a walk with his dog, but it turned dark and there has been no sign of him since. The dog came back without its master."

"Are they out looking for him already?" the commissario said.

The old man nodded. "The carabinieri and teams of volunteers are out on the hills." Magnani stood rooted to the spot, lost in his own thoughts. None of the others said a word, and the silence was expression enough of their disconcerted astonishment. Soneri went out into the mist now swirling across the streets of the village like clouds on mountain tops. The trepidation among the people standing under the flickering light of the lamp-posts on the piazza was almost palpable. The Comune was open and people were walking up and down under the narrow colonnade at the entrance. An ambulance with its emergency lights flashing, but proceeding very slowly, passed by.

"Either there's no-one inside, or else for the person they've got on board there's no point going at speed," said Rivara, who had also come out of his bar onto the street.

"An hour ago someone said they'd heard a shot," Maini said.

"Where did it come from?"

"From the direction of Gambetta, near the Croce path, but I couldn't say if that's true or not. Other people didn't hear anything."

"Are you saying it could have been a rifle shot from…?" Rivara asked, but he seemed afraid of finishing the sentence.

"It could've been anything."

A man in a wheelchair, wrapped in a heavy blanket, was repeating that they should talk to him, because he knew where Palmiro normally went. "We used to go hunting together," he kept repeating, but no-one paid him any attention.

"What about the dog? Maybe he could lead them to where he is," Rivara said.

"Perhaps, but he's an old dog and seems worn out."

"He could easily have got lost in this mist," Magnani said.

Everyone standing there waiting in the swirling fog was afflicted by the same sense of impotence. A carabiniere car swept past and drew up outside the Comune. Another set of headlights cut through the darkness in the direction of Rivara's *osteria*. Four young men from the village got out.

"Were you not needed?" Rivara asked.

"There're too many people there already," replied the driver. "They need people who know these woods. It's a foreign land to me."

"How are they getting on?"

"They'll never find him in this mist, at night time. It's insane. They'll end up losing somebody else."

"They can't just leave him to die of exposure."

"He won't be feeling the cold any more by now," said another of the young men from the car.

"The mist is much thicker up there," the driver said. "If you don't know your way, it's a struggle even to stay on the road."

"Are they working in teams?"

"A carabiniere truck went up and parked alongside the reservoir, near the aqueduct. The others have their radios."

Maini shook his head. "They're not going to find him tonight."

"You never know," Rivara said. "There are some people who know the woods like the back of their hands. And Palmiro, if he's still got any strength in his legs…"

"The carabinieri are relying on Ulisse, who's been wandering about Montelupo for forty years."

"Wouldn't he have had a mobile?" Soneri said.

"Palmiro!" Rivara exclaimed, taken aback by the sheer naivety of the question. "He wouldn't have anything to do with those things. He still did his accounts with a pencil! No, Palmiro is one of the old school. He reckoned you had to deal with pigs with your bare hands. He would grab them by the ears and turn them over as though they were sacks."

"And when the mood took him, he wouldn't think twice about giving you short weight." The words were spoken in acid tones by a squat man called Ghidini. His teeth were yellowing from the endless cigarettes he rolled himself.

An awkward silence fell and Soneri had the impression that the speaker had touched a delicate nerve. His words had brought to the surface a feeling no-one else would have dared to give voice to.

"We should go up there," Rivara said.

"To do what?" Maini said. "Either Palmiro comes back under his own steam or he stays in the woods."

"Maybe he's found somewhere to spend the night," Ghidini suggested. "In one of those huts on Montelupo, or in one of the shelters for drying out chestnuts."

"Those places are full of Albanians," Rivara said.

"That's nonsense," Maini said sharply.

"They must be. The huts are always full of cans and bottles, and every so often someone builds a fire."

"Well, Palmiro won't have gone out without his double-barrelled gun," Ghidini said.

"Just as well," Rivara said. "There are so many strange individuals on the mountains nowadays, and who knows what they're up to."

Soneri looked up towards Montelupo, but he could see nothing, not even the outline of the great mountain that loomed over the village. At that moment another car pulled up and the mayor, instantly recognisable, got out. He had a deeply worried expression.

"Well then?" Rivara said.

The mayor stopped. "Nothing, there's no sign of him."

Once again the man in the wheelchair started shouting

they should take him with them, but once again no-one paid him any heed.

"Ulisse hasn't found anything?"

"Montelupo is very big," the mayor said, removing his hat for a moment to straighten his hair. He was sweating in spite of the cold.

"And what about that rifle shot..." Ghidini said.

The mayor turned towards him with a venomous look. "I know nothing about it, but it wouldn't be the first time."

"They heard it before it got dark, and by that time Palmiro..."

The sentence was, as ever, left hanging. The mayor glared again at Rivara with irritation, but then his expression softened, and he spoke in a more measured tone: "It could be anything, if that's what you mean."

"They heard it as far away as Gambetta, over towards Croce," Maini informed him.

"It seems somebody is deliberately putting rumours about," the mayor said.

"But why ignore the possibility?"

The mayor's brusque shake of the head was an invitation to Maini to let the subject drop. He turned to Soneri, who had been taking it all in.

"Maybe you could help us," he said finally.

"The carabinieri are already involved. Once you're outside the city boundaries, it's all their territory," the commissario said.

The mayor looked deeply discouraged. "This is a very strange case and the maresciallo..." but he could not finish that sentence either.

"What does Crisafulli know about anything?" Ghidini sneered, putting into words what was in the mayor's mind. "They should send a senior officer."

"If it's a really serious case, they'll send someone," Soneri said.

The mayor turned back to him, but his expression was still downcast. He was uncertain what do to and he was looking for support. Silence fell once more. All the while, the mist was rubbing against the houses, a different mist from the mist in the cities: more swift-moving, rougher, more dense

"When all's said and done, nothing has actually happened," the commissario said. "What do you want me to get involved *in*? One man who hasn't come home, maybe because he had a quarrel with his wife? Another who got lost in the mountains, probably while hunting wild boar, illegally?"

"Could be," Ghidini said.

"Or is there something more to it?" Soneri said.

Silence again, the unsaid hanging constantly over their conversation.

"Nobody understands a thing," Maini said.

The mayor, however, seemed to absorb what was being said, and assumed an official pose, as though he were about to make a speech. "The commissario is quite right. After all, nothing has actually happened yet."

No-one was sure if the word had slipped out or if the mayor had said it on purpose. That "yet" seemed to have been uttered expressly to make the tension grow. And indeed it did grow, causing Soneri to lose patience.

"Speak clearly. If you know something more, tell us," he snapped.

The mayor looked at the group one by one, as though to give the impression that he could not speak freely in public. He shied away from saying whatever was on his mind. "Perhaps we're getting needlessly worked up," he said, turning away.

For a few moments a kind of electric charge hung in the air, until the car of the municipal police drew up on the piazza and Delrio got out. "We're getting nowhere," he said, shaking his head. He leaned sideways on his car and lit a cigarette.

"You'd be as well calling it off. At this hour, what's done is done," Ghidini said.

The policeman gave a shrug. "We have a duty to do all we can, assuming he's still alive."

"But surely you'd hear him shouting," Rivara said.

"If he has any voice left."

"Did any of you hear a shot from the direction of Gambetta?" It was Ghidini who spoke.

"No, not a shot. But something else," Delrio said.

"Great big animals," sniggered Rivara.

"Who knows? It's hard to make out." Delrio was being deliberately ambiguous.

"Maybe a two-legged animal." Rivara refused to let the subject drop.

"In this mist... It must have been a wild boar," Delrio said.

"Let's just pretend it was a couple of boar. No reason to be afraid of them," Rivara said, in an attempt to be ironic.

"Can Ulisse not help you?" Maini said.

"He's checking the paths lower down the hill, but he's moaning about having the carabinieri at his back. He says they are more trouble than the mist."

The policeman's radio crackled, and he put it to his ear. They were asking him to keep the ambulance in a state of readiness for dispatch to the reservoir. At the far side of the piazza, a light could just be made out at the window of the office where the mayor was waiting for developments. The four youths who had arrived a short time before made off again, the headlights of the car cutting twin circular openings in the darkness.

"He'll be shaking in his boots," Ghidini said, pointing to the one lighted window.

He received only grunts in response, but it was clear they had all understood and were in agreement. Soneri looked quizzical, but Ghidini and Rivara only smiled.

"Why should he be shaking?"

"If Rodolfi goes bust, the mayor's days are numbered. Here everything is linked to the pig-farming business, and even politicians come out smelling of pork and salame," Maini explained.

Ghidini raised his right hand, rubbing his thumb against his index and middle finger, the universal sign for money and wealth, a gesture which was at once eloquent and ambiguous. Soneri, innocent of professional involvement, was happy to remain a bystander. The now-customary silent pause followed, and just when it seemed that someone was about to launch into a speech, the first fireworks went off. Everyone turned towards the houses huddled around the church and peered into the mist as it took on different colours moment by moment. The explosions came slightly later, delayed like peals of thunder.

"Do you think that's such a good idea?" Maini said, referring to the fireworks.

"The mayor has decided it might help him get his bearings if he's lost," Delrio said.

"Assuming, of course, that Palmiro can see them," Ghidini said.

"Even if he can't see them, at least he'll hear them," Delrio said, staring at the flashes which appeared as opaque as coloured ice in a *granita*.

"I wouldn't count on it," Rivara said. "Sounds can be deceptive in these mountains, and can produce the very opposite effect from what you would expect."

"Palmiro knows what he's doing, and anyway he'll see the

lights," Delrio said, waving his hand in the air as a Roman candle was set off, its colours floating in the milky air.

"It's like being back at war, when Pippo and his reconnaissance plane circled the skies," Ghidini said.

Just then a sequence of bangs, similar to a burst of machine gun fire, rang out, followed by a loud report, like a deep cough issuing from enormous, tubercular lungs.

"We'd got used to the occasional gunshot..." Rivara said.

Each man's expression was grim and frowning but indecipherable. The bar owner, shivering in the damp air, broke up the meeting by suggesting they repair inside. They trooped in silence into the brightness, and still no-one spoke. Only a few stragglers and a couple of stray dogs were left on the piazza, but the solitary light in the Comune remained switched on while the last flashes from the fireworks died away, falling into an abyss of dampness. When the church bell struck eight, Soneri realised it was time for dinner, but just then his mobile rang. He went outside to reply, aware of the watchful eyes of the others gazing at him, as though he were a priest celebrating Mass.

"Is the mist as bad as ever?" Angela asked.

"In more senses than one."

"I deduce from that reply that the Rodolfi affair is beginning to intrigue you."

"There's more than one Rodolfi affair now. The father has gone missing as well."

"Palmiro?"

"How do you know his name?"

"Who doesn't know him? You're forgetting that I'm a lawyer. It was he who created the company."

"You think I didn't know that?"

"Well then, you must know that he can eat fire, he's as strong as a bull and afraid of nothing."

"I know, I know." The commissario cut her off sharply. "Anyway, right now he must be afraid of the dark and the cold, because he's lost somewhere on Montelupo."

"What is Montelupo?"

"It's the mountain facing the village. It's no place for day trippers, beautiful as it is in its own way. It's got a sinister feel because of all the legends associated with it."

"They're overdoing their disappearing act, these Rodolfis," Angela said.

"It's going to be a difficult business finding him. In this fog, either he makes his own way back or he stays up there for good."

"If you go climbing tomorrow, instead of finding mushrooms, maybe you'll find the old man."

"If this mist doesn't lift, I might get lost myself."

"No, you're like a cat. You always find your way home."

"I keep seeing myself as a boy, when I used to go searching for mushrooms with my father."

"If you go on like that, you'll only get depressed."

"He would teach me the names of the trees, but he wasn't given time enough to teach me all of them."

"Possibly Palmiro won't manage to teach his son all the tricks of the trade either."

"He might still turn up, but there's a really bad feeling abroad in this village."

"They're afraid the whole pack of cards will collapse. Anyway, you have work to do, Commissario."

"Yes, tomorrow, on Montelupo, among the beech trees," Soneri said.

When he went back into the bar, he was struck by the silence. All that could be heard was the plaintive tinkle of the videogame machine and the smack of billiard balls as two boys moved round the table.

"Are we going to have to wait up all night?" Maini asked the commissario.

"There's nothing we can do. We'd be better off going to bed," Ghidini said.

Rivara offered them all a drink, and they lined up at the bar like a detachment of soldiers, until their attention was diverted by the crackle of Delrio's radio.

"The ambulance? It's already here in the piazza. The doctor? Of course he's here. The one on stand-by duty." The radio crackled once more. "Yes, we're on full alert...You heard a voice?...Ah, you're not sure?...Well, we're ready in any case."

"They say they think they heard a voice, but it might have been the cry of a wild beast," Delrio advised his companions.

"There are some that sound almost human," Rivara said.

"Such as cats on heat," Ghidini added.

"You can never be sure of anything," the commissario said.

"It's not like being in the city. Sometimes these mountains seem to have been put there just to confuse people," Maini said.

"It's got nothing to do with the mountains, for God's sake," Soneri said.

"It could have been Palmiro calling for his dog. He can't have known it had long ago made its way home," Maini said.

"He was as fond of that dog as he was of his son," Volpi said.

"And the dog was more faithful," Ghidini said.

Soneri grew ever more uncomfortable listening to the conversation, laden as it was with allusions which escaped him. It was clear that there were layers of hidden meanings in the talk, confirmed by nods and little grins and winks. It was like a mime show put on for him, or like listening to a foreign language and it made him aware of a growing distance between himself and the people here with whom he would have liked to re-establish a fraternal cameraderie. He had deluded himself that he could easily re-enter the community, but now he felt as isolated as he felt in the questura, and as perhaps he always was.

He noticed that the conversation had stopped and that Maini and the others were staring at him. The same silence as before fell over the group. The waiting became more and more oppressive. He lit a cigar, more to mask his embarrassment than from any genuine wish to smoke. That intolerable silence was broken by the sound of a car screeching to a halt in the piazza. The youths who had been there a short time previously came running into the bar.

"Palmiro is home," the driver announced.

The tension evaporated in an instant. Rivara stepped forward. "Who found him?"

"No-one. He made it on his own. He bumped into the carabinieri at the reservoir and asked them if they were looking for him. Apparently, he didn't even want them to give him a lift back."

"Palmiro's made of iron!" Volpi said.

"They've made us waste all this time for nothing," Delrio grumbled. He picked up his radio-phone and bellowed into it, "OK?…It's all over?…Can we go now?"

He stood there listening for some time, while the others spoke in whispers so as not to disturb him. When he shut down the connection, he found all eyes trained on him.

"The fireworks did the trick. He says he saw them and was able to get his bearings, but he claims he would've found the road even without them."

"He must be nearly dead with exhaustion."

"I suppose so, but it's pitch black up there and they've only just found him."

"Did he have his rifle?"

"No, he was unarmed."

"Have they asked him how come he got lost?"

Delrio stretched out his arms. "His story is that he wanted to go as far as the mountain pass to see if there were any mushrooms there, but the mist came down without warning."

"And that was all he had to say?" Volpi sounded sceptical.

"He asked a couple of times about his dog, because it seems they were separated and he kept calling him."

"So that was the voice they heard."

"Sounds that way."

"The dog's getting old. He doesn't see too well now and doesn't like walking long distances," Ghidini said.

"So his chief anxiety was his dog," Delrio said.

"That's all he's got left," Rivara said.

One of the young men who had arrived in the car went over to the bar, placed both elbows on it and leaned over towards the barman. "Why do you think a lorry would be stopped on the main road at this time of night?" He spoke loudly enough to ensure that everyone could hear him.

"What lorry?" Rivara said.

"A refrigerator lorry with a foreign number plate. The driver seemed to have lost his bearings in the mist, and asked us for directions to the salame factory."

"He must have been picking up a load but was running late."

"The driver wasn't on his own. There were three of them, and we watched them go up to the factory."

"All three of them?" Rivara said.

The boy nodded, with the faintest of conspiratorial smiles. "If you want my opinion, they were planning to pick up a delivery right away."

"They must be in a great hurry," Ghidini sniggered.

"They certainly were. And why should that be?" the boy wondered aloud.

Nobody dared to utter a guess, and once more a silence fell. The young man said goodbye to the group and opened the door to go out, but he was stopped in his tracks by the sound of gunfire. Everyone followed him out onto the street.

"Was that from Greppo?" Delrio said.

"Couldn't tell. Either Greppo or Campogrande," Maini said.

"This is happening too often," Rivara said.

"At least we can all agree on that," Soneri said.

The mayor emerged from the Comune and strode determinedly across the piazza. Delrio went to meet him. The two men stood talking in the mist, then the policeman turned back and went into the bar.

"The mayor has told the carabinieri to go and see what they can find. This time the whole village heard the shot."

"It's high time they showed some interest," Volpi said.

"For all the difference it'll make! By the time they get there, whoever fired the shot will be long gone," Ghidini said, shaking his head.

"In this mist, you could lose an army," Rivara said.

"You never know. They're already in the right area," Delrio said.

Some twenty minutes later, the piazza was lit up by a flashing blue light which cut through the mist which was now even more treacherous. The carabiniere truck crossed the piazza and pulled up outside the Comune.

"Is that them on top of the job now?" Maini said.

No-one made a reply. Soneri was thinking only of the lorry parked on the main road and of the three people inside. He was keen to go and see whether or not it had gone to the salame factory, but once again his attention was diverted by Delrio's radio. He drew close to overhear what was being said.

"It was Palmiro who fired the shot," Delrio eventually relayed the news.

"Who at?" Rivara said.

"At the dog," Delrio said, but obviously he himself did not attribute much importance to it. There was another thought niggling him.

"So he's gone clean off his head," Ghidini said. "He has always been extremely fond of that dog."

"He told the carabinieri it was too old and the exertion had weakened its heart."

"Ever the unscrupulous bastard," Rivara said.

"If he was old...He would not have wanted him to suffer," Delrio suggested.

"I think there's more to it than that. He might have felt let down, if the dog had run off home leaving him on his own on Montelupo. There aren't that many people he could count on," Maini said.

"There wasn't much anybody could do. By the time the carabinieri got there, he was already burying it," Delrio said.

"All this trouble for nothing. Still, in the end everyone's alive and back home safely – apart from Palmiro's dog," Rivara said.

"What about the lorry at the factory?" said one of the young men who had stayed on after his companions had left.

The only response was a collective shrug.

3

It was still dark when Soneri came down for breakfast. The night before when he got back, he found the table still set. Sante had saved some vegetable stew for him, and when the commissario saw it arrive with an overturned plate on top to keep it warm, memories came flooding back of his mother in her dressing gown, of trains running late and of a house immersed in silence with the family already in bed. He had hoped to find the same peace and stability in the valley in the Apennines where his forebears had lived season after season, enduring the snows of winter and heat of summer, clearing the juniper bushes from the land and hauling timber down from the woods.

"In middle age, everyone yearns to return to the place they left when they were young to make their way in the world," Sante intoned.

For Sante, the world was the city. Anyone who moved away from the valley was a displaced person, and Soneri was coming round to this point of view. That was why he had come back, and now, as he stood looking through the windows of the *Scoiattolo* at the wooded slopes of Montelupo capped by woolly mist, he felt the tug of that mountain which had been the focus of so much attention in recent days. In a short while he would set off and clamber up its steep spine like a tiny, exploring parasite. He was intent on taking full advantage of the daylight hours and was only waiting for dawn to break.

Sante had prepared a box with a few slices of bread, some shavings of parmesan and a few thin slices of *prosciutto*. He put the box in a shoulder bag and got on his way, aware that he was retracing the steps of his father, his grandfather and of who knows how many others.

The ascent up the path from the village left him out of breath, but he was soon enough at the reservoir. Patches of mist drifted around him and trailed off all the way down to the village. He took the Boldara path, walking for another half an hour through a tunnel of branches on a mattress of fallen leaves, not looking back until he came to an opening in the woods. The houses were far off now, in a deep crevice where it seemed that they had ended up after falling down the mountainside, like all the other things which had tumbled down from the heights. He left the path and ventured into the woods, struggling with the undergrowth and slipping on the leaves. He spent some time probing the trunks on slopes where the tree fellers had been active, but he found nothing to interest him. The ground still had marks of having been disturbed, so it was clear that someone had passed that way not long before. He followed the footprints of the roe deer and the tracks of the boar for almost two hours until, in the shadow of a trunk nestling into the mountainside, he discovered a colony of "horn of plenty" mushrooms. Dark coloured and with a tapering stalk, they had a sinister appearance, but they made good eating for someone who knew how they required to be cooked.

All of a sudden, the light faded and the wood was shrouded in a dense mist. Soneri decided it was time to make his way back, but as he did so he became aware of the faint squelch of footsteps sinking into the damp leaves behind him. From time to time, the snap of a broken branch could be heard, seemingly from someone picking his way over dead wood in the shade of the beech trees. Soneri continued on his way, choosing carefully where to put his feet so as not to make the least inroad into the profound silence which seemed to amplify the slightest sound. He walked gingerly through a copse of oak trees, where the dry leaves still hanging on the branches made the surroundings even more gloomy. Somewhere lower down, he heard a sharp noise, the quick, alarmed movement of a prey that knew it was being hunted. He thought he made out the outline of a human being, barely glimpsed through the foliage. Perhaps someone had only just realised how close Soneri was and was vanishing into the mist, leaving no more than a tantalising shadow.

Soneri followed the course of the Macchiaferro stream until he emerged into an area of hornbeam and chestnut, ripe for the autumnal pruning. His mind was still filled with the image of that figure, little more than a shadow distorted by the dampness, which had made a momentary appearance before being swallowed up by the mist. As he turned onto the Boldara road, he recalled what he had been told about Albanians and others who supposedly moved about the mountainside. People spoke of them as a menace, in terms which made them the modern equivalent of the ancient fear of wild animals, lightning and hailstones. He took a rest at the reservoir and in the failing afternoon light sat down to enjoy his parmesan. He was taken aback when he realised how meagre were the fruits of his day's labour, no more than a few mushrooms, all of the "horn of plenty" variety, maybe a couple of ounces in total which would be reduced to half that when cooked.

Once he had eaten the cheese, he turned to the *prosciutto*. His flask contained a quarter litre of the Barbera which Sante had commended. He gazed up at Montelupo, which resembled an enormous, sweating beast, and thought back to the periods of rest permitted by his father during the hunting season when, seated on a rock or on a tree trunk, they partook of a frugal meal together. Everything was different now, except for Montelupo with its rocky outgrowth. His gaze shifted from mountain to mountain, each one well known to him, until his inspection came to a stop lower down, on the road leading to Villa del Greppo. An ambulance was making its way slowly along the road, and Soneri was reminded of Rivara's words: either it was going slowly because it had no-one on board or because the person on board was beyond help. Two cars followed close behind, and there appeared to be an unusual level of activity around the villa itself. Soneri took a sip of his wine and decided to go straight home, following the slope of the hill. Tiredness overcame him the moment he reached the plain, but by then he was only a stone's throw from the *Scoiattolo*, where Sante was pacing up and down on the courtyard, scarcely noticing his return. When he did see him, he looked at him with a distracted air. The commissario returned the gaze, but Sante continued staring straight ahead, like a blind man.

"All I have to show for a morning's work is about a quarter kilo of 'horns of plenty'."

"Is that what you call them? Do you know the names we use round here for that mushroom? 'The black chanterelle', or even 'the trumpet of death'. That's a better name after what has happened to Palmiro."

"What *has* happened to him? Has he gone missing again?"

"This time it's for good. This morning they found him hanging from a wooden beam in his loggia."

The commissario made no reply. He felt an instinctive need to reason, to put this news into some sort of context but he resisted it. "Do you think it was suicide, or is there more to it?"

Sante's grimace indicated that he did not know. "They say he hammered a huge nail into the wood, tied a rope round it and hanged himself. They found the hammer on the window-sill. He had contrived his own gallows."

"That takes guts," the commissario murmured.

"Palmiro never lacked guts. Once he'd made up his mind, no-one could shift him. He never allowed anything to stand in his way."

"He could have let the cold on Montelupo do the job," Soneri said, while images of the stolen coffin and the sound of shots in the woods played on his mind. Against his better judgement, curiosity was getting the upper hand and he began to put the various facts together. "What do you think made him do it?" he asked Sante.

Sante stopped pacing back and forth and stood still, his back turned to the commissario. He shrugged.

"You told me he was a decisive man, always sure of himself. Someone like that must have had a good reason for killing himself," Soneri said.

Sante turned slowly towards him, embarrassment written clearly on his face. "Who can say? Problems with his busi-ness…" The worries welling up inside Sante prevented him from expressing himself more clearly.

"The salame factory was not going well?"

The only response was another awkward gesture, a clumsy wave as though in an attempt to grab hold of some notion that was proving as elusive as a troublesome fly.

"There are so many rumours in this village. Who really knows what was going on in the Rodolfi household? This place is buzzing with gossip. You can draw your own conclu-sion. I've got a hard enough job keeping on top of my own business."

There was a tone of pain in the last words which Soneri sensed conveyed some deep, personal bitterness. For a few moments the two men stood facing each other in silence until

Ida called to her husband from the doorway of the dining room. She greeted the commissario, but without her customary warmth. He heard the couple exchange some words as they moved inside.

He went up to his room to change. As he came back out, his eyes fell on the basket with the "trumpets of death". He opened it and stared long and hard at the dark mushrooms with their long stems and wide-brimmed caps, not unlike instruments played by the town band. They had the eerie appearance of creatures that come out at dusk in northern climes, or in the dank parts of graveyards. They seemed to bear with them evil tidings, and troubled him so much that he tossed them into a ditch.

It was already growing dark when he went into the village. He saw Maini walking in the piazza, but before he could catch up with him he heard his name called out. It was the mayor coming quickly out of the pharmacy as though he had been lying in wait for him.

"So now something has happened," he began. "It's not just gossip any more."

"A suicide is a private deed. The most private of all," Soneri said.

The mayor was taken aback by this response, leaving the commissario with the strong impression that he did not consider the deed at all private.

"It's not an ordinary suicide. It couldn't be if the man who kills himself is Palmiro Rodolfi."

"In the face of death, we are all equal. As also in the face of despair."

"We've got to understand what drove Palmiro to despair. In my view, it was because of his grandson," the mayor said.

"His grandson?"

"He's turning out to be a problem. He thinks of nothing

but big, flashy cars. He spends money like water and won't do any work. And then lately…" The mayor lowered his voice to a whisper, as though he were in church. "It seems he has started taking drugs."

The commissario thought of the third-generation decadence, corrupted by wealth from birth. "Who found him?"

"His daughter-in-law. She used to go up to his room every morning to check that everything was alright. She loved him like a father."

"So where was his son?"

"It seems it was he who cut him down."

"Seems?"

The mayor spread out his hands. "That's what I've heard, but whether that's exactly what happened…"

"Have the carabinieri questioned Paride?"

"The maresciallo told me that by the time he got there, Paride had already left. They're looking for him, but there's no sign of him yet. His wife says that he's gone to their cabin in the woods, distraught."

"Did anyone see him?"

"Apparently so, but I couldn't tell you who."

Soneri lit a cigar to give himself time to think. The mayor had the same vaguely embarrassed expression he had noted on Sante, but perhaps it was really fear. "So what can I do? I don't get the impression that there's anything to investigate, except why did he do it."

"That's the question everybody's asking," the mayor said.

"In other words, it's a matter for priests or psychologists. Not my line at all."

The mayor made no move. The fog continued to swirl behind him on the far side of the piazza.

"Perhaps you are better informed than I am," Soneri said.

"No, no. I don't know a thing," the mayor said, but he spoke in the guilt-ridden tone of voice the commissario had heard countless times during interrogations in the questura. "All I am asking you to do is consult the maresciallo. I'm not asking you to make any commitments. A courtesy call, that's all."

"A soul in torment," Maini said, indicating the mayor as he walked off, with his crumpled, outsize raincoat flapping around him.

"I don't understand what he wants me to do," the commissario said.

"Everybody in the village wants to understand."

"Understand!" Soneri shook his head in bewilderment. "It seems to me you already know quite a lot. Maybe you're all simply afraid," he said, realising as he did so that he had made a distinction between himself and the rest. He had been aware of the limits of his relationship with them, but now it seemed like a barrier he could not cross. In some ways, he felt liberated from an ambiguity which had become increasingly cumbersome.

Maini pretended not to hear the commissario's words, the common reaction of mountain people to complicated sentiments. Everything would take its course, but every word spoken could be translated into another element of distrust. "He killed himself like the shopkeeper, Capelli," he said at last.

Soneri had heard about the case, but he could no longer remember the details. His amnesia reinforced his sense of being an outsider.

"He too hanged himself from a wooden beam," Maini said.

"He was a ruined man," the commissario said, grasping at some vague memory.

"It was the gambling. After the war he made some money, but it went to his head."

"Did he and Palmiro know each other?"

"That's the point. They were good friends."

At that moment, the commissario's mobile rang. "Angela, could you call me back in five minutes?"

The poor reception meant that he heard no more than a metallic murmur as he switched off his phone. Without either of them suggesting it, Maini and he moved into the *Rivara* bar. Rivara himself watched them take a seat, and joined in the conversation. "He took his own life in the same way as Capelli," he said, and then, turning to the commissario as though to a casual stranger, he added, "you know who I mean, the owner of the cheese shop."

Soneri felt the barrier between him and the villagers grow ever more impassable. "Even the letters they left say the same things," Maini said.

"Nobody knows who was the first to read Capelli's letter. Everyone knew he couldn't read or write, and that made it child's play for them to cheat him with the invoices," the barman said.

"At that time the maresciallo said he believed that Capelli had had it prepared some time before he hanged himself, but there are others who think that it was his creditors who wrote it."

"What does Palmiro's letter say?" Soneri said.

Rivara stretched out his arms, then leant forward and lowered his voice. "One of my regulars who knows a police officer says it was pretty succinct. 'Bury me up on Montelupo, under a juniper bush. That's where I want to be.' Not another word."

"The same as Capelli, who wanted to be taken up to Montelupo, but his wife had him buried in the cemetery, partly because the Comune got involved, and partly because love of money was the only love that kept them together," Maini said.

"Both men loved Montelupo. It was for them the whole world. They used to take their sheep to graze up there, up as far as the big house at Becco. The two of them and the guy known as the Woodsman."

"Ah yes, the famous Woodsman. Now he's the only survivor of that trio," Maini said.

"Because he didn't make any money. Money has been the downfall of so many people," Rivara chimed in.

"Capelli, on the other hand..." Maini said, seemingly rummaging about in his memory, "Capelli started out collecting milk from the farms in his hand cart, then he became a producer of cheese and got other people to do the hard work while he drove about in a Fiat 1500, wearing a tie and selling whole cheeses in the city. It was a huge risk, but he pulled it off."

"The fact is when you come into money all of a sudden, it can be the ruination of you. You think it'll never stop coming," Rivara said.

"It wasn't gambling that did for him so much as the paperwork and his sheer incompetence at it," Maini said. "He knew how much he could afford to lose and he stuck to that, but when they invited him to sign for things instead of paying in cash, he trusted them and they stripped the shirt off his back."

"Downright ignorance is always at the root of it," Rivara said. "Once upon a time they cheated you with phoney invoices, now it's with promissory notes from the bank, shares and bonds, that kind of thing. They tell you to buy and you end up with drawers full of waste paper."

"It's the same old story, the same swindle over and over again," Maini agreed.

"The fat cats devour the mice. Let's not forget that Capelli in his day –"

"Right after the war," Maini nodded.

Rivara threw back his head. "That wasn't the only time. He

did a deal with the Fascists so no detachment of Blackshirts ever went without parmesan to sprinkle on their minestrone. In return, he was left in peace to work the black market, selling his goods to anybody and everybody."

"And he made money hand over fist."

"It was a dirty business, but it always is," Maini said. "With money and the right friends, you can stuff justice."

"What about the Woodsman?" Soneri said.

Rivara laughed. "He had no head for business, and still doesn't. He's at home among the trees with his axe and rifle. That's how he came by the name. He has never moved away from the Madoni hills. He lives there on his own – in abandoned houses that are slowly falling apart. They'll come down altogether one of these winters."

"The original owners all moved away, to Turin, Milan or Parma," Maini said.

"Now he's as wild as the boar. The other two were as bad as he was, but their instinct was to go after money instead of wild animals. They made their fortunes, but then they hanged themselves."

Soneri lit another cigar, while the other two stared at him as though he were performing a conjuring trick.

"Capelli was the sharpest of the three. He was already a rich man at thirty. In the retail market in Parma, he would shift cheese by the ton, all deals done in advance. He had a nose for the business, had the patience to wait for the right moment to buy and sell," Maini said.

"In the last years," Rivara said, "he never actually touched cheese. He had his flunkeys to see to that side of things. He stuck to his office, but when you move away from the world you know and handle nothing but paperwork, you're done for."

"That's right," Maini said. "It was all that form filling that finished him."

Stefano, Rivara's son, came in, nodded in their direction and sat apart, on his own. He had nothing to say, it seemed, but all of a sudden he jumped to his feet and exclaimed, "That lorry, the one that was apparently lost yesterday evening, it loaded up after all, and went off this morning in the direction of the autostrada."

Rivara stopped wiping the bar and said, "He must have been held up by the weather, and no doubt had a deadline to meet."

Stefano shook his head doubtfully. "What about the other two? Were they in a rush as well?"

Rivara and Maini looked at each other in puzzlement, but said nothing.

"This story of the lorries, it's an odd business," the commissario said, in an attempt to keep the discussion going, but no-one had any inclination to break the silence until Maini changed the subject. "How did you get on? Did you fill a basket?"

"I only got a few 'trumpets of death'."

"I don't like them."

"Mushrooms in general or 'trumpets of death' specifically?"

"Neither."

"I can understand why, with a name like that. But they're very good," the commissario said.

"Things that grow in dark places, in the shadows," Maini said.

"Somebody must like them, considering the trouble I had to find any at all."

Maini shrugged. He had nothing else to say.

The mobile rang, relieving the embarrassed silence which had fallen over the group.

"I've waited a quarter of an hour." Angela sounded annoyed.

"We were talking about Palmiro."

"Again? Were you not supposed to be out looking for mushrooms?"

"He's hanged himself."

Angela did not speak for a few seconds. "I would never have expected that. It does not seem in his nature."

"Nobody expected it. It's a very odd business, and I can't make head nor tail of it."

"Well, if you don't understand it, and you're from there…"

"I *used to be* from here," the commissario corrected her. "So much has changed, it's as if I'd never lived here."

"It must be terrible to feel like an outsider in the place you come from. What about the people you know, your friends?"

A sudden, deep unease and a sense of utter futility so overwhelmed Soneri that he found himself lost for words. Angela's questions led him to reflect on the distrust he aroused among those he still considered his own townsfolk, and on the gulf that now existed between him and them. It was as though all those years of friendship and companionship had been snuffed out, even if their common interest in the affairs of the Rodolfi family could briefly disguise that unpleasant feeling of alienation.

"I would have been better escaping to a seaside resort where no-one knows me. I only like the sea in winter when there's nobody there apart from those who really love it."

"It's going to be hard not to get involved now," Angela said.

"The mayor is on at me to go and see the maresciallo, but I'm going to stay away from him at all costs. The fact is that there's nothing to investigate. Palmiro hanged himself and his son, so they say, has shut himself up in the house in the woods where he goes to be alone. Actually, it doesn't seem at all likely to me that he's there, otherwise the carabinieri would have been able to locate him. Anyway, these are hardly criminal acts, and if they were serious crimes, they would not be left to a mere maresciallo. Some high-flyer in the carabinieri would have been sent in forthwith."

"The whole thing stinks," Angela said.

"Like a rotting carcass. I expect developments."

"I could work on the lawyer who looks after the Rodolfi affairs, and pass any information on to you."

"What do you mean, 'work on the lawyer'?"

"How do you work on a man? You ought to know."

"Like you're doing just now, to make me jealous."

"A waste of time. You never fall for it. However, I have a good relationship with the lawyer in question and I could get him to tell me something. Tomorrow the papers will be full of Palmiro's suicide."

"Exactly, and your man of the law will button up."

"If he stays buttoned up, you've no reason to be jealous," Angela said slyly.

Soneri had no time to put his mobile away before seeing the maresciallo coming towards him. His first thought was to slip back into the bar and pretend he had not seen him, but the maresciallo gave him a wave, compelling Soneri to stop and wait for him.

The officer introduced himself with a jovial smile. "Maresciallo Crisafulli," he announced with an officer's precision and a cadet's stiff pose. He was the same height as the commissario, had dark skin, black hair and bright, sparkling eyes. "They tell me you're the only man who can find mushrooms in this season," he said.

"I'm not so sure about that," Soneri said with a smile, unsure of whether to interpret the remark as friendly or ingenuous.

"I know nothing about them. I can hardly tell the difference between lettuce and tomatoes. I'm a city man, from Naples."

"So how did you end up here?"

"If you want to get on and earn a bit more, you've got to put up with some time in Purgatory. At least it's quiet round here, and you don't run risks. Apart from the climate!"

"It's become a bit more risky of late, has it not?"

The maresciallo glanced over his shoulder before saying, "I *am* a bit worried about this situation."

"You'll know more about it than me."

"Not at all. When I was talking to the mayor, it occurred to me that I ought to ask your advice, seeing you're from these parts and you're off duty at the moment. After all, even if they all respect me, I'm still a carabiniere officer from the south of Italy. You get my point?"

Soneri nodded. "Don't imagine I'm any better off. The only advantage I have over you is that I understand the dialect and I know the names of the mountains and some of the places. I've been away from here too long."

Crisafulli pointed to the *Rivara*. "Would you like a coffee?"

Soneri gave a distracted nod before asking, "Have you seen Paride?"

"I haven't personally, but my colleagues are out looking for him. The family say he's in his house, but that he's too upset over his father's death and won't answer either the door or the telephone."

Soneri made no reply as the barman placed a cup of espresso before each of them.

The maresciallo started up again. "What worries me is not so much what has happened to the Rodolfis. It's all the rest."

"The village has the feel of a place awaiting sentence," the commissario said, lighting upon an image connected with the work of both men.

Crisafulli allowed a smile to flicker briefly on his lips. "They're all scared shitless. They're afraid of anything that might happen to the Rodolfis; and their well-being is tied up with the fate of the Rodolfi family."

"They're in deep trouble now that the old man has hanged himself."

"Palmiro hasn't been in charge for some while now. It's his son who's been running the business."

"And once he gets over the shock, he'll pick himself up and it's business as usual, isn't that right?"

The maresciallo drank his coffee in one gulp, put down the cup and looked out at the dying day. "Commissario, maybe it is as you say, but you know perfectly well that it doesn't add up. Don't those posters make you wonder? And wasn't it strange how the old man disappeared, then turned up, and then hanged himself from a noose he made for himself? And what about those gunshots? We're not deaf."

"I was witness myself to one of those shots only yesterday. It missed me by a couple of metres."

"Where?" said the maresciallo in evident alarm.

"Above Boldara," Soneri said, noting that the maresciallo had no idea where Boldara was.

"You see? And each time we've investigated, we have not been able to find one single clue. Never even an empty shell."

"Listen, Crisafulli, I agree with you that the whole business is troubling, but you know as well as I do that all this is just so much hot air until you have got proof that someone is actually committing a crime."

"Of course I know that, and that's exactly why I am asking you for advice, maybe even to give a hand. I am afraid that something really serious is going to happen here, do you understand?" He spoke in a whisper to prevent anyone overhearing. "Prevention is better than cure, don't you think?"

Soneri nodded. "If you're sick, you go and consult a doctor, but who is there for people around here to consult?"

"No-one. Maybe I worry too much, but if you could see your way to..."

Soneri finished his coffee, pushed the cup out of his way, put his elbows on the table, leaned over towards Crisafulli and said in a low voice, "What do you know about the Rodolfis?"

"I have been hearing that for a good while salaries have not been paid on time, but each and every one of the people who works for them denies that there's anything amiss. They say it's always been that way, that there's more work than ever, both in the abattoir and in the meat-curing plant. There was talk of speculations on the stock market going badly, but nothing has turned up in reports from colleagues who operate in the financial sector."

"What about Paride's son? They say he's a complete wastrel."

"People exaggerate. He's a spoiled brat who squanders money on cars and gets up to various kinds of mischief, but I don't think he's any different from other rich men's sons."

"Well then, what is there to investigate?" Soneri said, with a touch of relief in his voice. "I said as much to the mayor. It looks to me like a familiar situation. A village where gossip is rife and now it has a couple of mysteries to feed on."

Crisafulli wriggled uncomfortably in his seat, unconvinced but incapable of putting his doubts into words.

Maini, Rivara and his son were all silent too, giving Soneri the unpleasant feeling of being under observation. The maresciallo rose to his feet, picked up his cap and stretched out his hand. "It's been a pleasure," he said, but there was no concealing his disappointment. "Drop by the police station some time."

The commissario watched him leave, marching out as though he were on a parade ground. He thought about how deeply feelings counted in an enquiry. The problem was that even if your feelings kept you focused, they were liable to evaporate under cross-questioning. As he saw Crisafulli disappear in the mists on the piazza, he imagined his state of mind. He himself had often been in that same condition of anxiety, expecting something dire to happen. It was like waiting for a sneeze that did not come, feeling a symptom without an illness or groping for a handhold before a fall.

His stomach rumbled, causing him to jump to his feet. He looked over at the others and saw the bar in a new light, as if he had just awoken from a deep sleep. He remembered he had had only a light lunch of parmesan and *prosciutto*, and decided it was time to move on to the *Scoiattolo*.

Half the dining area was sunk in darkness. Two men were immersed in an intense conversation at one of the few tables which had been laid. Sante had the same worried air as that morning and displayed the same awkward concern. After finishing off their dish of wild boar and polenta, the only other two diners left. Sante was now fluttering nervously around Soneri like a planet on an irregular orbit. Finally, he sat down opposite him, looked hard at him and asked, "What did you do with your mushrooms?"

The commissario was taken aback by the question, particularly since it was spoken in a whisper, as though they were in a sacristy. "I threw them into a ditch," he said lightly.

He had the impression that Sante breathed a sigh of relief. "People believe that they're a warning of evil times, and with this business over Palmiro...I've never believed all that nonsense myself, but you're the first person who's found 'trumpets of death' this year, and on the very day he put a rope round his neck."

"I never thought of you as superstitious. They're just mushrooms like any others. And they're very tasty," Soneri sought to reassure him.

"A lot of people here in the village pull them out of the ground the moment they see them. They say it brings good luck and wards off misfortune."

"Rubbish!"

Sante stared at him, doubtful but desperate to be convinced. Soneri took out his cigars and offered one to Sante. They lit them from the same match, turning them slowly around the flame and then sitting in silence to savour the aroma. For the moment, no words were needed, but the silence soon became oppressive, and sitting face to face became embarrassing. If Sante chose to remain there, he must have a reason, but Soneri had no inkling of what he wanted to say. Once again, he was dealing with impressions, the very things which tormented Crisafulli. He was sure there was something Sante wanted to talk to him about, but he knew that if he asked him, he would immediately deny it, leaving the commissario, like Crisafulli, burdened by feelings but having no proof.

The arrival of Ida from the kitchen put an end to the awkwardness.

"Not much doing this evening," Soneri said.

"Everybody's in such a rush. There's not been much work for a few weeks now, but I've no idea why."

"A dead period."

"Well, who knows? There really never are dead periods, it just looks as though people have given up eating. There are even fewer lorry-drivers around. You would swear they've changed their routes."

"And this all happened only recently?"

The two of them looked at each other in silence, until Ida took the initiative. "The problems started when word got out about the Rodolfis."

"What have they got to do with it?"

"They're very important here, for the economy especially."

Soneri nodded, while Ida looked at her husband with growing anxiety. She was clearly in a hurry, but to do what? Sante peered at her nervously, but something prevented him from speaking.

"The money…" he began, but the words seemed to choke him. He blushed and his voice trailed off.

His wife was obviously keen to take up the story, but she bit her tongue. Respect for deep-seated traditions meant that it had to be the husband who did the talking. Sante made one more attempt, but seemed to be restrained by the complexity of what he had to say as well as by some sort of shame. Finally, his wife burst out, "Come on, tell him the whole story."

Under pressure, the man started to mumble. "I've been trying to tell him ever since he arrived."

The commissario made a gesture to encourage him to go on.

"It's to do with money," Sante said.

Another gesture from Soneri, meaning to convey that he had guessed as much all along. "Money or sex," was the endlessly repeated mantra of Nanetti, head of the forensic squad: that's what it always came down to.

"In this village, everyone knows everybody else, there's trust…" Sante began again, following a delicate line of thought which was probably so intricate it could not be set out without some confusion.

Ida gave her husband an angry look, and Soneri too found himself becoming impatient with this stopping and starting, but Sante still needed a long run up before he was able to leap forward.

"We all trust them," he said, picking his way with great care.

"The fact is, we gave him some money," Ida said, with an abruptness which sounded like a slap in the face.

Her husband was grateful for her help. "Have you ever heard of 'nursemaid' money?" he asked, finally free of embarrassment.

Soneri nodded. "A form of loan."

"That's right," Sante said, pointing with a finger as though the money were lying in front of them on the table.

"And now you're all worried about your money?"

"We still have trust, but all these rumours..."

"Did you give him a lot of money?"

Sante looked up at his wife, furrowing his brow as though he had endured a stab of pain.

"Yes, a lot," he said, without specifying the amount. "And we weren't the only ones," he added, as though that were an excuse.

"Who else?"

"Many people, more than you could imagine. But there's no point in you trying to draw up a list, because they'd never tell you."

"Why should they not?"

"People never talk about their own affairs."

"But you have."

"You're from these parts, even if you've no idea what life around here is like nowadays. Besides, we're relatives, distant relatives, but still relatives."

The commissario nodded again, knowing he would never have been able to trace the contorted links between the families.

"In spite of that, it's not easy for me to talk. It's that the very thought..."

"I don't see why."

"Because I feel I've made a wretched mess of everything," Sante burst out, with despair in his eyes.

"You told me you still had trust. Have you lost it now?"

"As long as Palmiro was there...He was the same as us. He spoke in dialect. But now...?"

"And we can't rest for thinking about how he died," Ida broke in. "We would never ever have dreamed that a man like Palmiro would have hanged himself."

"That's what they always say about suicides."

"Yes, but you didn't know the man! He was as much a ladies' man as when he was in his twenties. Some people would swear that he and his daughter-in-law..."

"Shut up!" Sante tried to interrupt his wife. "What are you saying?"

Ida stopped, but her expression was of out-and-out malice, and this was the most telling of judgments.

"Who was it who asked you for the money, Palmiro or Paride?"

"Paride keeps well away. It was Palmiro who came. It was his job to do the rounds. He'd kept in touch from the days when he started up the dairy business."

"What guarantees did he offer?"

Sante gave another shrug. "I told you. It's all to do with trust. We wrote the transactions and the dates down in a notebook and he added his scribble and that was that."

The commissario's expression must have shown his concern, because he saw Sante bow his head. "You do know that a mark like that is not worth a thing?"

Sante nodded.

"How long has this been going on?"

"Many years now," Ida said, accompanying the words with a wave of the hand which was meant to say that it was a long established practice.

"If it's been going so well for all this time, what makes you so scared now?" the commissario said.

Sante's expression lightened for a moment, but his dark mood returned as he started speaking. "As I've explained, because of Palmiro's death. Nobody thought...and that son of his who's never here…the few times we've actually seen him he would speak in big words we couldn't understand. He is used to discussions with bankers and financiers who handle money all day long. Many of them turned up at his villa and we were expected to bring them food we had made ourselves. We didn't get on with them."

"I can understand the question of trust, but to lend money blindly like that…"

Sante heaved a deep sigh and looked at his wife. It seemed that merely talking about it made him the more fearful of impending ruin.

"Palmiro had a way of convincing us. He repeated always the same thing. If we grow, you grow, the whole village grows. Who could quarrel with that? After the war, the poverty here was terrible. He made us feel like traitors if we refused him."

"Tell him about the interest," Ida hissed, without looking at her husband.

Sante sighed once more. "Well, he paid more than the banks."

"Much more?"

"It depends. You had to bargain with him as though you were buying a batch of cheese. If you seemed to hesitate, he would increase the rate he was offering, then he would do the sums in his head and tell you how much you would gain after five, ten or fifteen years. It was hard to resist."

"He was a right sly one in business," Ida said, cutting the air with her hand.

"Did you ever see any returns?"

"If you insisted, Palmiro would settle up. It did happen a few times, but in the majority of cases, he wouldn't let go. 'If you give me the money for five years more, I'll raise the rate by half a per cent,' he would say. Then he would churn out numbers that made your head spin."

"So you're saying that no-one withdrew their money?"

"Virtually everyone round here can manage, so the money they gave him was money they were putting by for their children, or to keep themselves in comfort in old age, or just out of prudence. In this village, they're great savers. They might live in hovels, but having some savings makes them feel more secure."

Soneri could hear his own father talk of his fears for some "tomorrow" when anything might happen. The peasants always feared hailstones, or drought, or an outbreak of foot and mouth disease. "I'm sure Paride will do the right thing," were the only words the commissario could find to reassure his hosts.

"Well, let us hope so," Sante groaned, without conviction.

Soneri rose to go to bed, but Sante's almost imploring look detained him a minute longer. "What can I do?" he said.

Sante murmured, "Nothing."

4

Even before daybreak, the skies seemed to have shed their earlier heaviness. Soneri left the road between the houses, keeping Montelupo, still cloaked in a thick mist, directly ahead of him. He walked past the shuttered houses in Groppo and turned off to start his climb towards Croce, hoping to find some ceps in the more shaded areas which would be still damp with the dew falling from leafless trees. He came in sight of the chapel of the Madonna del Rosario, a place of pilgrimage in the month of May, and proceeded through the tangled vegetation which flourished in the clay of the lower valley and gave off the pungent scents of the wild. Before moving into the hornbeam woods, he stopped to get his breath. The last houses were now out of sight, and within the woods he felt himself both hunter and prey. When he looked up, he could make out wisps of mist clinging so closely to the peaks as to resemble smoke from a fire. Above the path, a sandstone balcony had crumbled under the pressure of the mountain streams and had slipped down into the valley, creating a deep scar in the woods.

If he had had sufficient strength in his legs, he would have already been at the mountain huts and perhaps even at the bar on Lake Santo which was not far from the peak, but first he wanted to reconnoitre the hillside and the watery gullies where the weak winter sun could not penetrate. He gripped the trunks of trees as he clambered down, trying to recall movements he had learned so many years earlier in outings with his father. The third time he fell, he saw them: a colony of "trumpets of death" seeming to intone a *miserere* in the shadow of an enormous oak.

Sante's words rang in his ears, but he refused to be put off. His principal concern was finding someone able to cook those mushrooms the right way. He left them where they were when he heard the sound of something crashing about in the undergrowth close at hand, knocking into the lower branches of the trees. He decided it must be a wild boar, sniffing the air and detecting his presence. Soneri stood stock still, listening, and then, straight in front of him, he saw a strip of land which gave the appearance of having been ploughed. He swept aside the leaves and uncovered a second family of "trumpets of death", crushed into tiny pieces by blows from a club. Evidently there was someone who did believe they were omens of ill fortune. Shortly afterwards, he heard the brushwood breaking as the boar made off. Once he was sure the beast was well away, he returned to the path, from which it was now impossible to see down into the valley.

A thick blanket of mist came down, turning the countryside grey. The huts could not be far off, but he was fearful of getting lost, and afraid too of those shots fired at some target, whatever that target was meant to be. At last he saw the outlines of the stone buildings, sheds for climbing equipment and summer dwellings in the mountaineering season when the passes echoed with the many languages used in that borderland between sea and plain. Inside one of them rubbish was scattered all around – empty cans, broken bottles, plastic bags and the remains of tinned food – but the ash in the fireplace and the crumpled bedclothes on the wooden bench were evidence of some recent presence.

When he stepped back outside, the mist had lifted and this made him resolve to carry on. It was eleven o'clock, so he would have time to reach Lake Santo, see if the bar was open and make his way back, even if this meant another day without a single cep being picked. He quickened his pace along the mule path, coming out into the pure air of the clearing with the bar, high up the mountainside, beyond the point where the wood gave way to moss and stone. It was cold, and it occurred to Soneri that the first snows of winter could not be far off. This thought and the sight of the remote bar made him think of his father with that lurching gait of his, as if he were pushing himself forward by putting pressure on one leg, a habit which spoke of experience gained over a lifetime of grim, debilitating hardship.

Even in the dying days of autumn, the bar was open. Baldi, the owner, was still behind the counter, not yet ready to close up for the season. He was short and sturdy, with white hair and moustache.

The two men exchanged greetings, before Soneri said: "Are there still many hunters around?"

"The season's nearly over."

"What about the roe deer?"

"Not much doing. They've got cleverer and go down the valley into the reserve."

"And the trout in the lake?"

"They're not biting any more. You would swear they feel winter coming on."

"Same as us. When do you shut up shop?"

"Any day now. Or at the first snow fall – which is more or less the same thing."

"You think the snow's nearly here?"

"Feel the air. There's frost every morning now."

Two shabbily dressed men came into the bar. One of

them, in a heavy foreign accent, asked for two coffees and two grappas.

"Nowadays we have to put up with all kinds of foreign wildlife," Baldi said contemptuously, but speaking in dialect so that he would not be understood.

"What do they do here?" Soneri said. "I saw that other people had been down at the huts."

"Everything and nothing. They come from Liguria and Tuscany with all kinds of stuff. I've even seen some of them struggling up here with suitcases."

"Are the carabinieri aware of this?"

Baldi shrugged his shoulders. "Occasionally they come to make checks, but by the time they get here, everything seems to be in order. These people bury whatever they have in the woods."

"Who do they sell it to?"

"Well, you hear so many stories. They pass it on to other people who take it to the cities. Some of it's given to the kids in the village. They're at it now too."

"Drugs? Around here?"

Baldi gave another shrug. "Everything's changed. They get bored. The winters are long, there's nothing to occupy their minds, so they look for something different. If they'd ever known hunger, like this lot..." Baldi said, indicating the strangers with his chin.

Soneri's thoughts went back to his father, setting off for work with three pears and a crust of bread for his midday meal. He changed the subject. "Do you see the Woodsman from time to time?"

"He hasn't been here for a while. The woods are his world. Here, it's too open for his tastes. When you reach a certain altitude, the mountain's no good for keeping secrets. You can see everything that's going on, even if there are very few people watching."

Soneri took his time to decipher those words, the time needed to light a cigar, but he still failed fully to grasp their sense.

"What does he do that anyone might watch?" the commissario said, instinctively, without thinking.

Another shrug. "Nothing, but he wouldn't find out here what he finds in the woods."

"You mean the wild boar?"

Smiling, Baldi looked at him and murmured, "Yes, the boar."

Soneri understood there was more to it, but he chose not to ask. It would have been in vain, but he was left with the disagreeable feeling of having been outwitted.

"Nobody knows Montelupo like him. He reckons he owns it. Who's going to get the better of him? Delrio? Volpi?" Baldi spoke with a sneer in his voice.

The two foreigners got up, paid their bill and were gone. The commissario had watched as the one who had done the ordering took out a thick wodge of notes and peeled one off, as the fixers and middlemen who had once been active in those parts used to do.

"There's no telling who's coming and going on these mountains nowadays," Baldi said.

"Are you sometimes afraid?"

"I've got my gun under the counter, and my aim's as good as ever."

A light haze was hanging over the lake, like steam from a pot coming to the boil.

"Have you heard what's going on in the village?" Soneri said.

"Palmiro? It's terrible. I would never have thought of him hanging himself. Did you know that he and the Woodsman were good friends?"

The commissario shook his head. "I knew he was a friend of Capelli's, and he too ended up with his head in a noose."

"The only one of the trio left is the Woodsman. They were all from the Madoni hills, raised in the poorest families in the valleys. They knew what it was to go hungry, and they were all desperate to get out."

"Do you think the Woodsman too could kill himself?"

"Not unless he's cornered. When his time comes, he'll lie down in the woods and the worms will get to him before the dogs do. He's happy in his world and he's never cared for money."

"Where can I find him?"

"Somewhere on Montelupo. He only goes home when it's dark, that is, unless he decides to rough it in some hideout for the night. Your only hope is that you'll bump into him on some path. If he's in the mood, he'll talk to you, and if not he'll slip away the moment he catches sight of you."

"How does he live?"

"He's never short of meat," Baldi chuckled. "Apart from that, he sells firewood and charcoal. He's the only one left who can make it."

"Did he stay in touch with Palmiro?"

"I don't think there was much contact. They would run into each other on Montelupo, but they had grown apart. Money creates boundaries that aren't easy to cross. It's true that once they were inseparable, but then Palmiro married Evelina. The Woodsman and Capelli both had their eye on her, so the friendship between them was bust."

"The same old story, women…"

"There's more to it than that. Palmiro's money was what made up her mind. Not that Capelli was short of cash, but he spent it on whores."

"Was this Evelina really so beautiful?"

"They were all after her in those days, and the Woodsman completely lost his head over her. They say she was quite keen on him too. He had more of a spark to him than the other two, but then her parents persuaded her to make the most of her good looks. Was she really going to go off and live in a den in the woods when she had the chance of marrying a man who could show her the good life?"

"But you are sure she was more fond of the other one?"

Baldi gave a guffaw and rose to his feet. He produced a bottle of Malvasia and two glasses. "When they're pitched against self-interest, fine feelings are as much good as a two in a card game. A pretty face has its value, doesn't it? Why undersell it?"

This time it was the commissario's turn to shrug. "Money can't make up for an unhappy life."

"You get used to anything," snorted Baldi. "Humans are the most adaptable of all animals."

"Anyway, the Woodsman took it badly."

"Very badly. He believed she wanted him. And also because for the first time the companion with whom he had shared so much had stolen something important from him. But what really got him was the realisation that the two of them were different. Palmiro's thoughts were elsewhere, on his business in the big city, on buying pigs and selling *prosciutto*. The Woodsman, on the other hand, imagined that the bond formed when they both had nothing would never be broken. The result was that he never really grew out of adolescence, while Palmiro became harder and more dour as he focused more and more on his own interests."

"It's always that way with people who have feelings and people who only care about things," Soneri said, his eyes still fixed on the lake and its smooth surface with its light veil of mist.

Baldi gave another laugh. "I've never been persuaded by all this talk of feelings. The Woodsman was on heat for Evelina, and she had the same effect on the other two. That's all there was to it. Nobody in this world ever wants to call things by their proper name, so we have all this drivel about love and rubbish of that sort."

Soneri reflected for a moment, and was disconcerted to find himself largely in agreement. When he thought of Angela, he could not conceal from himself the physical desire he felt for her, but he had never really understood what love was and where it differed from simple liking. There was no more ambiguous or trite word in the language.

He sat lost in thought for a few moments, while Baldi poured them what was left of the Malvasia and put away the bottle before preparing to close. The commissario looked round the room. The clock on the wall told him it was already one o'clock.

"It's late. I'll need to head back down before it's too dark or too misty to see."

"You've got until four before the dark draws in. With the mist, it's a more of a gamble."

At the door, Soneri turned round. "Do you hear the gunshots up here too?"

"Nearly every day. Always from half way down the slope."

"Do you think it's poachers, or could it be the Woodsman?"

"Who knows? The Woodsman sets traps and the poachers won't go out in this mist."

"So?"

Baldi's face was expressionless as he gave yet another shrug. "Come back again," he shouted after him. "I'll be open for another week at least."

Soneri struggled to keep his footing. He slipped and slithered downhill towards the huts. The soft ground and the layer of fallen leaves muffled the sound of his footsteps. He glanced inside as he passed, but there was no sign of a living soul, so he pressed on almost at a run in the direction of the valley until he came to the path over the short grass of the upper mountain. He saw the woods a little way off, and when he entered them, a bank of mist made it almost impossible to see. Everything was a blur, and fear gripped him by the throat. He had no choice but to slow down. He remembered his father's advice: always keep moving downwards, because every descent leads to a valley where there will be either a stream or a riverbed; follow the water and you are bound to find a house. After walking for about half an hour, the mist suddenly lifted. He had strayed off the path but not by much, so he had no problem finding his way again. He made the best of the remaining daylight, even if it was fading as the afternoon wore on.

He was walking through a copse of chestnut trees when the mist came down again. The drops from the trees were like rainfall, and he could feel the moisture on his moustache. As he was pulling up the hood of his duffel coat, he heard an explosion on the far side of a ridge from which one rock stuck out like a wisdom tooth. The drifting mist parted a little and the commissario quickened his pace to get away from what looked to him like a firing range. He saw a light shining higher up and that increased his alarm. He crouched down, looking in the direction from which the shot seemed to have come, but all he saw were puffs of mist rising, tossing about in the breeze and rubbing against the tops of the trees. He set off again at a run and arrived in Groppo bathed in sweat. When he reached the road, he was exhausted and famished. Back at the *Scoiattolo*, he went straight up to his room.

He found Sante when he came down. He deduced from his expression that he did not have good news to impart. "A new carabiniere has arrived," he said.

"Officer or lower ranks?"

"A captain."

Soneri digested this news for a moment. "Does this mean there have been developments?"

"I know nothing, but if they've sent someone important, it means there must have been some big developments. And I have no reason to believe that's good news for us."

"Maybe Crisafulli wants to wash his hands of the whole business."

"Could be," Sante said, but he sounded doubtful. "In addition to all that, another two lorries were here last night and loaded up without the help of local labour."

"Who saw them?"

"I did. My head was buzzing with all those things I was telling you about, so I couldn't sleep. I went up to the loft and looked out of the window. I saw them arrive, load up and set off again. Six men in total. All over and done with in less than three hours."

"The ones who normally work there know nothing about what's going on?"

"They say it's business as usual. No change."

Soneri shook his head, indicating his bewilderment.

Sante changed the subject. "No mushrooms, then?"

"The only ones I found were the ones you don't like."

Sante furrowed his brow. "More 'trumpets of death'? They're the only ones anyone's found this year."

"You all detest them, but there's at least one person who won't leave them for the boar."

"They're a harbinger of bad times. And in fact..." Sante's voice trailed off as he raised his hand in an eloquent gesture.

Ida called him into the kitchen. The commissario stood where he was for a few moments, savouring the smells coming from the pots, then went out into the mist with its very different scents, the scents of the woods. He walked towards the piazza where he saw Maini in conversation with Volpi and Delrio at the window of the *Rivara* bar. Delrio was in uniform and gesticulating wildly. Soneri walked straight on in the hope of finding old Magnani in the *Olmo*. He could not get the story of the Woodsman out of his head, but before he got there, he ran into Crisafulli in the colonnade outside the Comune.

"Just the man I was looking for," the maresciallo began. "I went to the *Scoiattolo*, but you weren't there."

The commissario now understood how Sante had heard about the arrival of the captain. "I was foraging for mushrooms, and doing my best to avoid gunfire," he said, with a smile on his lips.

Crisafulli knew at once what he was referring to, and was obviously troubled by it. "We heard it too. At 3.24."

"Do you record them all?"

"We certainly do. We have a file. So far, we've counted sixteen, but there might be more. Whoever does the shooting always picks up the shells. We haven't yet managed to find even one. All we have are some marks on tree trunks made by large-calibre rounds from a hunting rifle."

"You've obviously looked into it deeply. These bullets are not toys. They're meant to kill."

"They're devastating. You should see the poor beasts when they've been hit by one. However, that's not the real news."

"I hear they've sent a captain."

The maresciallo looked at Soneri in surprise. "Who told you?"

"You told me to be alert, Maresciallo, did you not? I am only obeying orders."

"After reading my report, they've sent along a Captain Bovolenta." Crisafulli's tone made it clear that he had no wish to pursue the subject.

"Crisafulli, you are the very first investigator I have met who doesn't give a damn about his career. This might turn into a really big case, so you should have played it close to your chest. Do you have any idea of how this could all blow up? You might have ended up on television."

"I've got three children, Commissario. This is a great place to bring them up. They're happy here, and I'm always worried they might transfer me to some big city."

"You're right. Who gives a damn?" Soneri said, beginning to like the man. After all, they saw things the same way.

"There's another reason why the captain is here," Crisafulli said.

"I guessed as much. I know the carabinieri, and they would never send in an officer unless there was something more to it than an unspecific fear."

"It seems Paride Rodolfi can't pay back a loan."

"To the banks?"

"The banks in their turn have passed the loan on to their clients. Believe me, I'm out of my depth here. Bonds, defaults…it's Arabic to me. I can hardly understand my own current account."

"Nor can I. It's one of the most complicated things on earth," Soneri conceded. "Does this mean they're close to bankruptcy?"

"No, the family lawyer put out a statement saying that they will be able to pay. He says it's only a cash-flow problem and he gave an assurance that the money is there."

"What's the name of the Rodolfis' lawyer?"

"Mario Gennaro."

"Is there not a managing director, or a chairman?"

"The chairman was Palmiro Rodolfi, and the managing director is his son, Paride."

"And where is he?"

"To be honest, I have no idea. His wife is still saying he's in their house in the woods, but I think she's been lying to us from the outset. Either that, or she doesn't know herself, considering her stormy relations with her husband. Apparently they went weeks without seeing each other. Their lawyer thinks he might have gone somewhere to resolve this question of the bonds. He believes the company has money in a foreign account in one of those countries where you don't pay taxes, and he has gone to sort things out."

"Is it possible that no-one knows anything? Have you spoken to the people who work for the Rodolfis?"

"They say that everything's above board, and they do seem extraordinarily calm. I had a quiet word with the managers of the branches of the banks in the village and they all insist that the Rodolfi company is in solid shape and that if it gets more funds, it will be in a position to start expanding again. As recently as yesterday, they were selling bonds issued by the company and they were going like hot cakes."

"It's either one hell of a mess or else it's a bubble," Soneri said.

"At the moment, it's a bubble, but I'm going to leave it to Bovolenta. That way, if it bursts, he'll scuttle off, keeping his head down. If it's a mess, I'll be here to pick up the pieces," Crisafulli said, winking at Soneri.

The commissario had believed he was dealing with one of life's innocents, but now found himself facing a Neapolitan on the make.

The fragrance of the atmosphere in the *Olmo* was a pleasing mixture of the wood fire and the unfiltered cigarettes Magnani was smoking as he dozed behind the bar. This time there were more people there, some leaning their backs against the wall as if they were in the piazza in summer. When the commissario came in they all fell silent, like schoolboys at the appearance of the teacher. Their expressions were a combination of respect and distrust and that made him feel even more of an outsider in the village where everything made him think of his parents and his childhood. He looked around at faces he recognised, but on which time had laid a crust of suspicious hostility.

"No shortage of customers this evening," Soneri greeted Magnani.

"In these parts, there's no hospice so the *Olmo* takes its place," Magnani sniggered, with a touch of bitterness. "As for me, I'm half-way between the two."

The commissario waved away this solemn line of thought.

"I'm not much younger than your poor father," Magnani said.

The phrase struck Soneri. He saw himself once again as a boy in a bar full of young people, holding in his hand the chocolate ice-cream his father would buy him on Saturdays. He bent almost double, as though he had just been punched, and anxiety brought on a pain in his chest like an ache from a bruise, leaving him struggling for a moment to catch his breath.

Magnani noticed this and remained silent, waiting for it to pass. In the room, all the others had gone back to chatting or playing cards.

"This is the first day there's been no talk of the Rodolfis," Magnani said, to take Soneri's mind off his sorrows.

"Has the son been seen?"

"His wife has. She was at the pharmacy and it seems she said Paride would be back in a matter of days. He had to leave suddenly to attend to some urgent business, but he would rather have spent a few days on his own after his father's death."

"He's got problems repaying some loan or other," the commissario said.

"Huh, that's a risk we all run…" but he stopped short as another thought darkened his mood. "Last night, three youngsters were killed in a village near here."

"What happened?"

"Car accident. They were out their minds with drugs. Is there a more stupid way to die?"

"They had their whole lives ahead of them…" the commissario said, in a fatalistic tone. "And then they take some of that stuff…"

"So I've heard. I blame the immigrants who've brought us nothing but trouble."

"They can only sell what other people want to buy. I didn't know that sort of thing went on here."

"They've got everything they could want, but they get bored. The television does their heads in. They've never walked as far as the woods in their lives, and they won't even think about taking up their parents' businesses. As soon as they can, they're out of here, and the only ones that stay are the idiots, and not all of them either."

He broke off to take some wine from a glass he kept under the bar, but he had worked himself into a temper. "Montelupo's going to the dogs. There's no-one left who's willing to clear the ditches, to attend to the drains or look after the woodland. Instead of going to gather firewood, they switch on the gas. Do you know what it is? They have too much money and they spend it on things they could get for free, whereas the rest of us," he continued, sweeping his hand around the room, "we're not capable of anything any more, and we spend day after day yapping about nothing. That's our curse, and we'll die of it."

"There's still the Woodsman roaming about on Montelupo."

Magnani's face lit up. "He's the only one who's got any spunk, but he's surrounded by that rabble of foreigners. They should all be sent packing."

"I don't believe they ever meet up. Neither side is much good at conversation."

"They might not meet up, but he doesn't like them just the same. The woods are for working in. They're not a hiding place."

"I go searching for mushrooms. That's not work."

"Oh yes it is. There are men who earn their living looking for truffles, although this year..." Magnani said, shaking his head.

"All you can find this year are 'trumpets of death'," the commissario said.

"Nobody here eats them. They bring bad luck."

"Talking about deaths," Soneri said, changing the subject, "did anybody ever find anything about that coffin that turned up on San Martino?"

"No, nobody came forward to claim it. After a while the priest said it was cluttering up the chapel and that it had to be moved somewhere."

"So what became of it?"

Magnani appeared flustered and unsure of himself. He started to say something but then stopped. Faced with the commissario's calm but unflinching look, he muttered, "They put Palmiro in it."

It occurred to Soneri that there might be something more than coincidence at work here, but Magnani started up again: "They took full advantage...a beautiful casket, glossy chestnut wood...it was the daughter-in-law who gave permission, but it seems Paride was in agreement as well."

The commissario shook his head. The whole story seemed grotesque. Something ugly was unravelling, beneath the appearance of normality.

"It seemed a funny business to me too," Magnani said, guessing at what was in Soneri's mind. "But if you think about it, there's nothing really out of place. There's a coffin without an owner and nowhere to put it. There's a corpse which has to be buried. Why not put the two together? There are some people in this village who bought their coffins ten years ago, and in the meantime they use them to store wheat."

"It all seemed so random," Soneri said. "What's so strange is that the facts all line up, like the pearls on a necklace, and in real life that never happens."

Magnani shrugged. "Come on…when the devil gets to work…"

Soneri shook his head once more to indicate his resolute scepticism, then, as with Baldi, he asked Magnani, "Where can I find the Woodsman?"

Magnani waved his hands about. "Where would you find a buzzard? The skies might be bigger than Montelupo, but it is easier to hide on Montelupo."

"There must be one or two places where he is more likely to turn up?"

"I'd try the area round Lake Bicchiere, or Malpasso. Or you could try the cabins in Badignana."

"They're all quite a way off."

"He tramps around, and he has his own dens, where occasionally he spends the night. He's like a wild animal. He's not afraid of anything. His father once punched some high-ranking Fascist official to shut him up."

Magnani spoke of the incident with pride. Evidently the Woodsman was all he himself had never managed to be.

"What's he like? Physically, I mean."

"A beast, all one hundred and ten kilos of him. He could kill you with one punch. He's as solid as a safe."

"So it would be hard to miss him."

"He always wears the felt hat of the Alpino regiment, with the feather."

"Does he ever come here?"

"He leaves it to his daughter to come down to the village. He's completely antisocial."

"Ever since Palmiro and Capelli abandoned him. Is that right?" the commissario said, inhaling the smoke from the cigar he had lit while talking.

"Well, a great many things originate there. Before those two got rich, they were all as thick as thieves. Once the Woodsman saved Palmiro's life, up on Lake Bicchiere. He'd fallen in because he'd failed to notice a crack in the ice, which collapsed under him. The Woodsman stretched out full length on his belly, risking going under himself, and dragged Palmiro to safety by brute force. From that time on, Palmiro made him a present of some money every year, at Christmas, on the anniversary."

"Even recently? Seeing that things are not going too well?"

"What were a couple of coins to him? And anyway, who says things are not going so well? I've heard that the Rodolfis have millions and millions salted away in some fund somewhere."

"And he could always turn to the villagers," Soneri said.

Magnani stopped short, as though he had been stung by a wasp. "Not much hope there. You won't get much from a village of peasants and shopkeepers, and one way or another they all work for the Rodolfis now."

"Palmiro must have come here," the commissario said, tentatively.

"This was his bar. He always came here until the other one opened," Magnani said, with unmistakable resentment.

The door swung open and an old woman came in pushing a wheelchair with a man wrapped in a blanket, the one who on the night of Palmiro's disappearance had claimed to be a friend of his. The woman manoeuvred the chair round and positioned the man next to the heater. She lifted away the blanket, folded it neatly and turned to Magnani. "No wine, mind." She went out without another word, leaving her husband uttering curses behind her.

"Don't get annoyed, Berto," said one of the men in the group. "Women rule the roost the world over nowadays."

The old man, as impassive as a block of wood, said nothing.

"She brings him here every afternoon. That way she gets rid of him for a bit. He's off his head," Magnani said.

"Was he really all that friendly with Palmiro?"

"He was more than a friend. He was his faithful retainer. He turned his hand to everything for him – slaughterman, cheese maker, gardener, chauffeur. It wasn't the same with Capelli and the Woodsman. They treated Palmiro as an equal, but Berto took orders."

Soneri's cigar had gone out, and as he relit it he looked around the bar at all those ageing men, a company that could have included his father had he been blessed with only slightly better fortune. A deep weariness took hold of him. There were times and places where he was particularly and painfully susceptible to an awareness of the unstoppable march of time, of its inevitable ending and of the vanity of all things. He rose decisively to his feet and made for the door, meeting the glassy stare of Berto, who with difficulty raised a hand to him in greeting.

Once outside, he rang Angela. She answered in a drowsy voice. "Am I interrupting something? Are you in good company," he said, trying to sound ironic.

"Yes, of unreadable documents. You sound as though you are trying to be funny, which leads me to think you're not at your best. What's the matter?"

"Nothing. A mood that comes and goes."

"Comes and goes, as regularly as a bus service."

"Listen," he said, changing the subject. "You know a lawyer called Gennari, don't you?"

"We were at university together."

"He's the Rodolfis' lawyer."

"Well done, Commissario! Did you think I didn't know? I seem to remember telling you."

"I know. It was just to get the conversation going. The story here is that they are in a liquidity crisis, that they can't raise the cash to pay back a loan. In other words, they're on the brink of bankruptcy."

"You couldn't resist it, could you! You've been dragged into the investigation. So much for the dear old mushrooms."

"No, you've got it all wrong. The story's very mysterious, but very private. The only problem is that Sante, the boss of the *Scoiattolo*, is worried sick and has asked me to help him out."

"What's he got to do with it?"

"Palmiro asked the villagers for what they call 'nursemaid' money."

"What on earth is that?"

"It's a loan given in the way things used to be done in the old days in the villages. A few pages to jot down the transfer of cash, the interest agreed verbally, a signature and a hand-shake."

"And people still do that?"

"You know what it's like. In these parts, everybody knows everybody else, they trust each other and the Rodolfis are above all possible suspicion."

"If you were to go about telling people that story, nobody would believe you."

"It's a system which has worked for a long time and nothing

has ever happened. Honesty still counts up here," Soneri said, with a touch of pride.

"Are you sure of that? Things are much the same all over the world, I hear, and we've learned the worst vices from each other."

"This is a complicated story. There are some things I don't quite get."

"Gennari's putting a brave face on it all, but he hasn't got the whole picture, especially on the financial front."

"What has he told you?"

"I haven't had a chance to sit down with him properly, but when I simply mentioned the subject, he was hesitant and gave nothing away. Knowing him as I do, that is not a good sign."

"So there really is a crisis."

"Finally he admitted it. He gave me to understand that the outlook is grim, but he hasn't got to the bottom of it all yet. He says that no-one really understands the accounts, except, perhaps, Paride Rodolfi and those closest to him."

"Do you think the position can be saved? There's talk here about some account that could be unfrozen."

"I don't know. Talking to Gennari, my sense is that the whole show is going belly up. I'm telling you this based on impressions only. You know how women have a special intuition."

"It would be a catastrophe for the folk here. They'd be ruined and have no hope of other work."

"If you want my opinion, that account they're talking about simply doesn't exist. It's a trick to win time, to keep the creditors quiet while they search desperately for funds to paper over the cracks. It's not the first time the Rodolfis have pulled this stunt, did you know that?"

Soneri mumbled a "no" between his teeth, but once again

he felt himself overwhelmed by a strong emotion – like the one he had felt a short time before in the *Olmo*. The image of the Rodolfi trademark came back into his mind, an image which ever since his boyhood had been a symbol of security and solidity, but which now seemed to represent not only yesterday's lost world but also today's threat of destroying people with its collapse.

"Perhaps that's why the old man was going round collecting money," Angela said. "I don't understand even now why he didn't send his son. After all, it was he who caused the trouble in the first place."

"He's scarcely had any contact with the people in the village. He's seldom seen around the place, and he ponces about posing as a manager. He doesn't even speak the dialect. He's more comfortable with English."

"A typical social climber."

"Palmiro, on the other hand, remained one of them. He didn't intimidate them and they trusted him, because he drank wine and his hands were calloused. Do me a favour, try and find out when the company had its last crisis before this one."

"Anything you say, sir. I'll need to get my lawyer friend to unbutton."

"He can do all the unbuttoning he likes, but make sure you remain well buttoned up."

"Your fingers are not likely to be undoing my buttons any time soon, are they? You haven't even asked when we're going to see each other."

"Mountains make you depressed, you always say."

"If I'm there too long, but I have no intention of spending all my holidays there."

"Then come whenever you like. I have a double bed."

"O.K., Commissario, but don't start treating me as if I were your assistant, Juvara."

When he hung up, scents of minestrone were blown towards where he was standing. He glanced at his watch and decided to go back to the *Scoiattolo*. It was dinner time, and the streets were deserted. He walked though the lanes of the old town, but as he went, the sound of footsteps on the gravel in a garden gave him the feeling that, in the shadows of the trees, someone was following him. He spun round in time to see an imposing figure wrapped in a camel-coloured overcoat walking some thirty metres behind him. At first, he paid no heed, but he was quickly convinced that whoever it was had him in their sights. He turned into the piazza, saw the bell-tower looming over him and stopped beside the parapet which overlooked the lower valley where the new village slumbered. Its little villas and cabins were laid out in neat lines and right angles as though part of a re-forestation programme. His pursuer stopped too, feigning interest in the landscape which was finally clear of mist. Soneri decided to confront him, but when he drew up close, he discovered that the person following him was a woman. She was wearing a man's shoes, her hair was cut short, and the rest of her body was covered by the ill-fitting overcoat. She was tall, not particularly pretty but seemingly very sure of herself.

"Are you Commissario Soneri?" she asked.

He nodded, rolling in his fingers the cigar he had just taken from its box. "And who are you?"

"Gualerzi Lorenza," she said, putting her surname first, as though answering a school roll call. "My father asked me to tell you that he'll meet you tomorrow at Badignana because he has some things to tell you. He's sure you'll know the right place."

Soneri nodded again. "And who is your father?"

"I took it for granted that everyone knew. In fact in the village they know him only by his nickname."

The commissario, looking her squarely in the eye, began to suspect the truth. "Almost everyone has a nickname."

"My father is known as the Woodsman. Does that mean anything to you?"

That imposing physique was a giveaway. "What does he have to say to me?"

"I don't know. He doesn't say much even to me, but since I go to the village every day, he asked me to act as go-between."

"Did you shadow me?"

"I came out of my work and I saw you go into the *Olmo*. I waited in the garden and followed you."

"You might have come in. At least you'd have been out of the cold."

The woman shrugged. "If you lived in the Madoni, you wouldn't complain of the cold. Every night you'd go to bed in freezing rooms with no heating, but my father would never consider moving from there. He wouldn't even agree to making life easier with modern conveniences. We have a cooker but that's all."

As he looked at her, the commissario realised how primitively dressed she was. Apart from the outsize overcoat, her shoes were almost worn through and the mouse-coloured stockings would have been more suitable for a much older woman. He guessed she had been required to conform to the customs of an earlier time and saw her as one of life's unfortunates, an object of ridicule among her peers.

"Where do you work?"

"At the Rodolfi plant," she replied, as though it were the most obvious thing in the world. "Nearly everybody works for the Rodolfis."

"In an office?"

"I wish! No, in the salting and curing section."

"Does your father want to talk to me about the crisis? Is

he worried about your job or about the possibility you won't get paid?"

The woman's face darkened and, after a few moments' silence, she replied. "I told you I don't know. I never know what my father wants."

"They haven't been paying your salaries for months now, isn't that right?"

She shook her head in denial, but suddenly seemed to be in a hurry. "Papà will explain it all to you tomorrow. I've got to go now. I'm on my scooter and I'm afraid of being caught in the mists on the mountain."

He made no effort to detain her, and she strode off, taking the long paces only someone brought up in the mountains and used to life in the woods could manage. His thoughts turned to Badignana, to the cabins, to the shepherds down from the mountains, to the cheeses eaten in the company of his often taciturn and distracted father who kept his eyes trained on the hills, gazing at the things he felt closest to. Soneri sensed in that gaze, expressive of everything and nothing, the deep relationship between those mountains and the men born in their shadows, a relationship he could never know, having never suffered sufficiently on those rocks.

As he made his way to the *Scoiattolo*, he felt himself once more caught up in a mystery which involved him more deeply than any official enquiry ever could have. He opened the door of the *pensione*, took his seat at a table to wait for Sante to serve him the minestrone which had the same smell as that from the houses which had so delighted him a short time previously. He broke his bread and mixed it in his soup, and when he had finished eating, he poured some wine into his bowl, as his father used to do.

5

He woke from a deep sleep to hear a shutter banging. While still half-asleep and almost dreaming, he had the impression the sound came from far off, but the noise was repeated several times until he was fully awake. It was dark and the digital alarm on his bedside table showed 6.10. He sat up on the side of the bed, and it slowly dawned on him what had caused the shutter to flap. During the night a wind had got up and had cleared the sky, sweeping away all trace of mist. He washed and started to dress. As soon as he heard Sante moving about, he went down for breakfast.

He was served with his *caffelatte*, with fresh bread which he dipped in the coffee, and home-made plum jam. Without any preliminaries, Sante asked, "Any news?"

"The only news I have is neither good nor certain. I might know more by this evening," the commissario said, thinking of the coming meeting in Badignana which he now contemplated with growing curiosity.

Sante made no reply, but did not move. "That loan I was talking about," he began with a stutter, before pulling himself together. "I mean, have they really run out of cash?"

"It's too early to say. The Rodolfis maintain they do have the money."

"So where is Paride?" Sante said, raising his voice and close to losing his temper. Soneri knew this was the question they all wanted answered, the question that embodied the fears of a village where they were all creditors.

"Sante," began the commissario, looking directly upon him so as to sound more convincing, "the truth is I do not know. I'm here on holiday. The carabinieri know a lot more about it. They've sent in that captain. He must be on the case by now, mustn't he?"

"Yes, but I have more confidence in you. I saw you growing up here when I was not much older myself."

Soneri stood up and put his arm round Sante's shoulders. "You'll see: it will all turn out fine. I'll do what I can to find out more and of course I'll keep you informed."

Sante bowed his head. He tried to look grateful, but managed only to be a picture of anxiety.

When the commissario left the *pensione* he felt the force of the cold, biting wind as it swept along the valley. The freezing temperature was no longer confined to the higher ground, and even in the village the puddles had a thin covering of ice.

To save time, he made for the Case Rufaldi. There was a woodland track that would be hard going, but it went directly up almost to the ridge before turning onto the Badignana plain. The Woodsman's daughter had not given him a time for the meeting, or perhaps it had slipped his memory, but he would take no chances and be there early rather than risk missing out on the possibility of meeting her father.

After the Pietra fork, he stopped in a sheltered spot out of the wind to get his breath. The sun and the blue skies gave the woods a different appearance. He searched for mushrooms away from the path, coming across a colony of russolas, which he carefully picked, and then inside a broken tree trunk he found a cluster of chanterelles. The mist of recent days had made the undergrowth fertile, but the frost would render it sterile again. He followed the track through the beech wood, where the rising sun was reflected off the copper of the autumnal leaves. From nowhere, a dog came running to him barking, and immediately he heard its owner, still invisible among the trees, whistle. The dog was a *lagotto romagnolo* with a white, curly coat.

"It won't touch you," came a reassuring voice which sounded familiar to him. He turned to see Ghidini striding along a track beaten in the undergrowth by the wild boar.

The dog trotted back to its master, sniffing among the leaves as he went. "Poor thing," Ghidini said. "In this freezing weather, there are no scents for him to follow. We'll have to move round to the sunny side of the hill and hope it thaws soon."

"With the ice the way it is, it'll be a while before that happens here."

"I'm afraid so. I've come all this way for nothing so far. But I see you've been luckier," he said, pointing to the commissario's little bag of mushrooms.

"They're well hidden in places like this."

"It's all luck. But don't fool yourself. There are more eyes searching than you might think."

The commissario took a moment to puzzle over Ghidini's meaning. He was not pleased at the prospect of having his company to where he was going. He leant against the trunk of a beech tree and lit a cigar.

"That doesn't do anything for your breathing. I'm a forty-a-day man myself, so I'm only too aware of it," Ghidini said, taking a squashed packet of cigarettes from his pocket. "It's like having a hole in your petrol tank."

"It's O.K as long as you recognise your limits and don't overdo it, as with everything else."

"Now the Rodolfis," Ghidini said, giving Soneri the impression that this was where he had wanted to get to from the beginning. "I believe they really did overdo it."

"I don't know, could be," replied the commissario, trying to sound noncommittal.

"They've been good at blowing their own trumpets, but they've been a bit careless with other people's money. Not that that requires any great skill."

"Did you lend them any money?"

"Me? No. I've never had any. Which is why none of my kids was ever taken on at their factory. They all had to go into the city, but maybe they were better off in the end."

"Nobody has a bad word for the Rodolfis. Without them the village would have died long ago."

"The people here are a bunch of hypocrites. Pure self-interest makes them keep their mouths shut, because they don't want to stir up trouble for themselves. But now the chickens are coming home to roost. They're beginning to see themselves for what they've always been: a flock of sheep about to get fleeced. Year after year, they've dutifully voted the way the Rodolfis told them to. Aimi, the mayor, is on the pay-roll. Paride summons him to Villa del Greppo and gives him his orders. That's how they managed things when the villas in the new village were being built."

"You get the politicians you deserve," Soneri said curtly. Ghidini's tirade was beginning to get on his nerves.

"Maybe so, but what can you do when a whole community seems to be living under a spell?"

"Stand up to it. Make your voice heard in public. Just telling me about these things isn't going to make any difference."

"How could I change people's minds? The stakes are too high for most people," Ghidini said, shaking his head.

"Those are the rules of the game. You reach consensus by taking the stakes into account. I give you something and you give me something in return. Would you have voted for Aimi as mayor if the Rodolfis had taken on your sons?"

Ghidini reflected for a moment and then he gave a bitter smile. "Who knows? Maybe you're right and at the end of the day everyone is prepared to bend a little. I might have done so for the good of my sons, but I would never have changed my mind about the Rodolfis."

"The same as the rest," Soneri said dryly.

The dog started barking some way off in the woods. "Perhaps he's found something interesting," Ghidini said. Soneri took advantage of the distraction to continue on his way. Soon afterwards, he saw the sun emerge from behind the mountain top, and was afraid he was already late. At the Buca Nevosa fork, shortly before the turn for Badignana, he paused. He took a good look into the woods lower down, but decided he was being overcautious. If anyone had been spying on him, he would hardly have been able to miss him. Baldi was right: at a certain height, the mountain is no place for secrets. The plain with the shepherds' cabins at the far end was much wider than he remembered. Standing there in the bright autumnal sun, he felt completely disorientated. The dazzling light shining down from the clear, blue sky made it unlikely that the Woodsman would bother waiting for him, since waiting meant losing the best hours of a day when the sun would set early. He was almost running as he passed the pens abandoned only recently by the sheep and cows. Their pungent odours hung in the air. He was out of breath when he arrived.

He opened the doors onto rooms which still held the clammy heat of summer. He looked around to see if anyone was there in that small village occasionally populated by livestock and their shepherds, where now the chill was beginning to penetrate. He sat on a flat boulder and gazed at the mountain peaks behind which lay a different world of olive trees and holm oaks, trees whose presence announced the proximity of the sea. He re-lit his cigar and thought with irritation of the time he had wasted with Ghidini. As the sun melted the frost on the few stretches of earth visible between the rocks, he heard some stones roll in his direction. Looking up towards the Ticchiano pass, he saw two men walking past at an unhurried pace which told him they had been on the road for hours. Judging by their dress, they must be Arabs. They walked on without looking in his direction, and only once they had passed the cabins did they turn, like two frightened dogs, to look back. They carried on and disappeared behind the side of the mountain. It was then he heard a man's voice call out, a tired voice, little more than a mumble. He had been walking into the wind and had come up behind him without Soneri noticing, and now he stood there looking him calmly up and down. Soneri offered him a cigar but the other man refused with a shake of the head and took out tobacco and papers to roll his own cigarette.

"Is the Woodsman anywhere around?"

The man did not even look up from an inspection of his calloused hands, which seemed incapable of any refined work, and indicated that he had gone.

"We had an appointment to meet here," Soneri said.

There was no reply. The man seemed engrossed in the task of lighting his cigarette, shielding the match from the wind. Soneri waited until he completed the task. "He's on his own up here," he said, looking hard at the stranger.

The only reply was another gesture, which possibly indicated a vague coming and going.

"Does the Woodsman often pass this way?"

The other man, gazing along the line of rocks on the horizon, nodded through the smoke of his cigarette.

"Where will he be now?"

The only reply he received was yet another nod in the direction the two strangers had taken shortly before, but this time it was accompanied by a few words. "Over by Lake Palo."

"So I could find him there," Soneri said, unsure whether that was a question or a statement.

The man smiled, gave him a condescending look, then shook his head to dissuade him.

"I know my way round here," the commissario said, somewhat piqued.

"Nobody can keep up with the Woodsman," he whispered. He ran his hand over his face and Soneri thought he could hear the calluses rub against the stubble on his chin. For a moment he seemed embarrassed. Having to speak after a long period of silence and solitude in that wilderness must have required considerable effort.

"He told me to tell you to have a look around in the chestnut groves at Pratopiano."

"Nothing else?"

The man, holding the cigarette, now no more than a length of ash which he gripped between his thumb and index finger, indicated he had nothing more to add. He took one last draw and tossed the stub under a stone.

"Say to the Woodsman I do need to see him," Soneri told the man, as if he were one of his staff. The man did no more than briefly turn towards him, which Soneri took as a sign of assent.

"I will come back up to meet him. Will you be in these parts a bit longer?"

The man stretched out his arms tentatively. "That'll depend on the weather," he said. The commissario held up his hand in farewell and turned to go, but before he had taken a couple of steps, the man drew himself upright. "Go to Pratopiano right now. If you take the Malpasso path, you'll be there today before it gets dark."

There was a note of urgency in his voice, giving Soneri the feeling that he knew more than he was letting on. He looked at him for a few seconds, but decided there was no point in asking any more questions. The man moved off, springing nimbly over a cluster of rocks off which the rays of the midday sun seemed to be bouncing.

Soneri set off in the direction of Malpasso, trudging over stretches of stony ground behind peaks which crumbled away year after year at the onset of the winter freeze. Out of the wind in the valley, the heat of the sun was strong enough to make him believe that, after the days of mist, they were about to enjoy an Indian summer. Above, he saw a bright, clear sky with no more than traces of light clouds tossed about by the winds, and for a short time he felt at one with that sky, and as joyous and playful as a hawk swooping through the air. The solitariness – and the violence of the light – cleansed his mind of every thought, leaving it free to entertain only a primitive sense of belonging to those places.

As afternoon drew on, the light began to fail. The sun had passed its peak, its rays giving way to the rapidly falling November dusk. He passed below the summit of Monte Matto from which, on a bright winter day, it was possible to see the blue of the sea at La Spezia, and turned onto the steep path which snakes quickly down Malpasso. Half an hour later, he found himself in the woods, and calculating that there was no more than one and a half hours of light remaining, he quickened his step. He was still imbued with a sense of wellbeing and for the first time he realised he was free of all the petty annoyances of life in the police station. He reached the Macchiaferro stream which flowed over the path, and crossed it, jumping from rock to rock. He bent down and dipped his hand in the clear, ice-cold water purely to experience the sensation he had felt as a boy when, warm from his climbing and with the urgent desire to see and conquer the summits, he had wandered in those mountains.

At the end of Malpasso, he turned to take in the imposing bulk of Montelupo and the other peaks whose grey, rocky faces stood out against a sky which was growing darker by the minute. He could never be sure where the boundary lay between the hostile barrenness of the heights and the area where life flourished, even if it were only the timid life of the moss. The border was fluctuating, like the snows in late winter, or like that message passed on by the Woodsman at Badignana. From where he was, he could see the chestnut trees at Pratopiano, still given a gentle colouring by the last husks hanging on the branches. Everything was vague on the mountains, where a named place never had a precise location but drifted between dimensions traced out by the eye and the mind.

He was in the woods where the trees were already damp with the evening dew. As he stared around him, he wondered what he was supposed to find or look for in that place. He looked up at the sky and saw the swift dusk bringing to an end a day as short and as filled with light as a straw fire. He was startled to hear barking from somewhere below. From the edge of the path, he peered through the trees, which gave off the moist scents of dead leaves, but there was nothing to be seen. He heard a rustling in the bushes and someone summoned the dog with a precise, rhythmic whistle, clearly a recognised signal. It seemed the dog was coming up the slope, thrashing the undergrowth as it went, and his first thought was of Ghidini, but he could not see anyone. He continued his way down to Corticone, from where the path climbed from the west over Montelupo, and after a few minutes he was aware of following the sound of the barking but without having paid heed to the direction he was taking. When he realised he had lost his way, his nostrils were filled with a stench carried by a gust of wind. It was a stench he knew only too well from having many times in his career smelled it from locked apartments, from the boots of cars or from watery ditches littered with stones and rubble. He walked more quickly, and his nostrils dilated as he sniffed the air, like a setter. The growing strength of the smell guided him infallibly towards a point where the ground fell away to an almost inaccessible hollow where wild boar would shelter from the sun's heat on a summer afternoon. The air seemed heavier and damper, as though thickened by a veil of tiny drops of water issuing from a nearby waterfall. He climbed cautiously down into that freezing enclosure, holding on to protruding branches. When he was almost at the bottom, he saw it. Between two boulders which had rolled off the mountain, lay a decomposing and slightly swollen corpse, its face half-hidden in the slime. It seemed the earth wished to claim it and deny it any further burial. Judging by the number of pawmarks around it, dogs and wild boar must have mauled it and tugged at its arms and legs.

Holding his nose and balancing as well as he could on the rocks so as not to contaminate any possible clues, the commissario made his way over to the body. He could make out only a few of the victim's features, not the whole face, but clearly he had been a man who dressed with care and who had been equipped for an excursion on the mountain. His windcheater jacket had been ripped by animal teeth, and goose feathers, immobile in that windless hollow, lay scattered all around. Fangs had bitten into some parts of his legs, but there was no blood on the ground – a sure sign that the animals had only arrived on the scene a considerable time after death. When he completed his inspection of the body, Soneri regretted not being able to call on Nanetti, the head of his forensic squad. A metre away, behind a bush, he noted a dark patch where several animals had plainly clawed at the ground. He deduced that the patch was blood, and that after rolling down the slope the body had come to rest there. As he tried to remove the wallet from the hip pocket of the trousers he had a premonition, and when he opened it and saw the face of a woman and child, his fears were confirmed. The posters on San Martino had lied. Paride Rodolfi had not disappeared. He was there in the Pratopiano woods, dead, already swollen and rotting, like an ageing animal which had crawled into the darkness of its den to wait for its end.

The wallet was intact but there was no money in it, not even a coin. As the commissario studied the area around the body, darkness fell rapidly in the hollow. It would take an hour from there to the village, so he would not arrive before nightfall. He stood alone over the corpse, the fetid smell growing more and more offensive, and looked out at the dying light to the west. He felt the role of investigator thrust upon him once more, but he was determined to decline it, since he had no wish to deal with the troubles of a case as complex as this one threatened to be. He took out his mobile and called the carabiniere office. "Put me through to Maresciallo Crisafulli," he said to the operator, realising with a certain dismay that he had assumed the tone of voice of the officer on duty.

Crisafulli came onto the line, speaking in weary tones. "What can I do for you, Commissario?"

"I've found the body of Paride Rodolfi."

"Jesus!" Crisafulli said, before putting his hand over the mouthpiece to communicate with the people in the office. "And where is it?"

"In Pratopiano. Do you know the chestnut grove?"

The only response he received from the other end of the line was a groan. He remembered the advice given to him years before by an instructor in the police college: the most important thing is knowledge of the territory. In a place like that, everything now took place in the woods.

"You get there from the forest path to Boldara?" the maresciallo said.

"That's right, but you'll have to come by foot. It'll take about an hour."

"How are we going to manage in the dark?"

"I'll do my best to give you directions, but get a move on. The smell is unbearable."

"Alright. I'll need to inform Captain Bovolenta and the magistrate, but the magistrate will no doubt come in his own time."

Soneri moved some distance away to avoid the smell. There was a bitter, eerie chill at the bottom of the hollow, and in the silence it was impossible to miss the obscene swarming of insects as they fed on the corpse. He gave himself over to reflections on the fate of the human being who had been the richest man in the valley, a powerful industrialist whose word was law for politicians, financiers and bankers, categories of human being even more obscene than the insects buzzing in the dark. It was not the first time he had been affected by the presence of death, but it was the first time it had happened to him in the woods in his home town. There was more to it than pity. He felt inside himself a deep emptiness and an overwhelming bewilderment. Paride was dead, that gloriously splendid day had faded in the rapidly falling dusk, and all that remained to him was a useless weight of memories. Living for the moment, taking delight in the sun on the day of San Martino on the deserted plain of Badignana had filled him with joy, but only for a fleeting moment. Happiness had briefly blossomed but immediately withered, like a late-flowering bud. Fortunately, the moon was appearing behind the crags of Montelupo.

He clambered out of the hollow on all fours to put as much distance as possible between himself and the stench, and to be able to see down the valley. He made out the Boldara road and watched the carabiniere truck begin its ascent, its headlights reflected on the slopes on either side of the road. The wind carried the smell even to where he was standing. He focused on the branches swaying slightly under the moon as it rose in the star-filled sky. Suddenly he heard something rustling at the foot of the hollow where the body lay, but again there was nothing to be seen. He went down cautiously, stopping some twenty metres short, but from that distance all that could be seen were shadows, murky outlines to which the most fantastical identities could be attached. He stood waiting for the moon to light up the darkness, and then he saw a dog crouched beside the corpse, continuing a vigil which must have begun at the moment of death.

He approached the dog cautiously, stopping when it rose to its feet and stared at him. It was a bloodhound of medium height, lean and very dirty. Soneri crouched down and tried to call it. The dog wagged its tail with every appearance of friendliness and did not react as the commissario inched closer. It was a bitch. She sniffed at him from a safe distance, and allowed Soneri to pat her. She was wearing a collar with metal links and a medal with the name, Dolly. Soneri studied the dog, thinking she was the only living creature who had remained faithful to Paride. He took a sliver of parmesan from the pocket of his duffel coat, offered it to her and watched as she swallowed it whole as though it were a tablet. She went on sniffing him, and followed him when he moved to another spot to answer his mobile. It was Crisafulli asking for directions.

"From Boldara, you take the road to Malpasso," Soneri said.

"It's pitch black," came the complaint. "How are we to

identify the said road," he said, falling into the jargon of the military communiqué.

"I'll wait for you on the said road. There's no other way to go, and no doubt you'll be dying to see me," Soneri said, with heavy irony. "Anyway, I'll make out the torches, won't I?"

"You will. We're not attempting an ascent without lights."

Obviously Crisafulli was determined to show no weakness in the presence of Captain Bovolenta, who must have been right behind him. Other voices could be heard over that of the maresciallo, who was panting as he walked. After a while, Soneri saw the torches flickering in the more open spaces, but they were going as slowly as day trippers. The commissario sat down and felt Dolly's wet nose rubbing delicately against his neck. He took the bag with the cheese from his pocket and laid out what was left on the ground. The dog devoured it all in a few seconds. It must have been her first food in days, and that gave the commissario another means of measuring how long the body had been lying there. His mobile rang once more.

"Is there far to go?" the maresciallo wanted to know.

Soneri looked down and could see the torches swaying not far off. "You're nearly there. Another five minutes or so."

He heard a curse somewhere in the background, mingled with another "Jesus!" uttered by Crisafulli, whose breathing was growing more tortured.

The first men arrived a few minutes later, but Soneri could not make out how many, because the maresciallo shone the torch in his face. Soneri gestured to him to move it, but just then Dolly began to bark and growl. He calmed her with a caress, but the carabinieri drew back.

"What are you doing, Commissario? Is this a hunting trip?" Crisafulli asked.

"She was on a hunting trip," Soneri said, pointing to the dog. "That is, she was when her master was still alive."

"So you're saying that…"

"She was at his side."

The maresciallo looked at the dog, accidentally turning his torch into her eyes and causing her to start barking again. The commissario calmed her once more, and turned back to the carabinieri, recognising Crisafulli and the policeman he had seen previously. In the midst of them stood a small, neatly uniformed man who gave the appearance of having come straight from a barber's shop. This was Captain Bovolenta.

Soneri guided the group down to the hollow, and took some pleasure in noticing how gingerly they tackled the descent, taking hold of branches as they went down and slipping several times. Halfway down, Crisafulli was unable to restrain a cry of disgust at the stench when suddenly it hit him. When they reached the bottom, the torches lit up the area between the roots and the dead leaves. The commissario took the maresciallo's torch and shone it on the body. In the light, he noticed various details that had escaped him in the semi-darkness. The wounds inflicted by the bites of the wild animals were deeper than he had realised, and marks on the ground made it clear that the body had been hauled and dragged. Captain Bovolenta took the torch quite brusquely from an officer and ran it slowly along the corpse and the surrounding ground. When a ray of light illuminated the face half-sunk in the mud and slime, one half-opened eye stared sombrely back at them, showing death in all its obscenity.

"I doubt if there is much to be done tonight," Bovolenta said. "We have neither the equipment nor the appropriate lighting. Crisafulli, have the area sealed off and leave two officers on guard. Call for reinforcements from another company, to give the men here a break. To keep everything right, telephone the duty magistrate, but I think he'll agree with these measures. Tomorrow morning, at first light, we'll resume work. And get in touch with the Special Forensic Unit."

The captain issued his orders calmly and precisely, in a tone which brooked no contradiction. Before setting off, he turned back to the maresciallo. "Don't forget about the magistrate."

He addressed Soneri for the first time since Crisafulli had introduced them. "Are you coming back with us?"

The moment Soneri said yes, Bovolenta was off down the path with his torch lighting the way. The commissario set off after him but he had not gone ten metres before he heard Dolly's paws scrabbling on the rocks behind him. She followed him as far as Boldara and hesitated only when they reached the truck, as though she distrusted men in uniform. Soneri settled her in the back of the vehicle. As the truck moved off, Bovolenta turned to ask, "What do you think?"

"What everyone believed would happen, has happened," was Soneri's enigmatic reply.

"Everyone was convinced he was dead?"

"For some time, no-one would claim beyond peradventure that they had seen him alive. There was no shortage of rumours, but you know full well that..." Whatever was to be known full well petered out in a wave of the commissario's hand.

"His wife said he had gone abroad. She was lying," the captain stated with some emphasis.

"Perhaps Paride had lied to her, and never did leave."

The captain nodded, staring out at the countryside over which the moon spread a phosphorescent light.

"Tomorrow we'll find out how he was killed," Bovolenta said. "Have you any idea?"

Soneri shook his head. "I can't be sure. If I had to hazard a guess, I'd say gunshot. It seems to me the most obvious thing."

"Because of all the gunshots people have been complaining about? You think it was one of those?"

"Could be, but around here they use large-calibre hunting rounds. There was no sign I could see on the body of a bullet having passed right through."

Bovolenta grunted his assent, then leaned over towards Crisafulli who was driving in silence but listening intently. "Will you inform the family?"

"As you wish, Captain."

An owl hooted in the woods. Dolly got to her feet behind the seats and started growling.

"What are you going to do with her?" the captain said.

"I'll take her back home and see if she still has a master."

"Is there one left?"

"Paride's son, but he's crazy," the maresciallo said.

"What about the wife?"

"Yes, there's the wife," Crisafulli said, without further explanation.

"Anyway, they've got other dogs. They loved going hunting, as did their master," Soneri said.

"Dogs have an important part in this story. One was slaughtered in case it might turn out to be an inconvenient witness," Bovolenta said.

"If dogs could speak, we'd have solved the case already."

They arrived at the village. "Will you join me for dinner?" the captain proposed.

"Thank you, but I haven't told the *pensione* where I'm staying, and they'll have kept something for me. They make me at home there."

"You're from here, I was told," Bovolenta said, glancing at Crisafulli in the driving seat.

"Yes, but it doesn't feel like it. I still know the district and I have some memories of my own, but that's all," he said, overtaken by a sudden onrush of bitterness he could not manage to contain.

Bovolenta looked at him intently before replying. "I under-stand," he said, in a tone intended to convey some insight into Soneri's state of mind, but he changed the subject immediately. "Was there really no-one in the village who knew how bad things were for the Rodolfis?"

"If they knew, they found it convenient to keep their mouths shut. The bonds between the villagers and the Rodolfis are very close."

The captain nodded thoughtfully. Soneri shook his hand. "See you soon," he said, as he got out of the truck.

"Tomorrow," Bovolenta said. "We'll be up there at first light."

"It's nothing to do with me. It's your case."

"Well then, consider yourself summonsed as a witness. It was you who found the body, was it not?"

Crisafulli switched on the ignition and drove off before the commissario had the chance to reply. The captain sketched a quasi-military salute and the truck speeded up, but twenty metres up the road, it stopped. The maresciallo got out and opened the back door. Dolly jumped out and raced down the street towards Soneri. As he caressed the dog, he thought that she too had forgotten all about Paride Rodolfi. Life goes on, after all.

6

He was in the dining room well before dawn, and shortly afterwards was out in the chill of the morning. The shadow of the mountains made mornings seem duller than evenings, and that day the moon had gone down some time ago, leaving only the feeble light of the stars. Dolly picked up his scent immediately and galloped over to him with an enthusiasm which he found touching. He was surprised to hear Sante's voice from the doorway. "I gave her last night's leftovers," he said.

He went back inside to find his table set for breakfast, and Sante standing alongside it. "It's not shaping up well," he said, as the commissario took his seat. "Those lorries have been coming and going regularly for a couple of days now, carrying off anything they can before it's too late."

"The seasoned *prosciutto*?"

Sante nodded. "And the rest. Anything they can manage to take to pay off the debts. I'm told that includes the cars."

"It's an unfortunate business," Soneri said.

"I'm not going to get my money back. Nor is anyone else. I mean those who gave him loans," he said, in a tone which wavered between the tearful and the enraged.

"You won't see Paride either."

"He's dead, is he? I thought so, ever since they put up those posters."

"Killed up at Pratopiano."

"Pratopiano? What was he doing there?"

"No idea. He'd been dead for some days and the body was already stinking."

Sante stopped to reflect, then murmured, "It was bound to end up that way." The tone in which he uttered those words implied that Paride's death was in some way a substitute for the revenge he would never have. For the first time, Soneri grasped the depth of hatred Sante felt over the money lost, the deceit suffered and the trust betrayed.

"Don't say anything to anyone. It's up to the carabinieri to inform people. They'll carry out a full investigation."

"I saw a lot of to-ing and fro-ing yesterday, and I knew there must be something up."

"When did you see the lorries?"

"It was late, around midnight. They finished about four."

"You were still up at that hour?"

"How could I sleep with all that's going on in my head? Do you have any idea what it means to lose your life's savings?"

Soneri understood well enough, but he was lost for words. He never knew what to say when faced with life's misfortunes. The only expressions that came to him were meaningless or banal. He let a few seconds go by then picked up the basket and handed it to Sante.

"I found a fair number of russolas and chanterelles," he said, in an attempt to get off the subject. "Give them to Ida and see if she'd like to cook them."

Sante emptied the basket and filled it with Soneri's picnic lunch: salame, cheese, bread and fruit.

"You'll have no problem finding water at Pratopiano, and it's really good."

Soneri said goodbye and set off into the dark with Dolly at his heels. She would occasionally disappear into the undergrowth in pursuit of some trail, but would then make a sudden reappearance. He was well up the mountainside when he heard the noise of a truck coming up behind him, but by then he was almost at Boldara, from where there was no choice but to proceed on foot. Crisafulli brought the vehicle alongside and Captain Bovolenta leaned out of the window as he had done the previous evening. "You're strong on your feet, I see."

"You need strong feet for police investigations."

"I am afraid that's not true nowadays."

"On second thoughts, you might be right there," Soneri said, thinking of his assistant Juvara, who was forever glued to his computer. "But it's the case round here," he said, waving his hand in the direction of the woods and the rocky summit of Montelupo, where the rising sun offered the promise of another clear day.

As he continued on his way, he heard the roar of a four-by-four from further down the valley. Crisafulli announced, "That must be the magistrate. I got in touch with the ambulance service as well, for the removal of the body."

The two officers left on guard greeted Soneri and their colleagues with relief. They reported hearing strange noises during the night and said that on several occasions they had taken the safety catch off their weapons.

Soneri smiled at the two fresh-faced youths from the city, reared on dark tales of the forest. Finally the Special Forensic Unit and Percudani, the magistrate, turned up. The magistrate complained of having drawn the short straw, but he was from those parts and Soneri enjoyed good relations with him.

"Who's in charge here?" he asked, in mock bewilderment.

The commissario pointed to the carabinieri. "I was out hunting for mushrooms and I noticed the smell."

"What a coincidence!" Percudani said, without much conviction.

The first enquiries confirmed Soneri's suspicions. The dark

patch near where the body was lying was indeed blood, and the corpse had been dragged there by some animal.

Percudani gave the order to turn the body over and it was immediately evident that Paride Rodolfi had been killed by a bullet in the chest. Between the sternum and the stomach there was a little cavity with a mixture of coagulated blood, mud and fragments of clothing. The body, as rigid as a statue, was then wrapped in canvas. The stretcher-bearers struggled to lift it out of the hollow and carry it along the track. From time to time, those who remained could hear branches brush against the metal of the stretcher.

When the group disappeared down the slope, Bovolenta, Soneri, Crisafulli and the magistrate were left standing in a circle around the outline of body in the mud. Only then did they notice in the slime, which was still giving off an intolerable stench, the repulsive, writhing tangle of wax-coloured worms now deprived of their sustenance. The maresciallo turned his eyes away in disgust, while Percudani feigned interest in papers relating to the case, and engaged the agents from the Special Forensic Unit in conversation. The only one who remained undisturbed by that vision was Bovolenta, erect in his starched collar, eyes staring coldly out from under the peak of his cap.

"So this is death," he finally said. "It's even uglier than we imagine."

The commissario remained silent, continuing to stare at the worms wriggling about where the corpse had been.

"Just as well the cold…" the captain said before adding, either from cynicism or in an attempt to reduce the tension, "Remember this spot, Commissario. You'll get some fabulous mushrooms here."

Some other members of the Special Forensic Unit arrived, kitted out like speleologists and commanded by a bespectacled man who looked more like an accountant. They embarked on a finger-tip search of the sides of the hollow and the surrounding undergrowth.

"Any mushrooms that grow here will taste of fat," Soneri said bitterly, but he was overwhelmed by a deep sadness which affected his every thought.

"He met the same end as a street-corner drug pusher," Bovolenta said.

The commissario's mind filled with images of himself as a boy, of Palmiro Rodolfi distributing gifts from the company on the feast of the *Befana*, of the awkward display of gratitude from his father, and of the whole village united in admiration for a family which had shown the enterprise to create a flourishing business able to dispense such largesse.

"Could you have imagined anything like this?" Bovolenta said, his anger beginning to break through his attempts at restraint.

Soneri shook his head. "I told you, I'm a stranger here now. Everything has changed." He uttered the last words with a vehemence which disconcerted the captain. "My father worked for the Rodolfis, as did everyone else in the village."

"Met the same end as a small-time pusher," Bovolenta repeated quietly. "When there's that level of debt, the motive is clear, but there are so many potential killers. That's the problem."

The commissario made no reply. The question of motive was the last thing on his mind. He had never before been so close, physically, to a corpse and yet so mentally distant from an investigation.

"Found anything?" Bovolenta said to the head of the forensic squad.

"Not so much as half a shell. A few footprints," he said. The offhand tone made it clear he attached no importance to that discovery.

The stench was becoming overwhelming. Soneri watched the daylight spread through the leafless trees, each coloured in a different shade, but all he wanted was to get away from that stinking spot.

"If you need me, you know where to find me," he said.

Bovolenta stood up and shook his hand, but before Soneri had a chance to move off, he shot him a glance which was perhaps meant as confidential but which came over as merely embarrassed. "I'd like to invite you to have dinner with me one evening."

Soneri nodded his agreement and set off down the path with Dolly at his heels. She had made herself his shadow, and this worried him because he did not want the dog to grow too fond of him. Dolly had already lost one master and he had no wish to inflict more pain on her, but nor did he wish to hurt himself, since he had already become fond of her. With animals – as with people – his principal aim was to avoid inflicting hurt. He walked briskly down the track, too briskly, he decided, when he stumbled and almost fell. In a grove of fir trees, under whose canopy it seemed still to be night, he almost bumped into a detachment of carabinieri making their way up to Pratopiano, panting under the weight of the implements they were carrying. He stepped aside to let them pass, but as he did so, he felt a pang of anxiety and a lump in his throat. There were more carabinieri at Boldara. The whole of Montelupo seemed now to be crawling with them, and their presence brought back stories told by his father about the round-ups along the Gothic Line in '44. He recognised a group of journalists assembled alongside the reservoir, but he kept away from them.

He sought quiet to allow him to deal with the sense of melancholy which now pervaded his being. He also needed time, much as does the soil on the Apennines when saturated by too much rainfall. He felt this need all the more keenly when he came in sight of the village and became aware of the hubbub, a state of constant, agitated motion which from a distance resembled the fermentation of grape must. He imagined that the news of Paride's death must have reached the piazza, but as he approached he could identify no clear purpose in all that bustle. The scene reminded him of a pack of drunks staggering about. He crossed the piazza where bewildered, disconcerted people were standing around, seizing eagerly on any snatches of rumour. He took the Campogrande road which led to Villa del Greppo. In all his years in the village, he had never gone close to that intimidating place, but now he had a reason to go there. Dolly trotted along at this side, obviously very familiar with the path.

The closer he got, the more the villa disappeared behind the surrounding wall and the thick vegetation. One of the bolder pranks they would get up to as boys was to ride past on their bicycles, fire a couple of stones over the wall from their slings and then make off down the slope, leaving the Rodolfi dogs barking furiously in their wake. Now it seemed as though silence had fallen definitively on the villa. Even when he rang the bell he did not hear any sound within. Soneri allowed some time to pass before he tried again. As he waited, he lit a cigar and turned to observe the sunlit valley and Dolly wagging her tail, as excited as on the first day of the hunting season.

At last the gate was pulled back and a small Asian man with an expression of great melancholy appeared in the opening. He stood quite still, looking at Soneri without seeming to breathe.

"I came to bring back the dog," the commissario said.

The man glowered at him for a few moments, then turned his attention to the dog.

"Not know dog," he said in low voice.

"It belonged to Signor Rodolfi."

The Philippino made no reply, but he appeared to be surprised.

"Could you call the Signora?" Soneri said.

The man, still silent, walked in tiny steps across the courtyard in the direction of the house and disappeared inside. The commissario took advantage of his absence to move inside and look over the place which had been forbidden territory to him for so many years. He had expected to see signs of more conspicuous wealth than was on display. It was an old country house, with the barn and stables still recognisable even if now transformed into living quarters. The entire complex retained the unembellished, rustic style which reflected old Palmiro's peasant tastes.

The door opened and a middle-aged woman, whose severe beauty was tinged with sorrow, appeared. The long black hair which came down over her shoulders seemed to have been ruffled by the wind, and when he saw her from close up, Soneri had the feeling that a different kind of disorder resided in her inner being – or so he deduced from the clash between the haughtiness of her eyes and the brightness of her lips, her imperial bearing and certain listless gestures which were redolent of a languid sensuality. Traits of the abbess and the whore competed in her soul, combining without merging in the way she conducted herself. Even her immediate reaction was idiosyncratic and irrational. Her glance fell only fleetingly on Soneri, but she gave a more intense stare at Dolly, seated at his feet, moving only her tail. The woman's face lit up with the merest trace of a smile, quickly replaced by an expression of pain which she concealed by placing both hands over her face.

The commissario understood that there was no need to

explain anything to her. The presence of the dog was sufficient. "I thought it right to bring her back," he said.

She nodded, her hands still covering her face. "My husband was very fond of her," she said.

"She watched over him."

"She was better for him than any wife," she said, half laughing and half weeping, in words of bitter self-reproach.

"It's easier for dogs," Soneri said, by way of offering her a measure of comfort. "Life or death, love or hate. We get swamped by half measures. We are not as simple as they are."

The woman made no reply, but took her hands from her face, revealing an expression of suffering and resignation.

"However, I believe you were not unprepared..."

Her expression changed in an instant, as though she were removing one mask and putting on another. And in that instant, the haughty, almost arrogant, expression she had earlier worn, returned.

"We haven't even introduced ourselves. I am Manuela."

"Soneri," the commissario replied, shaking her outstretched hand. He noted that her body had stiffened and that she was now observing him more coolly.

"You're a policeman. I've heard talk of you in the village," she said, standing back.

"My family is from these parts, but I'm here for a holiday, not to carry out enquiries. I am just bringing back the dog," he concluded, with some embarrassment.

The woman did not share his embarrassment. "Did you find her?"

Soneri could do no more than nod.

"Where?"

"At Pratopiano."

Manuela seemed to be running over in her mind the various places in the valley that were known to her. "I don't know where that is, and I don't care. As far as I am concerned, all these places are the same –" She stopped all of a sudden, with a contemptuous sneer, but immediately, in another abrupt shift, she reverted to the gentle tone and asked timidly, "What state was he in?"

Soneri waited for a few moments before replying in a whisper, "You can imagine."

She lowered her eyes and looked at a clump of weeds at her feet. "Had it been long since …"

"A couple of days, judging by the condition of the body."

Manuela swallowed hard and stared once more into the distance. Her cheeks turned a gentle pink.

"Did he never speak to you about debts?"

She gave a sigh which swiftly became a scoff. She looked Soneri straight in the eye, and for a moment he thought she was about to faint.

"I'm going to escape from here," she said, in the tone of someone reciting a litany. "At long last I'll be free of these mountains…" – her voice rising to a hysterical scream – "I've lost everything: husband, inheritance, reputation and, what matters most, my life. My life. I threw it away when I chose to bury myself in this backwater. I played my cards badly," she said, with lucid cynicism.

Soneri could no longer meet Manuela's gaze, behind which he glimpsed an abyss of ugliness. He realised that many years devoted to detective work had not yet inoculated him against the sheer nastiness lurking beneath such a great variety of surfaces. It was in many ways a comforting discovery.

"Was it you that made them put up those posters on San Martino?" he said, coldly.

Manuela looked at him with a smile of distrust. "No, I know nothing about any posters. I was as surprised as anyone, but what does it matter? We're ruined and you can throw any accusation you like at us. You couldn't care less about knowing what really went on."

"Why don't you explain it to me?"

The response was a fresh peal of laughter that sounded more like a lament, but the woman quickly reverted to the expression of pain. "I found out only recently about the situation we're in. Palmiro told me when he realised there was no way we could get back on our feet. He was dignified in defeat. He was the only real man in this family. I was dragged towards ruination as ignorantly as a moth drawn to a flame," she said, with another cackle.

"When did your husband disappear?"

Manuela raised her hands, palms upwards to indicate that she did not know. "I hadn't seen him for two weeks, but I believed he was travelling somewhere. Anyway, when he was here, he spent nearly all his time in the other house in the woods."

"You were separated?"

"Astonishing! How on earth did you work that out?"

Only then, when his temper was aroused, did he realise that he was interrogating her as though he were on a case. "Nothing to do with me," he mumbled. "I only came to bring you the dog."

Manuela was clearly surprised by this, and shouted in the direction of the villa, "Chang!" The Philippino appeared almost at once, deferential and anxious to do her bidding.

"Take the bitch and put her with the others," she ordered, in a tone of contempt which could have been directed either at the man or the dog. The Philippino summoned Dolly, who made no attempt to move. He grabbed her by the collar and dragged her towards the house.

"Treat her well. She deserves it," Soneri said.

The woman shrugged. "She was treated better than me."

"Things have not gone too badly for you so far. You are still young and can make a life for yourself somewhere else. Would you rather have broken your back working in the stables?" he said acidly.

She looked at him with scorn. "They're all so concerned about the plight of the poor little peasant girls! Do you think ordinary people are pure of heart? You should see these peasant girls drool over their line managers for promotion or a pay rise. They'd happily let themselves be laid on a workbench if it would get them one more grade. And then there are all these pathetic males who used to line up to lick Paride's or Palmiro's arse if that's what it took to get a job for their sons or for some relative. And don't get me started on politicians, coming cap in hand. And not to forget the bankers, elegant pimps, sticky with sweat running down their starched collars. That's the sort we've had to deal with."

The sun was up and its brilliance assaulted them as they stood on the lawn. It was in Soneri's face, blinding him. Its dazzling light and the crudeness of Manuela's speech left him stunned.

"You're no better," he managed finally to say.

"No, we're no better, but we're no worse either. That lot, if they were in our shoes, who knows how they would have behaved."

"They're ruined as much as you," he reminded her.

"It was their greed that caused their downfall. Do you know why they gave us all that money? Because of the interest my father-in-law promised them. All this stuff about trust in the firm, or that we were all in it together…bollocks! Money, that's what they were after. They'd never have parted with as much as one cent if it hadn't been for the mirage of easy riches. They never gave a damn about the firm, and neither were they so stupid as to believe there was no risk. In the last couple of years, they were being promised rates of interest that would have shamed a usurer and not one of them stopped to ask: what's going on here?"

"Their trust was genuine."

Manuela shook her head vigorously, and her reply was scathing. "Once perhaps, but nowadays there are people here playing the stock market, and they know that trust gets you nowhere."

She took from her pocket a bottle of pills and swallowed a couple without any water. Soneri remembered being told in the village that she lived on tablets and pills. "It's time for me to be on my way," he said. He wanted to be gone as quickly as possible from that house and that woman.

"Off you go, Commissario, off you go. Back to those honest souls."

He decided not to answer, because he recognised a touch of despair in that injunction, but he had not gone very far when more harsh, unfriendly words reached his ears. "Just remember that your father came to see us as well."

The commissario stopped in his tracks, but as he was on the point of turning, he saw the Philippino scuttle inside and the gate close. As he walked towards the village, he wondered what Manuela had meant. Had she intended to put his father on the same level as the wretches who came begging for work, or was she pleading for clemency? He could not get the idea out of his mind. He had no time for the woman, but neither could he free himself of the doubt she had planted. She had polluted his memories. All the way to the town, he was troubled by feelings which the bright sunshine and the clear air could only partially lift, and when he reached the piazza, his unease grew stronger as he saw the coming and going of the carabiniere trucks and the chauffeur-driven cars from the Prosecutor's office carrying men whom he recognised.

There were also vans with television cameras and satellite dishes and packs of journalists ferreting about the village in search of someone to interview. A crowd had gathered round the Comune, chanting slogans. That was where the carabinieri were headed, since their colleagues were having a hard time holding back people pushing and shoving at the main entrance.

Other patrols were moving in a column for the salame factory where the only smiling face was that of the pork butcher on the Rodolfi label. Soneri looked up at the road running alongside the works and saw a mass of people there, carrying banners and being harangued by someone speaking into a megaphone. These must have been the striking workers protesting against the halting of production, but the whole thing had tumbled into a chaos where every law had been suspended. Once again Soneri had a flashback to the worms devouring Paride. There was the same frenetic activity in the village, and perhaps in a short time it would lead to the worms devouring one another. Soneri was trying to avoid the crush when he was interrupted by the ringing of his mobile.

"I tried ten times to contact you this morning," Angela began.

Soneri looked at his watch. One o'clock. He thought of his partner getting up from her desk after hours of work, adjusting as she did so the skirt which had climbed half way up her thighs. He experienced a thrill of desire, but her voice had a calming effect. It was primarily the voice of someone friendly and complicit, someone he could hold onto to avoid sinking in the quagmire. She noticed this. "Commissario, what's happening to you? You're like a seminarian at prayer."

Soneri blushed, annoyed at having revealed a hidden side of himself. "I've had a bad morning. I saw Paride eaten by worms."

Angela gave a snort of disgust.

"It was revolting, but we may as well resign ourselves to the end that's coming to us all," he said, donning his customary, tough exterior.

"The company has been declared bankrupt," she said, changing the subject.

"Not just the company, the whole village and maybe the council as well."

"There's a degree of sadness in your voice, Commissario. Didn't you say you were going to stay out of it?"

"It's not so easy. It seems everybody is caught up in it."

"But not you, and yet…"

"Angela, it's hard to remain indifferent when you're faced with the ruin of people you've known, people who speak the same dialect."

"Tell the truth. It's the idea you had of the place that's ruined. That's what's so upsetting."

Soneri refrained from telling her about the doubts concerning his father planted in him by Manuela. He said nothing for a few moments, then said, "The mistake was to come back."

"Maybe it would be different if I were there."

"Maybe," Soneri said. She had contacted him at the very moment when he was at his lowest ebb, and before he had the chance to change his mind, she grabbed at his half-invitation. "I'll turn up one of these evenings."

"I should tell you that the *Scoiattolo* is a fairly basic sort of place. There are cabinets beside the beds and a San Martino over the headboard, and that's the lot."

"I'll do my best to carry out an exorcism."

"Try to speak to the Rodolfis' lawyer."

"I'll try, but he too seems to have disappeared."

The commissario switched off the phone and walked towards the piazza. From a distance he could distinguish the yellow outline of the carabiniere H.Q., where there seemed to be a great deal of movement. As he approached, he recognised the journalists hanging about waiting for someone to invite them in. In front of the *Rivara*, he ran into Maini.

"It's all coming to the boil, but it's not quite at boiling point yet," Soneri said.

"There's still some way to go. I doubt if they know where to start," Maini said, nodding in the direction of the police station.

"They can hardly interrogate the whole village."

"Where would you start?"

The commissario shook his head. "I don't know. Every single person is a potential suspect, and each one of them could have more than one motive. There are all kinds of hatreds, passions... I'd want to talk to those who know about the skeletons in the various cupboards."

"In fact they've been to see Don Bruno."

"Of course, the priest. They always know a great deal, priests, but I'm not sure he's the most helpful starting point."

"They can't even find a wall to bang their heads against."

"Who's in charge of the interrogations?"

"The new man. Bovolenta I think he's called."

"There's a unpleasant atmosphere about the place," Soneri said, looking around at the stalls scattered across the piazza. "Do you think something's going to explode before the day is out?"

"Might do, but I wouldn't put money on it."

Both men observed the village in the bright light of the autumn sun. The fine vapour rising from the dampness of the woods gave the countryside a mellow haziness, but it seemed as though a menacing rumble, the first sign of an impending storm, could be heard in the background.

"Who has managed to save themselves from the disaster?" the commissario wondered. Maini failed to understand, so he went on, "I mean, who brought up the vehicles to empty the factory?"

"Who do you think? The banks. Who else would have the power to get the place opened? It's not likely to be a simple peasant or any one of those who bought the bonds. They tell me there's not a single *cotecchino* left inside."

A siren blared out and seconds later a carabiniere car, travelling at high speed, raced across the piazza. Some people came from the same direction, walking in small groups as though after Mass. Delrio, in plain clothes, was among them.

"The mayor has handed in his resignation," he announced, with a hint of nervousness in his voice.

"Was that him in the police car?"

Delrio nodded. "He's been receiving threats."

"Because of that rumour?" Maini said.

Delrio nodded again, leaving Soneri once more with the disagreeable feeling of being an outsider which had haunted him since his arrival in the village. "What rumour?"

"A bit of nonsense," Maini said. "They say he has managed to get back the money he had lent the Rodolfis. There's also a story that he's had one of the flats in the new development assigned to him, but in his daughter's name."

"Mere gossip," Delrio said. "In this village, every passing rumour immediately becomes a gospel truth."

"It's not only the mayor. There are others, some councillors, people in the same party as the mayor, who are supposed to have got their money out in time," Maini said.

"Aimi acted as a lightning conductor. They needed someone to blame, so they chose him as being a public figure. Nowadays, anyone in politics is automatically considered a thief," Delrio said.

"The real thieves are the bankers. Right up till yesterday, they were telling us the Rodolfis were in great shape, and they carried on selling bonds with a promise that it was good deal."

"People have piles of them this high," Delrio said, holding his hand about a metre off the ground. "Cartloads of waste paper."

"Are we supposed to believe it's pure chance they're closed today?" Maini said. "This morning there was a queue of people demanding their money back. Some of them still believe they're going to get it."

"I'd like to see any of them having the courage to show their faces in public now," Delrio said.

"Oh, they'll show their faces alright, only they won't open their mouths," Soneri said, lighting another cigar.

The other two remained silent, contemplating the truth in Soneri's words. "I suppose that's right," Maini said. "The majority will say nothing – out of a sense of shame. They'll prefer to face their ruin in silence rather than protest and let everyone know they've been duped."

The image of Sante, with all that repressed venom and resentful silence broken only by occasional snarls, sprang into Soneri's mind. He feared that years later the accumulated hatred would, like some toxic liquid corroding its container bit by bit, break out as an illness.

A few minutes later, when he found Sante standing beside his table, Soneri looked at him more closely than usual. Sante noticed this.

"My face is a mess. I haven't slept for a week," Sante said.

Soneri was tempted to say that his health should always come first, but he desisted.

"Ida cooked the russolas you picked. She's got plenty of time on her hands."

It was only then that Soneri realised that the dining room

was empty. He felt uncomfortable in that large room full of tables with no guests. Only half the lights were on, and the semi-darkness of the environment made it resemble an establishment in a seaside resort at the end of the holiday season, as the first storms were brewing.

After the *savarin di riso*, the mushrooms were brought in. Their taste was familiar and reawakened memories of his mother's cooking. A wave of emotion seemed to swell up from his stomach, carrying him back to a place he had no wish to recall for fear of falling into a displeasing state of melancholy. Those flavours reunited him, mouthful by mouthful, by methods beyond the reach of reason, with the past. Help came in the substantial form of Sante, who sat down on the chair opposite him.

"I expected a revolt, but there's actually less disturbance than on public holidays," Soneri said.

"What good has it done those who've got themselves all worked up? It only draws attention to the fact that they've been screwed. At least I want to avoid that. And anyway, they're all away."

"Who's away?"

"The directors of the company. All close friends of Paride. A gang of thieves."

"Until a short while ago, no-one would say a word against them," Soneri said.

Sante shrugged and Soneri noticed the exhaustion written on his pallid face. "I always heard the Rodolfis spoken of in reverential tones. Never a word of criticism, even when there were good grounds. It seemed there was nobody like them," Soneri said.

"Money puts a glitter on even the ugliest things. They've always been bandits." Sante spoke angrily, with a break in his voice, as though he were holding back a howl of pain.

"There's no other way if you really want to make a lot of money, is there?"

The commissario was inclined to agree, but said nothing.

"Bandits! And we all knew it all along. The number one was Palmiro himself. In the days of Fascism, he earned himself stacks of money by working on the black market. He used to go down from the mountains to La Spezia and buy up salt, fish, sugar and coffee which he then sold here at exorbitant prices. He knew the mountain paths like the back of his hand, so there no chance of him ever getting caught."

"It's still going on, but it's the Arabs now and it's not salt they're selling," Soneri said.

"Do you think I don't know? It's the same old story, with the difference that in the old days everybody knew who was coming and going on Montelupo with their black-market goods, while now there's no telling who's crawling about. Nobody knows, not even those who are squatting in the mountain huts or in the old drying rooms...well, maybe one person knows, the Woodsman."

"A childhood friend of Palmiro's."

"But he never dabbled in the black market. He never speculated on hunger, he never bought stolen pigs to make *prosciutto*, he never fed them on rubbish. After the war, you could get away with anything."

"I'm sure that's all true," Soneri said, becoming irritated. "But the fact remains that you all gave him your money. If he was really the bandit you now say he was..."

Sante sighed deeply, his great paunch bumping into the table. "We got along in business matters. He'd keep his bargain, as long as he was sure there was something in it for him."

"And that something was that he could fleece the lot of you."

"No, no. At the beginning, he needed to expand, to extend his salame factory, and then he wanted to pull it down and build a new one on the present site, because the old one in the village was no longer big enough. The banks would only give him so much, because most of his dealings were under the counter, and so the turnover was not impressive. That's why he turned to the people in the village."

"And you all opened your wallets. If he'd asked for your wife, you'd have handed her over as well."

Sante grimaced, but did not demur. He clearly had other thoughts in his mind. "In the early stages, he didn't go to every house because some people had hardly enough to buy themselves white bread. He only dealt with those who had managed to put something aside, and in exchange he promised to see their children alright. Sometimes, he arranged for them to study free with the priests in the city, but then when conditions in the village improved, he widened his circle. He got them to hand over anything they'd hidden under the bed, but he also took them on at the factory and guaranteed them a fixed wage. It was a perfect set-up."

This account worried Soneri. Could his father have been caught up in this web? Manuela's words continued to nag at him, but Sante's voice dragged him back to the present.

"You see, Palmiro was one of us. We spoke in dialect. He'd a good head for business, but he also knew how to rear pigs and produce high quality *prosciutto*. We knew what he was made of, but we could never work out what Paride was about. We had to address him as *Dottore*. He'd been to university and considered himself a cut above us all. He did favours for politicians, and they repaid him in kind. The money was manipulated in ways we couldn't understand," Sante lamented. "Our money."

The issue, as far as Soneri was concerned, was of a different order. He was not even sure how to define it. Honour? Principles? The integrity of the image of his father? A multitude of thoughts revolved in his mind, and they left him convinced he could no longer remain inactive in the story unfolding in the village. It seemed to him he had uncovered an old debt, and had no choice but to repay it.

Taking advantage of a moment's silence, he looked across to the door which opened onto the courtyard on the Montelupo side and saw the mountain bathed in the bright, early-afternoon light. He felt the need to get out of the semi-darkness of the room he was in. Sante was standing in front of him, cowed and stooped, like an old chestnut tree weighed down by rain-fall. Soneri sprang to his feet, but Sante remained immobile, shackled to a vision of his own ruin. As the commissario made to go out, Sante's voice called him back. "I denied myself so much to save that money. I gave up on living. They've taken away part of my life. It's worse than if they'd sent me to jail."

Soneri stopped in his tracks, struck by those words, and then said the first and most obvious thing that came into his head. "You have your job and your health. These are the most important things."

Only when walking in the sun did he think seriously about the rancour that was devouring Sante. That man was imploding day by day, at the same pace as the village which was now seething with silent hatred and stoking up a dying flame, as people do with the smouldering embers and ashes in which on autumn evenings they bake potatoes.

He crossed the piazza, still deserted after lunch, and climbed towards the church with one thought buzzing in his head. He went into the graveyard and saw elderly widows moving about among the tombs. Some were busy dusting off greying, sepia photographs and attending to the adjacent space waiting for them in the cemetery wall. He walked alongside those walls, noting familiar faces, each linked to him by some childhood memory. There they were now, side by side, still images from an uneven montage of some B-movie. He came to his parents' tomb. His mother smiled at him from one of the few photographs ever taken of her, but when he turned to the photograph of his father he received what felt like an electric shock. He had seen that image hundreds of times before, but his attention was drawn to a detail to which he had never previously given any importance, but which now left him transfixed. The gates in the background were the same as those to the Rodolfi establishment, and the piece of surrounding wall that could be glimpsed was the employees' entrance.

He had never before wondered where that photograph had been taken, but now he knew. The discovery was sufficient to bring back the doubt that his father too had gone to the Rodolfis for help, as Manuela had insinuated. He felt more implicated than ever in the case. As his mood grew darker, he saw Don Bruno coming out of the chapel, covered in dust, dressed in layman's clothes without even the Roman collar. He was kicking ahead of him some dried flowers which had become detached from old bouquets.

"I've even got to do the tidying up. There's not one single woman in the whole village who's prepared to give a hand. Not even part time."

"They've all turned anti-clerical, have they?" Soneri joked.

The priest was not amused. "They're all indifferent, which is even worse. Once there was a belief among them that they could make up for aridity of spirit by doing some service for the church, but now they can't even be bothered with that."

"Priests used to awaken consciences."

"In fact, we were accused of the opposite. Anyway, it is not like that any more. You can say anything you want. They'll listen silently and won't be ruffled in any way. That's the worst of it. They prefer to isolate themselves in the smallness of their own minds, wasting away in the pettiness of a few, utterly insignificant things. They haven't even reacted to all that's been going on. I'd rather have the anti-clericals back, the communists that I would debate with. At the very least you had the impression of hearts beating. But now I am left with a handful of old folk who come to Mass out of habit, or else with a nest of vipers who genuflect before the altar but who would cheerfully murder their husbands the minute they get home. And don't even talk to me about young people! To get the rest of my flock interested, I'd need to be a car sales-man or a banker."

"Bankers are not everybody's favourite at the moment," the commissario said.

"Oh, wait a while and it'll pass. Money is all they think about nowadays. And here am I devoted to the care of souls." The priest gave a bitter laugh before adding with an onrush of pride, "But I'm not giving up. They'll all come back to join the flock, I've no doubt about it. This catastrophe is the first sign that the things of this world will pass away and that sooner or later every human being has to settle his accounts with his Maker. His real accounts, I mean. Take Palmiro Rodolfi. He only cared about power, but at the end, all of a sudden, he realised it was all in vain. He settled his accounts alright, but the outcome was terrible."

"The outcome is always terrible, for everybody."

"That's not true. It's true only if you believe you can settle everything in this world."

"Were you getting the chapel ready for Palmiro?" Soneri asked.

The priest looked him straight in the eyes and nodded.

"But he committed suicide."

"God's mercy is infinite. We will pray for him too. I hap-pen to believe that his final act implies repentance, do you not agree?"

"Perhaps. He no longer had the strength to show himself to those he had betrayed, but neither did he have the strength to show himself to God and beg forgiveness. This might mean he did not recognise him."

Don Bruno paused in silence for a moment, then said, "We'll never know what went on, but the Almighty Father does."

The commissario reflected that this was true of his own father as well. Perhaps he would never know what went on between him and the Rodolfis.

"I heard you came to look for mushrooms." This time it was the priest who changed the subject. "Your father shared that passion."

"So did you," Soneri said.

"Once upon a time, yes, but now my legs have let me down."

The priest was short but had heavy bones. Only the metal-framed glasses undermined the image of a man of the mountains and woodlands. He was bow-legged, like a jockey, but the bend was due to the weight of his body.

"Who told you I was here to gather mushrooms?"

"Priests get to know everything, sooner than the carabinieri, who in fact come to us for information."

"Were you summoned to the police station?"

Don Bruno made a gesture which was half fatalism, half resignation. "They're not aware that we have precise obligations."

"They didn't actually ask you for the name of the person who had confessed to the crime?"

The priest laughed. "Hardly anyone comes to confession nowadays. Maybe that is because we obstinately continue to take an interest in other people and go round sticking our noses into their business."

"And they have no idea which saint to pray to."

"I understand they are following a definite lead."

"Yes. Revenge for the fraud. But so many people have the same motive," Soneri said.

"There's also the question of the gunfire that was heard on Montelupo on the day after the feast, and which you can still hear occasionally," the priest said. "But it could have been a poacher. There are so many guns around."

Soneri looked puzzled but said nothing, so the priest went on. "I'm afraid they're closing in on the Woodsman. They started digging up things from his past and they've uncovered something about an old rivalry over a woman. They must have some sort of proof."

Soneri could not help thinking that if he had been in charge of the case, he too would have wanted to know more about the Woodsman. But then, why had he sent his daughter to make that appointment?

"Who called you in? Was it Bovolenta?"

"Yes. Crisafulli's been sidelined."

"What did he ask you?"

"Are you involved in the investigation?"

"No, I'm on holiday, but everything here brings up personal issues."

"Of course. You're part of this community."

"Not any more, Don Bruno. In part because I've been away for years and in part because I'm finding everything different from how I remember it."

"Bovolenta is expecting some assistance. He likes to appear sure of himself, but he admitted to me that he cannot fathom this village. It's different for you. You're *from* here."

"The less I get involved, the better for everybody. My father worked for the Rodolfis, remember."

"Of course, and I gather he had a good relationship with them."

"What do you mean, a good relationship?"

"He didn't see them just as employers. He was happy to work there and was fully committed to the company."

"I was only a child then, and later I went off to study in the city. I don't know much about my father's work," Soneri said.

"Neither do I, but I heard that's how things were, at least until he threw it all up and moved into the city himself. But there's no point in asking me what brought that about, because I simply don't know. Perhaps there was some kind of argument, or maybe he just made up his mind it was time to go. Maybe he got fed up with village life. Or maybe he saw a better opportunity."

The commissario thought of his father's work as an accountant, but also of his love of the woods and of Montelupo and found it difficult to imagine that life in the city would have been in any way better for him. He found his father's past more and more difficult to understand. He realised they had never spoken about his time as an employee of the Rodolfis. At most, he had thrown out a couple of hints, free of rancour or nostalgia. Any time he mentioned it, he used the phrase, "when I was under the Rodolfis". Soneri found himself regretting for the hundredth time opportunities missed.

"Have you seen the Woodsman again?" Soneri said.

"He never comes down to the village, and if he did he would not come to church."

"I know. He's not a believer."

"It's not his fault. Palmiro wasn't either. The pair of them were brought up in the Madoni hills among the beasts, and the only object was survival. It's not much different now."

"He lives like a savage and yet he's the master of Montelupo," Soneri said, with a trace of envy in his voice.

"I wouldn't be too sure of that. Up there many strange things go on, and they're getting stranger by the day. On a clear night, you can see lights that look like fires flare up in the clearings, but they go out quite suddenly only to reappear further up. There are lots of people living on Montelupo now, and they're liable not to be officially registered."

"Foreigners. They come and go from Liguria," Soneri said.

"Not only foreigners. There are all sorts who turn up there. They come from far and wide and they don't look like holiday-makers."

"When do you see these lights?"

"At night, if there's no mist. All you need is patience, and keeping your eyes peeled. I'm not a good sleeper."

"Have you reported this to the carabinieri?"

"I told Crisafulli some time ago, but he gave me the same answer as when I spoke about the gunfire. There is nothing he can do about it."

Dusk was falling rapidly and Soneri regretted he had not made better use of that sunny day. Don Bruno got into his old Fiat, leaving Soneri to stroll back to the piazza. He arrived as the streetlights were being switched on. A stronger light suddenly cut through the twilight, shining a bluish beam onto the surrounding houses. The carabinieri's Alfa Romeo was coming up the street from the new village on its way to the police station. Soneri recognised Captain Bovolenta in the rear seat.

"They've got someone," he was told by Maini, who had been watching developments from the *Rivara*. "They say it's a foreigner, a dealer who operates on Montelupo."

The bar and the piazza were suddenly sunk in the silence of the falling night. The tragedy, with its ramifications of lost money and unexpressed shame, was now unfolding behind closed doors in every household. Soneri glanced at the thin, wiry figure of his friend, remembering races run along path-ways and first cigarettes smoked furtively in mountain huts, and felt confident enough to ask him about his own private affairs. "Did you trust the Rodolfis with your cash?"

Maini turned quickly, blinking rapidly in embarrassment. He gave him a wink, but on his face the commissario could read deep hurt mingled with a plea for absolution. Again Soneri felt ill at ease, but Crisafulli, with his prancing gait, turned up at that moment to spare them further awkwardness. "Good evening, Commissario. The captain would like to see you."

Soneri nodded to Maini, whose expression was growing more and more melancholy.

"Am I under suspicion?" a decidedly displeased Soneri asked the maresciallo. He could not stand anyone interfering with the planning of his days. He liked to be in charge and decide for himself, moment by moment, how the day should go.

"Oh no! What do you mean? We've got somebody."

"So what?" Soneri said, brusquely.

Crisafulli turned to him, shaken by this reaction. "Was that an important conversation?"

"A business matter," Soneri said.

The maresciallo did not pursue it any further. "A Romanian. We found Paride Rodolfi's mobile on him."

The commissario shrugged.

"Isn't that an important clue?" Crisafulli asked.

"It's a clue of sorts, but I'd proceed cautiously."

"Bovolenta, I have to say, is taking it very seriously." Crisafulli winked at the commissario.

There was something treacherous in that remark which did not go down well with Soneri. "How did you get him?"

"Luck. You need a bit of luck, don't you? We sent a fax to all the police forces in the Apennines, and we came up trumps."

"Where was he picked up?"

"In Sarzana. He sells things in the street to camouflage other kinds of dealing, if you see what I mean. Maresciallo Zanoni gave him the once over and found the mobile hidden in his car."

Soneri nodded to say he had understood. They were at the police station and Crisafulli accompanied him to Bovolenta's office.

When they were seated, the captain looked disapprovingly at Crisafulli, then turned to Soneri. "No doubt the maresciallo will have informed you..." he began, with a touch of irony in his voice.

"Yes, the Romanian."

"Exactly, the Romanian. That's why I asked you here. When you found the body, did you do a search of the surroundings? Even the most cursory of searches?"

"No, it was nearly dark and I didn't want to grope around too much. I only took out the wallet to ascertain the identity."

To Soneri's annoyance, the captain uttered an "Ah". It was not clear if this was a reproach or merely an aside, so he added, "It was completely empty."

Bovolenta paused for a moment to reflect. "The man we have arrested claims to have found the mobile in the woods. From his description of the spot, it would not seem to be not too far from where the body was discovered."

"Was he the one who removed everything from it?"

"Probably, but he's never going to admit it. His story is that he found the mobile by chance, as though someone had lost it. He swears he never set eyes on the body."

"There are so many people wandering about on Montelupo."

"Exactly, so many. That's why I have my doubts as to whether..." but he left the sentence unfinished.

"If I were in your position, assuming your doubts refer to the Romanian, I would share them."

"But he talked at great length about Montelupo. And, as you said, there are lots of people moving about up there."

"Always have been. But in the old days, they were a different type."

"I know what you mean. But it's not only foreigners. The Romanian spoke about a huge, tall fellow with a beard, who goes about armed and sometimes fires off his gun. He and his friends are terrified."

"There are plenty of people who fire guns."

"I know that too. But this is an Italian, a local man. We know his name, Gualerzi." Bovolenta's expression was almost venomous, an Inquisitor's expression. "Do you know him?"

"Of course I do. The Woodsman. But what's he got to do with it?"

"Do you think it normal for someone to go round armed, firing when he feels like it? The Romanian claims that twice, on separate occasions, bullets passed very close to him."

"He's a man of the woods. He's spent his life on Monte-lupo, and as for poaching, they've always done it up there."

"Where can I find him?"

"To the best of my knowledge, he lives in the Madoni hills," Soneri said, feeling he was taking on a role which he had not initially wished to assume.

The captain turned to Crisafulli, having no idea where the Madoni hills were.

"Drop it," the commissario said. "This is a matter for game-keepers."

Bovolenta stared at him intently. "We can't afford to neglect any angle."

"And the Romanian?" Soneri said.

"He's in custody. He had stolen objects in his car. For the moment, we've got him for handling stolen goods, and mean-time we'll proceed with this line of enquiry."

Before the captain could make a move, Soneri jumped to his feet as rapidly as a private soldier.

"The invitation to dinner is still open," Bovolenta said.

The commissario nodded and said goodbye. Crisafulli went with him to show him out. At the front door, looking over his shoulder to make sure no-one was within hearing distance, the maresciallo, as though offering an excuse, said to Soneri, "He's new. He's still got a lot to pick up." As he spoke, he waved his hands eloquently in the air, as only a Neapolitan can.

For some ten minutes, Soneri wandered aimlessly through the narrow streets, still sunk in a tense silence. When he came out on the piazza, he noticed a bright light. It was coming from a fiercely burning fire, near a house outside the village, on the road to Montelupo. Livid flames engulfed the tops of the chestnut trees some way higher up. A few moments later the fire exploded and the flames leapt up towards the skies. He heard the carabinieri rush from the station, and imagined the curses of Crisafulli, forced out his office chair. Shortly afterwards, the strident sirens of the fire engines filled the valley, violating the peace of the evening. No-one in the village made a move, as had happened in times of war, when the curfew protected the solitude of the victims.

The vehicle of the municipal police, with Delrio at the wheel, moved off from the Comune. The usual group of evening customers was gathered outside the *Rivara*.

"Is that the Branchis' farm?" Soneri said.

"They've been gone a good while. It belongs now to a family called Monica," Rivara said.

"They burned the Branchis' barn in '65," Volpi said.

"And in '44. But that was the Germans," Ghidini said, with an exaggerated precision which sounded malicious.

The flames were now through the roof, and already the fire-fighters were working from the neighbouring fields which were as bright as day. Someone was running to free the desperately bellowing cattle tied up in the stalls. One cow was running in terror towards the woods, while others were scattered over the slopes.

"Poor beasts. It's not their fault," Volpi said.

Soneri would have liked to enquire exactly whose fault it was, but the profound indifference he saw etched on every face made him decide that this was not the best time. Maini took him by the arm and led him away from the group.

"They hate the Monicas here," he said, when they had moved far enough away.

Soneri made a questioning sign with the fingers holding the cigar.

"The son is one of the Rodolfi accountants, and they say he's salted a lot of the money away."

"So it's revenge?"

"Probably. Burning barns is an ancient custom."

The commissario remembered various tales told locally, especially one about a house outside the village where a blackened skeleton lay for many years.

"Monica himself went to school with Paride. They dabbled in finance – investments in the stock exchange, shares, asset-stripping, that sort of thing. They were the first generation in a poor village who'd gone to university, and they thought they were untouchable," Maini said.

"You thought you were too."

"I believed in Palmiro. How could anybody know it was all built on a fraud like this?"

"You're right. When you get down to it, it's always hard to believe how appalling reality is. It invariably takes you by surprise."

Neither man had anything more to say. They watched the barn burn down in spite of the best efforts of the fire-fighters, and contemplated the senseless tragedy of the fire as it rose diabolically up against the indifferent bulk of Montelupo. From time to time, a light breeze carried towards them gusts of tepid air and the scent of burning hay, creating an improbable spring-like heat.

The commissario turned towards the houses and became aware of furtive movements behind the shutters. He could detect the malevolent joy of revenge on faces fleetingly visible in a glimmer of light behind curtains or grilles. Bells began to toll like hammer blows, but the village remained imperturbable.

"It's gone. They could divert the river Macchiaferro onto it and they still wouldn't extinguish the blaze," Ghidini said.

The flames seemed longer, higher and unaffected by the water, which had as little effect as if it were tumbling down a crack in the rocks. No-one bothered any more to make an effort to save the barn, except for a few dispirited firefighters holding the hosepipes. There was only one man who had rolled up his sleeves and it seemed he wanted to leap into the burning building. There was no longer any sign of the animals. They must have all run off, perhaps up the mountain path they had only recently been brought down.

"The embers will smoulder for two days," was Rivara's reckoning, delivered with a sarcastic half-smile.

The breeze dropped quite suddenly and a shower of ash fell on their heads.

"Is it Ash Wednesday again?" Ghidini sniggered.

"I don't see any sign of penitence," Soneri snapped.

"It wasn't us."

"No, but you're all quite pleased just the same."

Maini looked at him sternly but imploringly. Soneri was setting himself up against them all, and he did not care. Ghidini and the others did not react. They held their peace, but exchanged sharp glances.

"As you sow, so shall you reap. Monica's son was one of those who did the accounts up there," Ghidini said, pointing to the salame factory. "He knew everything that was going on, but he got above himself with the money he'd stolen. If you play dirty, sooner or later someone is going to make you pay. He's lost this hand." He looked around, expecting the approval of the group.

"Playing dirty suited you all," was all Soneri said by way of reply.

"The people in the village were not responsible. The banks should have put a stop to it once they'd run up all those debts. They could see the whole game," Rivara said.

"The banks are hand in glove with the politicians, and the Rodolfis wallowed in political schemes," Ghidini said.

"You voted for those politicians, don't forget. Who was it who returned Aimi with majorities hardly seen outside Bulgaria?"

Soneri's tone was calm but biting. Maini stayed on the sidelines, trying unsuccessfully to move the conversation to safer ground, even after it had turned bitter. Rivara stuttered that they were not all in agreement and that many had understood only now, but he did not carry conviction. The debate dragged on and ended in a hostile silence. The commissario was familiar with that state of mind among the mountain men, because at least in part it was his own. He was only too aware that when faced with a direct accusation, they invariably preferred evasion. Their silence transformed the words they would have liked to voice into apparent indifference and detachment.

The siren from a fire-engine winding its way along the twisting road in the valley had a mournful sound. It was sufficient to ease the tension which had been created.

"Another one on the way," Volpi said.

"They'd have been better off staying at home at this stage," Ghidini said.

Soneri took his leave with the excuse that he wanted to observe the operations at close hand, but as he left the group, he was conscious of a strange, niggling sense of embarrassment. Maini came after him, but as he caught up Soneri's mobile rang. Angela's voice came and went, but he could hear her when she shouted "I'm on my way."

"Where are you?"

"I'm looking at a sign that says twenty kilometres. Are you asking me because you want to warn me off?"

"Not at all. It's to know when to expect you. You're arriving in a moment of particular turmoil."

"That's not surprising, with all that's been going on."

"Apart from all that, there's been a fire. A barn went up in flames."

"Arson?"

"It belonged to the family who were Paride's closest collaborators, so draw your own conclusions."

"I've a lot to tell you. I spoke to Gennari, the Rodolfi's lawyer. Once he found out you were on holiday and not engaged on the case, he opened up. Obviously, I omitted to mention that you were holidaying in their home village."

Soneri agreed to meet her in half an hour. When he turned to talk to Maini, he had disappeared. The village bells stopped ringing and the fire-fighters made no noise as they moved back and forth, so everything was plunged once more into silence. The barn was a smouldering wreck now, with only an occasional tongue of flame shooting up into the darkness. The crackle of the beams collapsing under the intense heat, dragging down sections of the wall with it, could be heard quite distinctly. It was the end, the final death spasm of a section of the village. The commissario decided the spectacle was over and set off for the *Scoiattolo* through the narrow streets of the old quarter. He glanced into the *Olmo*, where some of the older customers were at their cards, watched by others leaning against the walls. Magnani was behind the bar, only half-awake but with a cigarette in his mouth. The contented calm of the older generation signalled that all was as it should be on any normal evening.

He walked on, leaving that cluster of houses behind and coming out on the road which overlooked the valley. The lights from the houses there seemed like reflected starlight. He continued quickly on his way until he saw the sign of the *pensione*, but at that moment he heard the gentle scrape of a dog's paws on the road. He turned to see Dolly, wagging her tail. She had been waiting for him at a spot where she knew he would pass by.

7

"I'll never understand what made you come to this place," Angela said, as she got out of her car and looked around, still unsure of herself in the dark.

"It wasn't a wonderful idea, I have to admit," Soneri said.

"So move on. You're on holiday, not in custody."

At which the commissario, plainly uncomfortable, stretched out his arms.

"Oh God, is this you at it again, struggling with ghosts from the past? You manage to get free of the big chief in the office, but fetch up under an even more thuggish boss." Angela gave him a hug, but Soneri remained impassive. "When I first met you, you never thought about the past. You were too caught up in your work."

"Maybe that's why the past weighs so heavily on me now. I feel the years grinding me down. Sometimes I think I'm without memory and I've wasted too much time on pointless things."

"You'll waste even more if you go on thinking that way. It'll do you no good at all."

"I regret everything I didn't say, and all the time I could have spent with my father."

Angela sighed but, guessing at what lay behind Soneri's mood, she went on, "Never mind all these rumours. They're nearly always malicious lies."

This time it was Soneri who embraced her, with feeling,

holding the cigar away from her. But as he was kissing her, Dolly's wet nose rubbed against the hand at his side with the cigar between his fingers.

"Don't tell me you've acquired a dog. You're getting more and more like a maiden aunt."

"It was *she* who acquired *me*. She was Paride's dog."

"It's either her or me," Angela said, in a tone of playful jealousy.

"I'm going to take her back to her owner tomorrow. It'll be the second time."

"She obviously adores you."

"I'm not the right man for her. She's already suffered one loss, and I don't want to put her through another one."

"Definitely not, but she ran away to be with you again."

Soneri determined not to grow too fond of Dolly, but he could not help patting her gently.

"Anyway, Angela, tell me about the Rodolfis' lawyer."

"The situation is more serious than anyone realised."

"Isn't every situation?"

"Paride and his accountants have been getting away with false accounting for years. The balance sheets were just so much fluff. In some cases, they invented credit by fabricating phoney documents and then using them as collateral for more borrowings. The thing came unstuck when they couldn't redeem a parcel of bonds that fell due. They won a little time by making out that there was a fund where they had assets stashed away, but when that turned out to be a fiction, the whole house of cards collapsed."

"And nobody had a clue. Not even the banks," Soneri said sarcastically

"They couldn't care less. They've loaded the majority of the debts onto the savers by selling them junk bonds."

"Who's investigating this mess?"

"The guardia di finanza, but it's hard to find the way through an accountancy labyrinth where legal and illegal operations overlap. There's no telling how big the final black hole will be. Add to that the fact that before they threw in their hand, the directors shredded the archives and wiped the computer files."

"Who are the accountants?"

"Friends of Paride from school days."

"A village gang! And nobody could stop them in time?"

"It's been going on for at least ten years. They thought they could cheat everybody *ad infinitum*. They believed they were omnipotent, but that's often the way with these get-rich-quick people."

The commissario bowed his head. Although they were by now frozen to the bone, they were still sitting on the wall alongside the street, watching the moon travel across the sky. Dolly was lying at their feet, looking up hopefully from time to time to see when the next caress was coming. They walked towards the village until they drew level with the Monicas' barn, now reduced to a gigantic, smoking ember.

"An act of revenge," Soneri said.

"Has it got something to do with the fraud?"

"It belongs to the Monicas."

Angela gave a start. "The son is another one of Paride's friends."

"Feuds new and old are passed on. I'm sorry to say it's an old custom."

"Like setting fire to barns."

"Sooner or later the past falls on top of you."

"If anything's going to fall on top of me, I want it to be you," she said, snuggling close to him.

They returned to the *Scoiattolo*, where Angela smiled at the dull ornaments and plain furniture in a *pensione* where rustic bad taste was the order of the day. Soneri was hard put to it to convince her of the cleanliness of the bathroom and the sheets, and had to make three separate searches of the bedroom to get rid of spiders, beetles and other insects. He then ruined the effect by informing her that this was the season for bedbugs, awakening a fresh round of alarm. In spite of all this, he was secretly proud of how true he had remained to his country origins in comparison to Angela, who had perhaps never spent one entire day away from the city. Possibly on account of these apprehensions, she fell asleep holding him close and when he awoke in the morning the commissario had various aches and pains caused by that lengthy contact. His thoughts, however, were still where they were the night before.

"The fraud is clear enough," he announced at breakfast. Sante served them in silence, seemingly intimidated by Angela's presence. "But the murder of Paride is anything but clear. Neither is Palmiro's suicide, although he had every reason to kill himself."

"Revenge, the same as with the barn."

"Perhaps, but we have to find out what manner of revenge."

"You've always told me that human actions are prompted by very simple motivations: first money, then power or sex. It's not hard to guess which one it is in this case, is it?"

"That's what the carabinieri think too."

"Who wouldn't? But there's some personal factor at work here. For you, I mean."

"There always is, in any investigation. I've got to imagine myself into the mind of the murderer, and then the victim. It's indispensable for me to get under their skin, to relive the state of mind of each one."

"Have you managed that with Paride?"

"No. There was one sentence spoken by his wife. An unfortunate choice of words about my father."

"What did she say?"

"That he had been to knock at their door, the same as everybody else."

"That's not a crime."

"No, but it almost makes one an accomplice. Everybody knew and everybody exploited the situation for their own ends. In a certain sense, that's the whole story."

"But you knew nothing about it?"

"I was away at college in the city. My father never spoke about his work and I never asked anything about it. We didn't have deep conversations, although we got on well, especially when we were out hunting or searching for mushrooms. Later the whole family moved to the city. As far as I knew, it was because my mother was unwell and had to be near a hospital. Now what I think is that something must have happened between my father and the Rodolfi family, but I have no idea what."

"And that's what's been bubbling away inside you?"

"No, it's more than that. I'm afraid Papà was in cahoots with that bunch of swindlers. Or maybe he was one of those who knew everything all along but found it convenient to keep his mouth shut, like the rest of them in this village. Don Bruno told me my father was on good terms with Palmiro. It's one of those phrases that might mean everything or nothing."

Angela gave him a look which was both affectionate and reflective. "An investigation for you is like a visit to a shrink."

"I've got to do everything by myself," were his final words as Angela got into her car.

They went their ways in opposite directions, Angela along the twisting road down the valley and Soneri towards the slopes of Montelupo. Just beyond Boldara, he ran into Volpi coming up from the Croce path, the one which crossed the red jasper rocks over to the west. He had a rifle slung around his neck, leaving his hands free. Soneri kept his eyes on him until they were face to face. He was wearing corduroy trousers with green, knee-high wellington boots.

"Found any poachers?" Soneri said.

"There's no shortage of them. They're not the problem. Hunting has started up again."

"For the wild boar?"

"If only. For the Woodsman."

Just at that moment, from near Montelupo they heard men shouting and calling out to their dogs. Dolly, who had followed Soneri, cocked her ears.

"It's a big hunting party. There must be at least thirty carabinieri scattered through the woods," Volpi said.

Soneri thought of Bovolenta, who had obviously only been pretending to consult him while going the way he had already decided to go. "They're going to have a hard time of it with the Woodsman," he chuckled, realising that his exasperation with the captain had put him on the Woodsman's side.

"They're out of their depth," grunted the gamekeeper with contempt. "They'll end up injuring themselves or else they'll get shot if they have the misfortune actually to locate the Woodsman. He doesn't fool about."

"He'll play with them for a day or two, till they get tired. Montelupo is too big for people who don't know it."

Once again they heard whistles and once again Dolly bristled.

"Have they got dogs with them?"

"Three or four, but out in the wild there are scents all round them, so they don't know which one to follow and they go dashing off in all directions," Volpi said. He pointed to Dolly. "You shouldn't take dogs out with all this going on."

"She belongs to the Rodolfis. She was standing watch over Paride when I found her, and since then she's been following me everywhere."

"You're going to have the devil of a job getting rid of her. When hunting dogs attach themselves to a master, they'd get themselves killed rather than leave him."

"I've taken her back to the villa once."

"They're all on the run from there now." Volpi looked through his binoculars in the direction of the woods where the shouting was coming from.

"Did Palmiro still go in for poaching?" Soneri asked when he found Volpi facing at him again.

"Easier to say who didn't go in for poaching. Palmiro and the Woodsman both come from the Madoni hills and felt they were masters here, in their woods."

"What was he hunting, the wild boar or roe deer?"

"As far as I know, he preferred to shoot birds. He put them in his polenta, Venetian style. But if some other animal crossed his path..."

"You need a different sort of ammunition."

"Certainly, but there are rifles equipped for all kinds of charges."

The voices were drawing closer. Some carabinieri, wearing camouflage, passed them in a treeless clearing. It looked like a wartime scene.

"They asked me to accompany them as their guide, but I told them I hunt poachers and I'm not a policeman," Volpi said.

"Then what happens to the Woodsman should be your business."

"That's not what they had in mind. I'm not a spy."

"Just as well. It seems everybody in the village supports the Woodsman."

Volpi shrugged. "That captain can attend to his own affairs. Gualerzi must have had a good reason for doing what he did, if it was him. And so would have many other people."

They heard whistles again as the dog-handlers tried to rein

in their dogs, but this time the echoes came from higher up, where the terrain was more harsh and rocky.

"They're going all out," Soneri said, as he attempted to restrain Dolly.

"They'd be better off holding back and thinking it through. They're flapping about like grouse. Do you know they've staked out his house?"

"They must be hoping to wear him down."

"That'll be the day! He'll have seven or eight refuges dotted about in the woods, and that man can hunt with or without a rifle."

"You seem to know a lot about him. Is that because of your job?" Soneri said, smiling.

"Laws have to be applied with common sense. Men like the Woodsman or Palmiro Rodolfi were used to going hungry when they were growing up, so poaching was a matter of survival for them. It's in their blood and they're too old to change now," Volpi said.

The conversation was interrupted by a burst of rifle fire, followed by other gunshots.

"Has the battle begun?"

"The wrong kind of weapon," Volpi said, listening intently. "Someone must have got a boar."

"They've never gone hungry, but they're out shooting just the same. You'd be as well to ignore it this time as well."

"No," Volpi replied calmly, still listening to the sounds. "They must have gone too close to the den of some female with her young, and she attacked them. They're a fierce sight when they charge."

Soneri nodded and turned to continue his ascent towards the mountain bar. His path would take him through the chestnut grove in the direction of Malpasso, but away from the shooting.

"Take care," the gamekeeper shouted after him.

"I run risks for a living."

Montelupo looked different to him today. The whistles and shouts in the distance all seemed part of a tension throbbing in the shadows or springing from unseen life in the undergrowth. He hurried on, impelled by an anxiety to which he could give no name. His path took him past the deserted, rubbish-filled huts and out onto the small clearing in front of the bar. The sun had been up for some time, and in areas free of vegetation the rocks felt warm. Baldi was busying himself with the stove, and had placed the heavy beech chairs upside down on the tables. Soneri waved to him and pointed questioningly at the bar-room.

"It's over for the season. Maybe for good, I'm not sure," Baldi said.

"You're on the young side to be thinking about retiring. Your best days are still ahead of you."

Baldi looked at him doubtfully. "Was it the Woodsman they were firing at this morning?"

"No. They seem to have blundered on a female boar who then charged at them. You could hear the yells."

"They've obviously got the firepower, but they've got to hit the right spot to bring down an animal that size."

Soneri nodded. "Do you think he killed Paride?"

Baldi looked up and held Soneri's gaze, shaking his white hair. "He's capable of it, but the whole thing seems strange to me."

"Maybe he owed him money."

Baldi lifted up the round lids over the stove, releasing a burst of flame and a cloud of sparks. "It's possible. He's not a man who'd peacefully put up with any injustice done to him, but somehow it doesn't add up."

The commissario kept his eyes fixed on Baldi, who was

on his feet now and stood facing him, as bulky as a haystack. "It's more likely he bumped off Palmiro. It was him who collected the cash in the village, while the son dealt with the banks. And then he'd grown up with Palmiro. They were like brothers, Palmiro, the Woodsman and poor Capelli. What a threesome!"

"That might be why he felt betrayed."

"Well…" was all Baldi could say. "Anyway, what does it matter what I think? The only ones that matter are the carabinieri. It's them who have to change their minds, isn't it?"

"That's true."

"They'll never catch him. They don't know the kind of man they're dealing with. The Woodsman's got more cunning than a wildcat. Even the S.S. never managed to trap him, so do you see a handful of carabinieri succeeding? In a couple of days, their teeth'll start chattering with the cold, they'll get lost in the mists and they'll end up whining into their walkie-talkies for someone to come and take them home. The mountain is hard and pitiless. You need a tough hide."

The wind carried the sound of dogs barking in the distance on Monte Matto and, outside, Dolly started growling. Even Baldi stopped for a moment to listen to the chorus from the hunting pack.

"They're over at Bragalata. They've been moving very fast, so they'll get tired of it quickly."

There was only one table without upturned seats, and Baldi sat on top of it. "The one good thing to come out of this is that all those foreigners who used to go up and down to La Spezia have cleared off. They're afraid of being picked up."

Baldi got to his feet and took two glasses and a bottle from the bar which now had nothing on it. He poured a measure for himself and one for Soneri. "Your father had a tough hide. He liked the mountains. He applied for a job in the woods, but it didn't work out. You needed someone to put in a word for you, so they ended up with people from the Veneto or the South."

"You needed the party card, or else a letter from the parish priest," Soneri said.

"And your father was a red, and not only that, a partisan in the Garibaldi brigades."

"Didn't the Rodolfis care about these things?"

"They certainly did! They were always hand in glove with the priests. Every sacristy or church in need of restoration could count on their support. It was all bluff, of course. Palmiro was only interested in money, and Paride was even more of a phoney."

"So how come my father..."

"I've never understood that."

"Paride's wife gave me to understand that..." The commissario could not go on. Anger gripped him by the throat.

"She's mad," Baldi cut in. "She married for money, but the moment she discovered it was all coming crashing down, she went right off her head. And then Palmiro's death..."

"Did she get on well with him?"

Baldi burst out laughing, his eyes sparkling with malice. "Get on well with him! Everybody for miles around knew she was in his bed. Paride was living up at the Boschi house, leaving Villa del Greppo to her and Palmiro. It was obvious it was going to end up that way. A woman like her needs to feel reassured and protected, and Palmiro gave her all she wanted. In spite of his age, he was still full of vigour. Paride could hardly give her security. He didn't feel secure in himself."

"But he knew?"

"Of course he knew, but he didn't give a damn. When he felt the urge, he'd pick up one of those women available in rich men's clubs. A quick encounter, no time wasted."

Soneri was about to ask more about his father, but he was

interrupted by a shot. Others followed in quick succession, like an irregular burst of machine-gun fire. Each shot was separate and distinct.

"That's a real battle now." Baldi rose to his feet and went to the window looking out towards Bragalata. "They must have found the Woodsman, but he fired first."

"Are you sure?" Soneri said, coming to join him. He looked over the grey wasteland of rock, below which a green undergrowth of myrtles flourished, with the beech wood further down.

"The first shot was from a Beretta. Then there was rifle fire."

Silence fell again for a few moments, then another round of shots rang out from somewhere among the tangle of beech trees.

"Rifles. Like in the war."

"Have they got him, do you think?" Soneri said.

"It's strange that he fired fist."

"They probably told him to surrender and he reacted."

"Could be. He wouldn't think twice. Or maybe he's got one of the carabinieri."

"Why would he do that? He has to keep out of the way. If he shoots one of them, it'll make them the more determined."

Dolly came to the window and sought out Soneri's hand.

"She's agitated, and that tells you there's electricity in the air. Animals sense these things before we do. They can smell our fear," Baldi said.

There was not another sound to be heard. Even the dogs had stopped barking.

Baldi was unnerved by the sound of the gunfire and moved away from the window, but the commissario remained, listening intently. Dolly was sitting beside him, but she was clearly uneasy and even looked as though she wanted to run away.

"The dog senses something," Soneri said, looking anxiously around the room.

"Maybe she's picking up a voice, or the noise of the carabinieri moving in the undergrowth. We'll never see them in the woods from here."

The commissario moved back from the window. The sun was high enough in the sky to melt the frost on the roof, so water was dripping steadily. Baldi, still shaken, was staring into his glass with the expression of a man in a drunken depression. He got up and started packing away things which were still lying about. The commissario was making an effort to interpret the deep silence which had fallen after the shots, but failed to make sense of it. He was on the point of rising to his feet, even if only to escape the sense of impotence which had come over him, when Dolly, starting to bark, stopped him.

"Someone's coming," Baldi said. He relaxed when Ghidini appeared in the doorway.

"They're on friendly terms," Ghidini said, grinning at Dolly and his *lagotto*. "Is she on heat?"

Soneri shrugged to indicate that he had no idea.

"Where have you been?" Baldi said.

"Where the battle is raging."

Baldi could not hide his curiosity.

"The Woodsman has fucked them all up, good and proper," Ghidini said. "I was over at Groppizioso, on the slopes looking out over Bragalata, when I saw the carabiniere detachments coming up. I got my dog to stay quiet and moved off the path. They stopped to have a bite to eat near the drying plant at Pratoguasto, sitting in a neat circle like school kids, each one with his picnic box open between his legs. At that point, who should appear from behind the Macchiaferro waterfalls but the Woodsman himself? He didn't want to pick them off there and then. He fired at a beech tree and the splinters flew all over the carabinieri. Then he disappeared up the gorge and out of sight."

"But they must have fired thirty or forty rounds."

"Yes, but at mosquitoes. They had no idea where he was."

"That was a stupid thing for him to do. Now they'll call in reinforcements," Soneri said.

"That's the Woodsman for you," Ghidini said. "He's in a rage because they've put guards on his house in the Madoni. They even smashed one of the huts where he kept all the cheese he'd got in August."

"This is going to end in disaster," Baldi said.

"One of the carabinieri has been taken to hospital already," Ghidini said.

"Who?" Soneri asked.

"God knows, but he was shot by one of his own men. They're not well trained and don't know about the use of firearms. In the chaos, one of them must have slipped and the gun went off."

"Is he seriously injured?"

"I don't know. He was holding his arm, and then he must have fainted. A rifle shot could go right through you."

The commissario got up. The sun was shining through the window, and had formed a halo round the Bragalata peak. It was a call which Soneri was, as ever, incapable of resisting. He bade farewell to Baldi and shouted to Dolly who was fighting off the amorous approaches of Ghidini's *lagotto*. Ghidini himself followed Soneri out, and when he turned towards him, the commissario could not help noticing Ghidini's embarrassment.

"There's something I've got to tell you. I should've told you ages ago, but it seemed too trivial."

The commissario took out a cigar and matches.

"It was something the Woodsman said about your father."

Soneri's attention was so concentrated that he allowed the match to burn out in his hand.

"He said that Palmiro was very grateful to him for resolving some question during the war, but he didn't want too many people to know about it. It was to be a secret between the two of them and only a few others. The Woodsman was one of those few."

"Something to do with the partisans?"

"Perhaps. I never really understood. Gualerzi is one of those people who never gives a straight answer to a question. If you ask him things directly, he clams up."

Soneri experienced another wave of impotence. He felt like dropping it all and leaving, but this mood dissolved on the instant. He had no choice but to continue with this bizarre investigation. Ghidini went back into the bar, and Soneri turned towards Malpasso.

He stopped at the stables next to the summer grazing lands, hoping to meet the man who had acted as messenger the day before, but he found the doors locked and bolted against drifting snow. He was about to take the path down the mountain when his mobile rang. Angela seemed flustered, or perhaps she had some important information to communicate.

"Monica, the one whose barn they burned, he's put all the blame on the banks and on the Rodolfis."

"So?" Soneri said, sitting on a rock to savour the heat of the sun.

"He says the banks had been perfectly aware for some time of the company's plight, and for that reason should never have advised their customers to buy the bonds, nor should they have sold them themselves."

"That's true as far as it goes, but if the company had never run up all those debts…"

"You could equally say that about the savers. They knew, and continued to invest in junk bonds because the rates of interest were much higher than usual."

"They all knew and they all went along with it, hoping it would all turn out right in the end. There wasn't a single one with the courage to dig his heels in, or just say no!"

"It wouldn't have resolved anything. There were too many snouts in the trough. You're always digging your heels in at the police station, and what have you got to show for it?"

"I've got an ulcer. But at least I'm at peace with my conscience. Do you think it's enjoyable eating shit and then having to say how lovely it was? I choose the lesser evil."

Angela snorted and, pretending not to have heard, carried on. "As regards the hole in the company's accounts, Monica puts the whole blame on the Rodolfis, and specifically on his former friend, Paride. He says he made a lot of mistakes. He was guilty of selling at too narrow margins, with the result that he ended up with a gaping chasm in the balance sheets. So as not to go bankrupt, he asked him to cover the debts with fictitious operations, or with false, offshore financial instruments in phantom companies."

The commissario grunted something to imply he could not take any more. He felt depressed, weighed down by a deep sadness. He thought back to his carefree childhood on the streets of the village, and reflected that there had been more happiness when everyone was poor. He found himself, by some obscure mechanism, recalling philosophical precepts he had learned at school, and particularly a definition of happiness as the cessation of suffering. That said it all; people are happy when they no longer suffer.

He heard Angela calling out to him repeatedly. "Did you roll off the path?"

"No, I was just thinking of suffering and happiness."

"You're a great one for contradictions. Maybe that's why you're such a bitter-sweet man."

After he switched off his phone, he decided that basically she was right. He was quite downcast, but at the same time he was relishing the straw-coloured, autumn sunshine. Before plunging into the shadow of the woods, he waited till the light took on a copper hue as the sun set behind Bragalata.

8

There was about half an hour of daylight left when Soneri took the road to Villa del Greppo for the second time. Dolly trotted faithfully behind him, evidently having no idea that she was facing another separation. Only when they were at the gates did she betray any sign of recognising the place, and began to sniff about and growl. The commissario pressed the bell and this time heard a hollow ring inside. After a minute, the Philippino arrived and looked unwelcomingly at him.

"The Signora not here. Out. Car."

"I've brought the dog back. She ran away the last time."

"Always run. Not want here."

"She's young. She needs exercise, so if you keep her in a pound…"

"Used to Signor Palmiro. His dog dead, so took this one."

"Wasn't it Paride's?"

"Yes, but he not go shoot. This dog good, very good."

"Did Palmiro always take his rifle with him in the evening?"

The Philippino blushed, and Soneri realised he had touched a nerve. The servant waved his hands about him as though he were losing his balance and was struggling, with his limited vocabulary, to find the right words.

"I can ask the gamekeeper," Soneri said.

"He said it only pleasure left," the Philippino said, relieved at being allowed to give an indirect reply.

"I agree," Soneri said, looking at Dolly. "Take her to her kennel."

The servant called to Dolly, who kept her eyes on Soneri and did not move. Feeling painfully churlish, he had to turn away from those imploring eyes which seemed to be requesting an explanation. The Philippino took Dolly by the collar and dragged her in. When he heard the lock click shut, he turned towards the village. From where he was standing, it looked like a brazier flickering in the dark.

"Just down from the villa?" Maini said.

Soneri nodded.

"I saw you coming back without the dog."

"I had to give her back, but the visit was worthwhile."

Maini looked at him blankly, but did not seek further elucidation. "Paride's wife wasn't there."

"So the Philippino told me, but maybe it was only a way of getting rid of me," Soneri said.

"No, she's in Parma. Her son's had a car accident."

"Did he hurt himself playing with his toy?"

"It seems he was drunk and drugged up to the eyeballs, but he didn't do himself much damage."

"Drunk? There's a surprise. Not the best of times for the Rodolfis."

"Not just for them. Have you heard what's happened in the village?"

"What now?"

"Somebody took a knife to Biavardi. His daughter was Paride's secretary."

"Who was it?"

"Nobody knows. They attacked him at home, but possibly they were after the girl."

"Have the carabinieri been told?"

Maini's gesture implied that the matter was of no interest to him. "It took them two hours to get there because they're all searching for the Woodsman. Nobody wants to talk, and they don't exactly trust the carabinieri."

"Until a couple of days ago, Crisafulli was playing cards in the village bars."

"The general view is that the Woodsman was quite right. Paride was never popular and he cheated everybody."

"But it was Palmiro who collected the cash."

"They believe Paride deceived him as well, and that by hanging himself the old man confirmed it. He was ashamed and that was his only way out."

"It was obvious to him that they were all backing the Woodsman."

"He's only doing what they'd all have liked to do, if they had the courage."

Several people were leaving the *Rivara*, but in the gathering dusk in the piazza the commissario could not make out who they were. The sun was going down, giving way to the freezing air which crumpled the few leaves left on the branches. All along the Montelupo valley, the mist was growing thicker, making the night darker. At that moment, some lights appeared on the path above Boldara, half way up the mountainside. About a dozen torches were swaying rhythmically as the men marched back. The carabinieri, clearly having mistimed nightfall, were returning to the village.

"If we were at war, I'd say that was unwise," Maini said.

"They're abandoning the field to the Woodsman – if they'd won it in the first place," Soneri agreed.

Their conversation was abruptly interrupted by the sound of gunfire, sudden shots blasted out to disturb the peace of the valley. It seemed almost possible to see flashes as they dispelled the darkness in the foliage and cut through the evening mists, or perhaps it was the torches fanning out in search of the source of the volley. The first salvo was followed by the rifles' angry retort. Other shots rang out in quick succession, or simultaneously, from many angles, it seemed. It was clear the carabinieri were firing blindly, more in the hope of neutralising the threat than of hitting their target.

"Good God! He's firing like a devil." Soneri recognised Volpi's voice in the middle of the group that rushed out from the *Rivara*. "He's attacking them in the dark to scare them off."

Confused shouts came drifting down. Someone could be heard bawling out an order intended to restore discipline in the ranks. The favourable wind carried indistinct sounds, not intelligible words.

"He's trying to wear them down with these ambushes," Volpi said.

"It's stupid. He'd have worn them down more quickly if he'd simply kept out of their way," Soneri said. At that moment, an image of Captain Bovolenta came into his mind: all military stiffness and ingrained stubbornness, his head filled with notions of honour.

"He feels sure of himself and he's bursting with rage. If you ask me, I don't think that what Gualerzi did deserves so much as a fine," Delrio said.

"It's the reaction of a man who's been ruined." It was Rivara who spoke. "His brother once kept a regiment of Germans at bay at Badignana with nothing more than a Sten gun."

"And he was at his brother's side."

"He's not even afraid of tanks."

The carabinieri had switched off their torches so as not to provide their enemy with an easy target. They appeared to have spread out in the woods, waiting. Everything settled into an unnatural calm. Not even the hoot of an owl could be heard. They too had been silenced by the shots cutting through the air.

"If they get too far off the path, one of those boys is going to get lost, and if the Woodsman finds him, he could finish him off with a single punch," Delrio said.

"Do you remember that time at the San Matteo fair when he stunned a cow with one blow between the horns?" Rivara said.

At that moment, the firing started again, this time further up the mountain, among the chestnut trees at Campogrande.

"He's moved. He wants them to know he can attack them anywhere he likes," Maini said, his voice almost drowned out by a new volley. The bullets seemed to fly across the valley, a whistling sound followed by a bang.

"That's the Woodsman's Beretta alright," Volpi said.

He was presumably firing in the air, since his objective seemed to be to frighten them, not to hit them. Bullets sailed through the trees, snapping off branches as they passed, and Soneri imagined a shower of bark falling on the crouching carabinieri. Suddenly, they returned fire from several different positions, all aiming in the direction where they believed the Woodsman was. They had allowed him to shoot at will, but they were now obeying orders to open fire in unison, like an execution squad. The valley shook to the terrible roar of the guns, the woodland was lit up by brief flashes as rifle fire was concentrated on a ten-metre range where the breaking of branches and the thud of bullets against tree trunks was the only sound heard.

"They're focusing on the one zone, but they're covering a wide front. They hope they'll get him that way," Delrio said.

There was a sinister silence, a lull before another storm, and then an explosion, this time from some hundred metres above the carabiniere position. The wind from the blast once again ripped through the village at gale force. The Woodsman had lowered his sights and was firing into the woods. The carabinieri replied immediately, but with staggered shots which sounded like firecrackers. It was now a skirmish among the trees, fought blindly, the outcome dependent on the vagaries of chance. The trees alone provided a certain target, the wood crumbling as each bullet impacted.

Soneri shook his head. "He couldn't have done anything more stupid."

The others turned to him in disbelief, and for the first time he had the sensation of really being a policeman.

"You'd have to be there in the middle of it," Rivara said, in an almost hostile tone.

"All he had to do was keep away from them. He could have led them on a merry dance for months."

"They won't let him go back home and his wife is ill," Volpi said. This news plainly came as a surprise to the others.

"The Woodsman's made that way. When he's in a rage, he behaves like a charging boar," Rivara said.

"His wife is seriously ill." The speaker again was Volpi.

"Isn't her daughter there to look after her?" Soneri said.

"She's doing all she can, but with the carabinieri always in the house...She has got to go regularly to the hospital to be kept under observation." Volpi was keen to let it be known that he was well informed, and the group listened attentively. He spoke slowly, choosing his words with the same patience as a hunter stalking his prey. He was dressed in a heavy green jacket with many pockets, which made him look stouter.

They stayed there another quarter of an hour, listening for more exchanges of fire. There might have been bodies lying in the woods, but none of them cared. More time went by, then they heard trucks starting up and they made out the headlights shining over the reservoir. The carabinieri drove swiftly down the path through the woods and accelerated when they reached the road. The vehicles came into the piazza at speed, one behind the other. As they passed, everyone could see an officer in the front of one of the trucks holding a bandage to his forehead. Rivara announced that he saw blood flowing. "There was one taken to the hospital this morning, and now he's shot another one," he said. The vehicles did not head for the hospital, but drew up at the police station, ignored by the few bystanders.

The group outside the *Rivara* broke up, one after the other drifting off without the usual goodbyes. Indifference and passivity seemed to have infected the community, and a dull hatred lurked among the cluster of houses. In the centre of the village, the *Olmo* played host to its veterans, spectators at a drama whose latest act was unknown to them. When the commissario passed by, Magnani appeared at the door. He stubbed his cigarette out on the road, giving the impression he had been listening to all that had been said until then.

"Fine battle, eh?" he said.

"It's war now."

"If you know that captain, tell him to steer clear of the Woodsman. His chances of capturing him are slight, but the chances of Gualerzi putting a bullet in some carabiniere's head are considerable. If you tread on his toes, he won't think twice."

"I'll be sure to pass the word on, but the Woodsman is doing one crass thing after another."

"One good thing he did do, get rid of Paride."

"If it was him. But he had good reason."

"I agree the whole business is odd. Unless Rodolfi really did ruin him."

"He did the same to a lot of people."

"It was different with the Woodsman. There was nothing about Palmiro he didn't know. He could have landed him in the shit any time he wanted."

"Because he went to bed with his son's wife?"

"Lusts, desires, nothing more." Magnani was not interested in this aspect. "There were more important things. It seems there was some kind of pact between Palmiro and Gualerzi. They were both men of the woods, and men of that sort understand each other by smell alone."

"He did fix his daughter up with a job at the Rodolfi factory."

"I have an idea they used to meet on Montelupo and when they were there, they went back to being boys together. When you get right down to it, Palmiro had no idea what his business had become. Finance, stock exchange... these words reduced him to a babbling wreck. His son more or less shut him out of all the dealings, and he was none too pleased about that."

"From what I hear, they didn't even seem like members of the same family."

"Paride took after his mother. She was frail, fearful, very nervous and had never enjoyed good health. In her last years, she wouldn't even sleep with her husband, because she couldn't cope with his colossal virility. They say Palmiro was a bull of a man."

By some sort of conditioned reflex which pitched the brutal reality against the gentle image, the Rodolfi trademark, with its smiling pork butcher and the pig at his side, came back to Soneri. As the commissario felt many of his most deeply held convictions and memories disintegrate, Magnani, standing with the door ajar behind him, went on: "Don't get the idea that it was all plain sailing for Palmiro, as they believe here in the village. Nor was it all Paride's fault, even if he wasn't exactly guiltless."

"It's always easier to be forgiving about times past, and in many ways Palmiro belonged to a different world."

"I'm not nostalgic about the past. I know what it is to suffer hunger and poverty. What Palmiro's story proves is that the arrogant and unscrupulous always come out on top. Like in wartime."

"Around here he was treated as a saint."

"By people with small minds, or those who were dependent on him. That's all there is to it. They make out they don't remember how he made his money. He dealt with both the Fascists and the partisans. He was an expert at keeping a foot in both camps. He used to do what the immigrants do today, black marketeering. He never did drugs, just foodstuffs. He had a stranglehold over the peasants, but once the Americans turned up, there he was hand in glove with them. He even betrayed a couple of boys in their twenties to the Fascists, in '44. Not people from around here, because he would have been wary of the villagers."

Soneri lit a cigar to calm himself as Magnani continued, "What's at the root of the Rodolfi fortune? Greed, bullying and a fair bit of outright theft. The same as with anybody who makes money in this world. They're treated with respect, people grovel out of fear, and all their dirty tricks are forgotten. But then, even with the most beautiful animal at large in these woods, slit open their bellies and what do you find? Gore and shit."

"Until recently, the Rodolfis were still up to what you call 'dirty tricks'."

"They all are. The Rodolfis were caught out. Do you really believe that other companies are not up to their eyes in debt, and that they don't get up to the same kind of underhand dealings? The difference is that they're cleverer and have a little more style."

"Or more effective political cover."

"Politicians don't count for anything any more. Take Aimi. He was no more than a middle man, but he had to flee the village like a thief. Maybe the real mistake the Rodolfis made was to bet on politics, and to think that politicians were still major players. They gargle ideas and ideologies in public, but it's cash that counts nowadays. Financiers, bankers and industrialists, these are the men who pay the piper, and they toss a few crumbs to the politicians to keep them quiet, the way you toss a dog a bone."

"The Woodsman was one of the partisans and he must have known all this."

Magnani nodded, deep in thought. His face was flushed, perhaps because what he had been saying had made him agitated. They both remained silent, until the wife of the old man who had been Palmiro's assistant came down the street, pushing the wheelchair

"Here's another one who saw it all but found it convenient to keep his mouth shut," Magnani said. He stood out of the way to let them pass. The husband, forcibly removed by his wife from the company of his peers, was cursing her loudly, but she remained impassive. The commissario helped her lift the wheelchair over the entrance, bending down so that his face was level with man's as he did so.

"Give me a cigar," the man whispered.

His wife intervened peremptorily. "He's not allowed to smoke. Doctor's orders."

She spoke as though her husband were not there, but he persisted. Soneri got the impression that if he had been able to rise, he would have slapped her. Without warning, he changed the subject. His mind leaped from one topic to another, particularly concerning the past.

"If you want to know where Palmiro used to go, I'll tell you," the old man said. The subject was plainly an obsession with him. The commissario could not tell if he was aware that his ex-employer was dead. Perhaps at that moment he had forgotten.

"We used to go to Malpasso, Badignana, then on to Monte Matto and Bragalata in summer, if we had time or if we were out hunting. In the evening, we would sometimes walk along the Croce path with the dogs. That was a shorter walk," he mumbled, the saliva running over his chin.

With the zeal of a nurse, his ever-vigilant wife bent over to clean round his mouth, cutting off the final words and provoking a fresh spasm of impotent rage. She proceeded to push the wheelchair forward, preventing further conversation, but as she was doing so, the old man turned his head to the side and managed to utter one more sentence which, from what he heard, Soneri worked out had something to do with full baskets. He took it from the pride with which the old man expressed himself that they had both been excellent hunters.

Magnani shook his head. "It'd be far better to end it all rather than live like that, a burden to yourself and those around you."

Soneri was thinking of Palmiro's walks and of the fact that he had not stopped going to the woods even when he had been left on his own, totally isolated inside his company and alone in life, apart from the Woodsman with whom he continued to have mysterious, fleeting encounters, and Manuela, with whom he shared a bed.

"They should give him a pill. I'm sure he'd prefer that if he was still lucid. I've no doubt he would do the same as his old boss if he could," Magnani said. He turned on his heel, pushed open the door and without another word went back into the bar.

Soneri walked through the village to the *Scoiattolo*. He found Sante, pacing anxiously up and down in the courtyard. "There's that carabiniere in there waiting for you," he announced.

"The maresciallo?"

"Not him. The officer, his superior."

"Bovolenta, the captain."

"That'll be the one. I asked him when Palmiro's funeral is to take place, and he told me the magistrate has now given authorisation. It could be tomorrow afternoon, but they've nothing to do with it any more. It's the family's responsibility, and if you ask my opinion, they'll want it done quietly."

Bovolenta got up when he saw Soneri come in. He seemed exhausted, but was keen to maintain his military bearing. "If I'm ever to have you as my guest at dinner, I've got to come to your den."

"After a day like you've had, you must have something really important to tell me. By the way," Soneri added hurriedly, "how are the wounded officers?"

Bovolenta put on a serious expression. He was clearly very worried. "One is in hospital. Nearly lost his forearm. The other man is only concussed. He was hit on the forehead by a huge branch."

"So all in all, it wasn't too bad, considering the number of shots that were exchanged."

"He's mad. He seemed to be everywhere at once. He was out to kill us all."

"Mad he may be, but he didn't want to kill anyone. He was deliberately firing into the air."

Sante came over to ask what they wanted to eat. Bovolenta chose the *anolini in brodo,* and Soneri did the same.

"We've lost face over this."

"Don't look at it that way. It's not a duel, and your honour's not at stake. The Woodsman's on his home ground and Montelupo is difficult terrain."

"A lot of them don't want to go back up there. They're scared stiff. A couple of my men went completely berserk and started screaming. I think he heard it."

Soneri tried to think back to when he had been in a similar position, with bullets whistling around him and not much cover. He remembered an armed robbery in Milan when huge bullets pierced the doors of his Alfa Romeo, leaving the shattered metal looking like a cheese grater. The shots had missed him by a whisker. Half a degree more one way or the other and he would not be there now addressing an angry policeman.

"You're not likely to take home any prizes from this hunting trip," the commissario warned him.

Bovolenta looked at him and was close to agreeing, but he said, "I have no choice."

"Are you quite sure it was the Woodsman?"

"His wife's seriously ill with diabetes and he needs to get back the money he lent the elder Rodolfi to pay for her treatment. Does that not seem to you motive enough?"

"Then why didn't he kill Palmiro?"

"Who says he didn't try? Who else could have been responsible for all those shots fired in recent days? And anyway, Palmiro did away with himself." The captain dipped his spoon deep into the plate and picked out some of the *anolini* from the soup. He must have gone without his lunch, since only hunger could have made him forget military etiquette to that extent. After a few minutes, he cleaned his mouth and looked Soneri in the face. "You're not convinced, are you?"

The commissario, his mouth full, shrugged.

"I came here to ask you for some advice," Bovolenta said.

"I don't really know much about it."

"We cannot continue to move about in a herd, as we did today. Gualerzi would hear us from a long way off and he'd have all the time in the world to hide until we got within range. We'll have to use his tactics, hit and run. The problem is we don't know where to find him."

"There I can't help you. There's not a man around here, even if he knows the woods, who would know where to find the Woodsman."

"He must have enemies."

"That may be, but no-one would dare stand up against him. Anyway, everybody in the village is on his side."

"He's mad and he has to be stopped," Bovolenta said, stretching across the table to grab the bottle of Gutturnio, an act of rudeness which definitely ended any pretence at good manners. "A desperate lunatic who's playing his last card."

"Gualerzi's always been like that. He's a savage with a code of honour."

"I don't believe he has the slightest interest in honour. He's desperate and capable of anything."

"You're wrong there. Granted he can be ruthless, but he's not the bastard you make him out to be."

"In the past, maybe not, but he's got cancer. Did you know that?"

Soneri stopped and would have liked to say that was the only thing which would make him surrender, but he had no wish to irritate the captain further. "How do you know that?" he said.

"We searched his house and we found the tests."

"If that's so, what's the point of trying to ambush him? All you have to do is wait."

"If we were monks, we could, but we're carabinieri."

"I don't see any other way out. Don't kid yourselves that the Woodsman is going to let himself be captured like a common criminal. That's one thing he's not."

"He shot at us."

"If you carry on pursuing him, he'll take one of you out. But he'll keep the last bullet for himself."

Bovolenta appeared deep in thought. For a few seconds there was a brightness in his eyes, before weariness made them cloud over again.

"Listen to me," Soneri said. "Scale down your operations to patrolling Montelupo. Leave him in charge of the territory, and he might even come round. Otherwise it's going to end badly. He's not a man for compromises, not even with himself."

"If it were up to me…Headquarters have decreed…I obey orders."

The commissario felt some sympathy for Bovolenta. He was subject to the unsubtlety of higher command, to a primitive vision which divided the world into two, friends and enemies, victories and defeats. "Tell your superiors that to wring one chicken's neck there's no need to knock the whole hen-run down," he said, in an attempt to reduce the tension.

"There may be no way out for the Woodsman, but there isn't for me either. How will he cope with that? That last bullet you were talking about might be for me."

"I'm afraid that's true. If your life's at stake, stand up to them. This time the game is worth the candle."

"I can't."

The commissario let his impatience get the better of him. He had never had any sympathy with irrational conduct, even when he understood its origins. "One of the things I have learned is that there are times when you have to say No, because otherwise there's no difference between us and the peasants here who knew what was going on but put up no fight. In their own way, they too were obeying orders, orders of self-interest. They ended up ruined."

Bovolenta sat bolt upright against the back of the chair,

saying nothing, facing the bottle he had emptied almost by himself. There was real humanity under the uniform, but it was the uniform which carried the day. Soneri felt disappointment rise from deep inside him.

"God save us all," murmured the captain, and it occurred to Soneri that he was as well to put his trust in the Almighty since he lacked the will to make use of reason.

Bovolenta put on his cap with the silver flame, symbol of the carabinieri, at the front. He held out his hand to the commissario. "I'm grateful to you. You've been my guest, even if this is your home."

Soneri followed him to the door. He intended to take a walk before going to bed. They walked side by side for a little way, in silence, until they reached the piazza. The captain said goodbye once more, but he stood facing him, plainly pursuing some line of thought. "Among the Woodsman's papers, we found your father's name. I didn't know he'd been a partisan."

Soneri nodded, doing his best to conceal his agitation. "What paper was that?"

"A chart giving the names of the Garibaldi brigade in this locality. Your father was political commissioner."

"He was anxious to keep well away from gunfire."

"You're the first police officer I have met whose parents were Communists." Bovolenta smiled. "Did they not make things difficult at H.Q.? Not so long ago, it would not have been easy with a background like yours."

"I've had my problems. Was there anything else about my father?"

The captain realised he had opened a subject of some importance, and indicated to Soneri that he understood. "I'll get my men to have a look. Or maybe I should attend to it myself. Yes, I think that would be better."

He walked off and Soneri, although confused, realised that,

in spite of everything, he had formed a favourable opinion of Bovolenta, and that was something that did not happen too often. His thoughts turned to the papers the captain had found in the Madoni hills. They were not likely to contain anything he did not already know, but then again there might be something new. Perhaps they would provide the key to his father's relations with the Rodolfis.

He did not realise that he was walking towards Villa del Greppo until he became aware of the deepening darkness on the road leading to the fields. He turned and saw beneath him the roofs of the village, beyond which the vast, empty spaces of the valley stretched into the distance. He looked closely at the piazza, deserted at that hour, the lighted window of the *Rivara* and the lamp-posts lining the narrow streets. Anyone chancing upon the village without knowing what was going on there would have decided that it was a tranquil enough spot in which to spend a week searching for mushrooms. He lit a cigar, took out his mobile and dialled Angela's number.

"I've just had dinner with Bovolenta."

"Whom do you prefer, him or me?"

"He told me that the Woodsman is on his last legs."

"Is he surrounded?"

"No, he's got cancer."

Angela sighed. "A person in that condition is capable of anything."

"Precisely. I think that's the case with him. So far the shots he's fired at the carabinieri have only been to scare them, but if they go on hunting him down..."

"If he no longer cares what happens to him, why should he care about other people?"

Soneri changed the subject abruptly. "The captain has found some papers concerning my father in the Woodsman's house."

"Are you back on that hobby-horse of yours?"

"Don't you want to know what he said?"

"Maybe that woman was talking nonsense. Maybe she made the whole thing up."

"So much the better if she did," Soneri said, cutting her short.

At that same moment, he heard a dog bark, and the bark was familiar. He interrupted the conversation with Angela to listen. It came from the mountain, from the path which led from Greppo to Campogrande. He stood still for a few moments, keeping his mind clear as though he were afraid his thoughts might make a noise. Everything was peaceful, apart from the hoot of an owl in the depths of the woods.

"You still there?" Angela said.

"I thought I'd picked up a sound in the trees."

No sooner had he spoken than he heard the dog bark again, this time from lower down. The animal was coming closer. Just a few paces more and, if the wind was in the right direction, it would pick up his scent.

"Where are you?" Angela said.

"Near the Rodolfis' place. I think there's something going on down there."

This time there was no possible doubt. A dog was racing in his direction.

"I am glad I called you," Soneri said, already guessing which dog it was.

"I always bring good luck," Angela said, but without any idea of what was going on.

The dog emerged from the brush a few moments later and came bounding down the road. Soneri felt its tongue lick his hands, and when he bent down to rub it behind the ears, he had all the confirmation he needed that this was Dolly. There was no way of knowing why she was on the road which led from Campogrande to the uplands of Croce. He walked on until the villa appeared ahead of him. He committed to memory the position of the mule-track, but he could not see the whole track from where he was standing, since it turned into a small gorge before climbing up to Greppo. It was then that he heard a low whistle. Dolly heard it too and stiffened, making no movement, standing as still as a hunting dog about to put a flock of partridges to flight. So she had not run away. Someone was with her. The commissario looked in the same direction as Dolly and noticed she was staring down the path. Shortly afterwards, a faint light appeared – perhaps a torch – and moved about. Then it disappeared and the whistle was blown again.

Someone was searching for Dolly further along the path, but she had heard Soneri talk on the phone and had come looking for him, or perhaps she had picked up the scent of his cigar. The commissario thought of going over to the mule-track but he worried that whoever was there might hear him. He was also constrained by memories of tales he had been told in his childhood about that path, where "strange things" could be seen and "stranger things" heard. At night-time, the path was lit by lights which appeared and disappeared, while indistinct whispers and laments were carried on the wind.

He decided to wait close to the villa. He struggled to keep Dolly quiet, as she whined and tried to snuggle under the hem of his duffle coat. He hoped to see someone emerge along the path, even if he was not clear who that someone might be. For a while he thought it might be Manuela, but the more he pictured her with all the airs and graces of a *gran signora*, the less plausible did it seem that she would be out in the woods at night. So he remained where he was, in the company of Dolly in the pitch black of a moonless night, the stars invisible above the dense, damp air.

An hour later, when it was evident that no-one would be coming, he set off. He wondered what had become of that nocturnal presence, made manifest in whistles and faint lights, which seemed only to confirm the truth of the old legends. He walked into the village, escorted by Dolly, stopped in the piazza and took a seat on the wall. The dog stood facing him, looking up and wagging her tail. Her eyes were shining with a trust and devotion which he found deeply affecting. He tried to imagine what life would be like with Dolly at his side. The very thought was a novelty, but all of a sudden he saw a custard-coloured brightness in the form of a huge candle swell up before him.

A bright light and the acrid smell of burning rubber came from the lower part of the village. Out of the darkness, an enormous funnel of smoke ascended into the night sky, then stretched like a giant mushroom as it moved in the direction of Montelupo. Soneri raced down the deserted streets until, in the square overlooking the new town, he saw a car in flames. There was no-one there to make any attempt to extinguish the fire – although there was nothing that could now be saved. Behind the shutters, whispered voices and the sound of bolts being drawn could be heard, but as the fire died down, silence again fell on the village. The commissario stood watching as the flames turned to glowing embers. Only the rubber of the tyres and the plastics were still burning. Finally the carabinieri arrived.

Crisafulli had the dishevelled look of a man who had fallen asleep at his desk. "After a day like the one I've had, this was all I needed," he moaned in Neapolitan.

"It must have been half an hour ago," Soneri told him. "It could have been a slow fuse in a petrol can. The whole thing was over in a couple of minutes."

The maresciallo walked round the burned-out wreck.

"Do you know whose it is?" the commissario said. "All I can make out is that it was a Ford."

Crisafulli nodded. "It belongs to the mayor's son. I thought this sort of thing only happened in Naples."

The maresciallo ordered his assistant to take down all the details and to call in the Special Forensic squad who were still in the village investigating Paride's death. "Who knows? They might come up with something interesting," he said, but he sounded doubtful.

"That Romanian, the one who was found with Rodolfi's mobile, do you still have him in your cells?"

"The magistrate has authorised an extension of the period of custody. You never know."

They both looked again at the car, still burning but no longer fiercely. Neither had anything more to say. From time to time the steel of the chassis made a crackling sound as it buckled in the heat.

"When is the funeral of the two Rodolfis?"

Crisafulli gave him an embarrassed glance from under the peak of his cap, and shivered. He must have been frozen standing about in the cold. "Tomorrow at dawn. Paride's wife fixed the time and the only ones who know about it are Don Bruno and us."

"What are they afraid of? The villagers have been quiet up till now and they'll stay that way."

"There are other people not from here who feel cheated as well. People from the city, for example, and they always make more fuss. And then," Crisafulli said, lowering his voice, "the Rodolfis are ashamed of being seen in public."

The commissario winked at Crisafulli and put his hand on his shoulder. "I'm going to bed. And you're out hunting again tomorrow."

"Commissario, we're not hunters. We're the hunted."

9

In his dreams, Soneri saw the chestnut groves of Campo-grande, and saw himself careering half way down the hill, zig-zagging from tree trunk to tree trunk on the steep slopes at whose foot stood the new town with its workshops and wide road, buzzing with activity. Once more he saw himself with his father, once more he heard good advice delivered in half-phrases accompanied by vague gestures, but as he lay half-asleep and half-awake, he felt a sense of anguish creep over him. His father walked ahead round the trunks of fallen trees, indifferent to his son's inability to keep up. Soneri saw himself tumble and roll madly downhill, bumping into tree after tree, but at that point he awoke with a start to see Ida standing beside his bed, shaking him, bending over him, holding the blankets with both hands as though she were kneading *sfoglia*.

When he switched on the light, he saw her face clearly, but it was a face deformed by panic. "Sante's very ill, very ill," she repeated, over and over.

Finally she let go, allowing him to get up. He peered at the alarm clock, which read half-past four. Once out of bed, he was assailed by the biting cold, and this, together with the dream, the restless night and the abrupt awakening, knocked him back on his heels as effectively as a punch on the nose. He put on his slippers and slowly began to come to his senses.

Ida led the way, proceeding sideways, almost skipping

down the stairs. When she reached the landing on the floor below, she turned into the room where she and her husband slept. Sante's eyes were glazed over. He seemed to be staring at the ceiling, but with a look of disbelief. A slight wheeze was the only sign of life. Ida and Soneri positioned themselves at either side of the bed, as powerless as if attending a wake.

"I kept telling him to calm down. He couldn't sleep and he wouldn't take the pills to reduce his stress," Ida said, through tears.

Soneri was lost for words as he passively assisted at the undoing of another image from his past, the one featuring the relaxed and jolly Sante, the inn-keeper who made everyone feel at home. It was at that point he made the decision never to return again to the places where he had grown up.

A few minutes later the ambulance siren rang out and the stretcher bearers rushed in. Before carrying him out, a paramedic attached a drip to his arm, immobilised him with a collar and put a tube down his throat. A machine seemed to keep time with the patient's precarious, irregular heartbeat. While this was going on, Ida went on explaining obsessively what had happened, but no-one paid any heed to her. She said that Sante had been in a state of agitation for days, that he had not gone to bed at all on recent nights but had padded about from sunset till dawn. He had done the same the previous night, but this time he had wanted to be ready early to go to the Rodolfis' funeral.

"I don't know what he wanted to do, doctor," she went on, "but I'm afraid he was planning something crazy. 'I want to go and spit in his face,' he kept saying. I was doing my best to calm him down, but the rage poisoned his blood."

Ida repeated that he was no longer taking his pills, and at that the paramedic briefly raised his head. Sante was lifted up and carried cautiously to the front door where the ambulance was waiting. Soneri watched him leave his *pensione*, but it appeared he was also taking leave of his mind. A new image, that of a defenceless body trussed up like a chicken, was being superimposed on the image of the man Soneri had known.

He got dressed and went out without waiting for breakfast. The first light of day showed up the white of the countryside hardened by the frost. As he walked, he heard the crystals crackle under his feet with the same sound as a footfall on sand, while Dolly's paws struck lightly and rhythmically against the asphalt. There was no-one in the graveyard chapel other than Don Bruno, busily arranging a bouquet sent anonymously, with no name on the accompanying card. In a corner, there was a brush standing guard over a pile of dust with some dry petals and stems.

"Is this where the funeral is taking place?"

The priest looked up and turned an expressionless face to Soneri. "It's already taken place," he said, pointing over to the Rodolfi family tomb.

"When?"

"It finished half an hour ago," replied the priest, shaking his head. "You didn't miss anything."

"Who was there?"

"Only his wife, the son on crutches and the Philippino servant. A dozen or so old men turned up, but they were here only for Palmiro. Nobody so much as looked at Paride's coffin."

"He didn't go out of his way to make himself liked. He's caused some people, like Sante Righelli, to suffer a heart attack."

"Sante?" Don Bruno repeated incredulously. "He seemed the most well-balanced man in the world."

"If they cheat you out of everything you own, it's not easy to maintain your composure."

"That's because people no longer focus on the things which really matter. Look here," he said, pointing to the rows of crosses. "All these people lived as though death were not part of their lives. When you believe you're immortal, you only think of yourself."

Soneri reacted with impatience, as Don Bruno noticed. He came over to where the commissario was standing, fixing his black, slightly malicious eyes on him. "This village has grown more and more corrupt ever since money, real money, started circulating here. Material possessions have become the centre of people's world, meaning that everything is treated as merchandise or as a means to an end. Instead – how did Plato put it – you must attend first to your soul."

"If you want to put it like that," Soneri said, sceptically, "but that kind of philosophy sounds better in a sermon."

Don Bruno looked at him darkly. "They'll all realise eventually that they're on the wrong path. When they're near the end, I've heard them damning everything they've spent their lives pursuing, and spitting on the very things they believed in blindly for many, many years. My sermons are not enough, but death will convince them to look on all the baubles of this world as vanity."

"I'm no intellectual, and my explanation would be much simpler. When a person is poor, he knows he might need other people, and so he's prepared to give a hand because one day he might be in trouble himself. It's got nothing to do with goodness of heart. What moves people is fear and need."

The priest looked perplexed. "There's some truth in that. Poverty induces prudence and humility, while wealth leads to arrogance. You might say that these things too are the fruits of fear, but I insist that respect and human understanding are also factors."

Don Bruno lowered his voice as he came to the end of his speech, as though he were in the confessional. Soneri saw written on his face the concern that must have been tearing him apart inside, and he thought of all the various spiritual exercises the priest must have practised to stem that haemorrhage of trust. Soneri, on the other hand, was falling in a void where there was no safety net.

"Think about it the way your father did. He too believed that people were motivated only by their needs, including people on his side. He used to say they struggled for a cause because they had no choice, because they'd been humiliated and wanted to redeem themselves, but, so he said, once they were free of poverty they would think the same way as the boss class. When you look at the situation today, he wasn't far wrong. He believed in what he said, and he understood the difference between a man with ideals and a man with a full belly."

"How did my father get on with the Rodolfis?"

"You've already asked me that and I don't know what to say."

"There are some weird rumours going about."

"Pay no heed to them," Don Bruno said, waving a hand to clear the air.

"No, I have to resolve this, even if the conclusion is that the whole story is rubbish."

"Look, all I can tell you is that it was something to do with a piece of paper, a document, but don't ask me what kind of document, because I couldn't tell you. I also know that it's an old story, going back at least as far as the war."

Soneri immediately thought of the papers Bovolenta had found in the Woodsman's house, and was tempted to hurry off and find him. Don Bruno noticed this reaction and turned away to get on with cleaning the chapel. The commissario thanked him and went out to find it was already daylight and the sun was rising over the mountains. No sooner had he left the graveyard than he heard the sound of gunfire. It came

from somewhere above Boldara, and no doubt took the carabinieri, who were barely ten minutes along the footpath, by
surprise. Plainly the Woodsman was intent on warning them
what was in store for them that day. At the same moment, a
ray of sunlight shone over the peaks and lit up Montelupo.

Soneri walked quickly down to the village and went
into Rivara's for breakfast. "Any news of Sante?" he asked
immediately.

"The ambulance men who took him to hospital say his
condition is critical. They think it was a stroke, and he might
be paralysed."

The commissario said nothing, but he thought it might be
the end for Sante. "It's like half-dying," he finally said.

"Better to go altogether than to linger on," Rivara said.
"Did you hear that?" he added, nodding in the direction of
Montelupo.

"The war's started again."

"The Woodsman's bidding them good-morning," Delrio
said, appearing behind Soneri.

"Where's his daughter?"

"Sometimes at home with her mother and sometimes at
the Rodolfi factory. The workers are keeping guard on the
salame factory," Delrio said, before asking, "What's Paride's
dog doing here?"

"She ran away from the villa, and ever since I found her
beside her master's body she follows me everywhere."

"Ran away? They must be keeping her in the courtyard."

"I wouldn't know, but she isn't the first dog to run away."

"The Rodolfis have a pound with a high wall and metal
bars. I went up there with an official from the Health Board to
check it out because they'd built the pound without a permit.
Anyway, you've got a good deal with that dog. She's an excep-
tional animal. She can sniff out game from kilometres away."

The commissario patted Dolly as they went out. "Unfortunately I can't be keeping her. She's not mine and, besides, I haven't the space."

"If you want her, just keep her. What's the widow going to do with a dog? She's certainly not going hunting, and nor is that Philippino she's got in her house," he said, without hiding his contempt.

"Latterly it was Palmiro who took Dolly out."

"His own hound was getting on a bit. He couldn't even catch a bitch on heat."

In the piazza they passed some carabinieri from the Special Forensic unit with a pack of journalists and photographers at their heels. "What with the Woodsman, the Romanian, the fires and the stabbings, they don't know where to turn," Rivara said.

"Let's hope it doesn't drag on too long," Delrio said. Soneri detected a longing for normality and a desire to get back to a peaceful life lived in an out-of-the-way place in the shadow of the mountains. Even if he could see the advantages of the "take life as it comes" mentality, Soneri failed to understand how anyone could aspire to that kind of narcosis, and it occurred to him that perhaps it was that same unbearable emptiness which had forced his father to leave. There comes a point when wandering in the mountains is not enough, and when the discontents of middle age highlight only a series of disappointments.

He went out into the ice-cold air to chase away those thoughts, but he thought of Angela, who was perhaps at that very moment getting ready for the office. He looked too at Dolly with her heart-warming devotion and decided it was time to stop being miserable.

He climbed towards Greppo and then turned onto the Croce path. Bright sunlight alternated with the shade of less exposed stretches where the stagnant damp and cold were a warning of the imminence of the first snows. He searched for confirmation that someone had been there the previous night, but since the mule-track was covered by a layer of frost there were no footprints. He continued on to the hollow where he had found Paride's body. He saw signs of the work done by the forensic experts and remembered that access had been permitted in that area only the day before. He called Dolly and let her sniff around, even if the frost had sterilised the smells on the ground. The commissario was aware that he was roaming aimlessly, following Dolly anywhere her sense of smell happened to take her. Only for her was there any purpose to that wandering in the undergrowth among the trees.

He walked on, persuaded that exercise would clear his mind. He felt alive climbing up and down slopes, as when he was searching for mushrooms, but there was something else at the back of his mind, the beginnings of a thought, if less than an idea. He decided to put himself in the shoes of that mysterious person who had been walking after dark with Dolly towards Croce. In the distance, he could hear the shouts of the carabinieri on the trail of the Woodsman, followed by the rifle shots which rang out along the hillside.

He heard Dolly, at the bottom of a ditch, bark in the high-pitched tone of dogs confronted by a larger animal. He ran to find her and, without being aware, found himself back on the pathway. Dolly went on growling, but Soneri drew up, seeing Baldi appear ten metres ahead of him.

"She's found something interesting," he said, pointing into the ditch.

The commissario nodded. "She'll have to deal with it by herself. As you can see, I don't have a gun."

"I think she's standing still. If it was a boar or a deer, she'd be off after it."

"What about you? Have you shut up your place?" Soneri said.

"It doesn't thaw during the day any more. It's time to get out before I'm buried by a storm."

"So now all you have to do is wait for spring. Will you back by the Feast of the Liberation in April?"

Baldi stood in silence, looking in the direction from which Dolly's barks were still coming. "I doubt it," he said quietly.

"So what about the bar?"

Baldi shrugged, but he said nothing. Soneri was once again overcome by melancholy.

"It's no longer a world I know," Baldi said, still talking in a low voice. Leaving the place where he had worked all his life evidently caused him some distress. "I was born among shepherds, cows and the smell of cheese. Once, I used to live up there among people I knew, not crooks, smugglers and drug dealers who don't speak my dialect. Sundays used to be feast days for the villagers themselves, not like nowadays when people arrive from the city scowling, with big boots showing off the brand name, people who don't take even a drop of wine, who are on diets and who sit out in the sun all day long. No, that's not my world any more. The only one that's left is the Woodsman and look what's happening to him, hunted across his own lands like a boar. And then this illness," he interrupted himself to cough. "Those carabinieri ..." he spluttered, before running out of words.

"It's not their fault. If only he'd turned himself in, everything would've been cleared up, but now, this way, he makes himself look guilty."

Baldi frowned. "You obviously don't know Gualerzi." His tone was designed to make the commissario aware how much of an outsider he was. "What chance was there of him surrendering to the carabinieri? In his whole life, he has never taken orders, not from anyone. Do you think a couple of carabinieri would be going to change that?"

"But they won't give in either."

"Then it's going to end in disaster. The Woodsman's got nothing to lose. He's done for, so's his wife, and his daughter will have to look after herself."

Other shots rang out, and this time they were closer.

"They're coming from this side. I don't understand where he's leading them," Baldi said.

"He's not firing."

"Who knows what's on his mind? Maybe he thinks it's going to be a long battle and he's saving his ammunition."

Dolly had stopped barking and from the rustling in the undergrowth near the path it seemed she was coming back. When she emerged, she bristled, looking in the direction from which the shots were coming. At that moment, the shouts of a detachment which had come down across the Macchiaferro on the Malpasso side could be clearly heard.

"They're somewhere above us," Baldi said, mildly alarmed. "They're at Fontanazzo," he added, referring to a place unknown to Soneri.

"I think we'd better get out of here," Soneri said.

"You're right. We could end up as sitting ducks."

The commissario called to Dolly, who was caught up in the thrill of the hunt and growing more excited by the minute, and they set off swiftly. The voices pursuing them seemed to be getting closer.

"I wonder where the Woodsman is," Soneri said as they emerged onto a clearing from where in the distance, beyond a thicket of chestnut trees, they could see Greppo.

"If you ask me," Baldi said, "he's leading them over to Badignana so he can take up a position on the ridge. And if he gets there, it's going to be tough for the carabinieri."

"He's going to do something else stupid," Soneri said.

Baldi's expression turned serious and this time he agreed with the commissario. "I fear you're right. By now he must be sick and tired of being hunted."

"Do you mean he'll fire wildly, and to hell with the consequences?"

"The fact that he's not returning fire makes me fear the worst. At first he was trying to scare them off, but now since they're still pursuing him..."

Another volley crashed into a cliffside, causing the brittle Apennines sandstone to crumble.

"They're firing out of fear," Baldi said with derision. "They see a shadow and they shoot at it. They have no balls."

"That's another reason for getting out. That lot'll fire at you the moment they set eyes on you."

They hurried down to the small plateau at Campogrande. As they ran through the trees, they heard the whistle of a stray bullet as it passed high over the branches, followed by shouts which seemed to come from close by. Their fear was that they had ended up between the pursuers and their prey, and Soneri thought of squatting down in a gulley so as not to offer a target. Finally they reached a clearing not far from Greppo. Without warning, Ghidini's dog ran out towards them.

"Are you mad? You're going to get a bullet in your skulls!" Ghidini shouted at them. "I heard the Woodsman pass by up at Pietra. I was there an hour ago. Maybe he saw you and that's why he led the carabinieri this way, to put them off his trail and put them onto yours."

It was true that the carabinieri seemed to be making for the point where Baldi and Soneri were. The yells of the officers, together with the precise orders issued by Bovolenta could be quite distinctly heard.

"Better make a break for it before they catch up with us," Ghidini said, calling his dog to his side.

Soneri and Baldi moved off without another word, moving swiftly over the open spaces. They stopped further down when they were within sight of the road and completely out of breath. Silence had fallen again, making it impossible to say exactly how the manhunt was going. They heard an isolated cry, followed by others in response, and calculated that the carabinieri had swung round to the east to make the ascent to Badignana from that side.

"I told you so," Baldi said. "He's leading them up there."

"The Woodsman is a beast. He's leading them into a trap," Ghidini said.

Soneri ran over in his mind the path up to the crags. On the upper slopes the mountain became more forbidding and provided less cover metre by metre. "He must be well ahead of them, or he's going to be an easy target on the final stretch."

Baldi shook his head. "Relax, Gualerzi will have everything worked out. He's not going to provide them with target practice."

The commissario tried to imagine where the Woodsman would want to make a stand, and remembered how he and his brother had held a detachment of Nazis at bay with their one Sten gun. The Woodsman was now in the same situation, making his last stand in defence of the last piece of the mountain he considered his own.

As they spread out over a wider expanse, the shouts from the carabinieri became more isolated. Everything seemed calmer. The sun was up causing the ice to melt and giving a glitter to the tufts of frosty grass.

"I'd like to go and see what's going on," Ghidini said. "It'll be alright as long as you keep your distance, maybe from the Malpasso path."

"I'm not going back up there. The spectacle won't exactly be edifying," Baldi said.

"From Campogrande it should be possible to see how it all unfolds," Soneri said.

Baldi appeared hesitant, but at the same time he was evidently curious to see what would happen. "I might go with you as far as Campogrande."

"It's the only place where you'd get a proper view," Ghidini said.

They set off back up the slope, but this time they had the impression of being the hunters. The carabinieri seemed to be following the Woodsman at the same distance as before, but they were also producing some kind of unrecognisable background noise. At Campogrande, the three men ran into Volpi who was looking through his binoculars. He was not distracted by their approach, and did not take his eyes off the rocks.

"Do you see anything?" Baldi said

"He's taking them to Badignana," the gamekeeper replied in his clipped tones, not turning round.

"That's not a good sign."

"No, it's not," Volpi agreed. "They still think they're dealing with an ordinary fugitive from justice. They just don't realise…"

They all understood. "Did you see him make his way up?" Ghidini said.

Volpi shook his head. "I think he followed the course of the stream, against the current."

"You mean he climbed up the Macchiaferro?" Baldi said.

"He must have done. He might well have a cache of ammunition hidden somewhere in the cabins. He got there first, and so he's had time to collect it. All he has to do now is wait for the carabinieri."

They got confirmation soon afterwards that this was so.

A volley of shots rang out from the Badignana ridge aimed down into the lower valley. The beech trees seemed to shake.

"That's Gualerzi! That's his Beretta," Volpi said.

Immediately afterwards, all hell broke loose. The carabinieri pointed their weapons upwards, more to cover their advance than in any organised attempt to hit their enemy. They had not expected to find themselves under fire in a clearing with no shelter apart from a few shrubs and stacks of brushwood. Angry orders were yelled out and Soneri imagined they came from Bovolenta, enraged at having fallen into a trap. Then once more the baritone boom of the Woodsman's rifle thundered along the mountainside.

"Oh, shit!" Volpi screamed, his eyes glued to his binoculars. "He's got one of them."

The carabinieri returned fire, shooting wildly, while at Badignana a cloud of white smoke rose up.

"They're bringing the wounded man down," Volpi informed them. "He looks like a broken mannequin. All the rest are keeping them covered."

Soneri became aware he was sweating with tension. He had tried to warn Bovolenta, and was appalled at the stupidity of his pushing on to the point where the two sides were shooting at each other, but time after time he had found himself obliged to give way in the face of irrationality.

It was easy to make out the shots fired by the Woodsman, since they had a darker and deeper tone. "What kind of bullet is he using?" Volpi wondered aloud, still looking through his binoculars. "They make huge holes in the ground where they land."

"Imagine what they would do if they hit a carabiniere."

"The carabinieri are moving back, into the undergrowth," Volpi said.

Meantime, they continued blasting away at the Badignana

ridge. The cloud of dust which had formed above the rocks where the Woodsman was hidden was becoming even more impressive, but after a time the shooting stopped.

"They've reached the woods," Volpi said, putting down the binoculars. "The show is over – for the time being…"

"I'm going down," Baldi said, setting off for Greppo. Ghidini and Soneri followed him, but Volpi stayed where he was. "Some of the carabinieri will be in the village in about an hour. If they've got a wounded colleague, they'll have to hurry."

When they got to Greppo, there was a great deal of activity in the piazza. There were three ambulances, the same pack of journalists and a detachment of men from the Special Forensic unit bustling about shouting instructions. As they carried on down, the sun's light faded until it took on the colour of a *zabaione*. They reached the piazza ten minutes later, just in time to hear the police trucks manoeuvre along the winding road from the reservoir. Shortly afterwards, the trucks roared into the village and pulled up at the kerb under the lampposts. A helicopter hovered overhead, and as it came in to land on the piazza, everyone moved over to one side, pushed by the force of the wind from the propeller. A stretcher bearing a police officer in a tattered, blood-covered uniform was carried off the tailgate of one of the vehicles. Two other carabinieri, supported on both sides by colleagues, were helped into the ambulances.

The helicopter took off, blowing up dust. Soneri went over to the *Rivara*, where the few people who had been watching this scene were standing.

"One of them is done for," Maini told him. "The Woodsman got him on the chest. It went through him as if he was a piece of paper."

"What about the other two?"

"Not too serious. One got some lumps of rock in the face and the other was hit by a bullet ricocheting off the stones on the ground."

"It was pure hell up there," Soneri said, lighting a cigar. "That captain is mad."

"He hasn't understood what he's up against."

The commissario felt drained. His watch told him it was half-past two, and he had not yet had any lunch. He went into the *Rivara* and ordered a sandwich with *prosciutto*, as though he were back in his office.

"You can eat here if you want, now that Sante is…" Rivara suggested.

He had not thought of it. He would need to find alternative accommodation. "Perhaps this evening. Anyway, I'm not going to be staying much longer." He was addressing the words more to himself than to the barman.

"As far as I am concerned, you can stay as long as you like," Rivara said, offering Dolly some slices of fat from the *prosciutto*. "Nobody wants fat any more."

"*Prosciutto* without fat is like an egg with no yoke," Soneri said, while his attention was distracted by Bovolenta's drawn face at the window of the car turning into the police station

"That's it for today. They've got enough problems to be going on with," Rivara said.

Soneri's mind was on the document he had discussed with Don Bruno. With all that had been going on, he would need to put off the time when he could seek clarification. He gulped down a glass of Malvasia, and went out to watch the shadow of Montelupo lengthen in the setting sun. He dialled Angela's number. "The Woodsman has killed one carabiniere and has wounded two others," he told her.

"In the state he's in, why should he care about anything?"

"He knows he hasn't long to live, and he's not going to give up. Palmiro took the woman he loved, and took his money as well. Now the carabinieri want to take Montelupo from him, and into the bargain he has cancer and he reckons he has nothing to lose."

"You still don't believe that he murdered Paride, do you?"

"I don't believe he had anything to do with it."

"So why is he shooting at the carabinieri?"

"They want to take him in. They're convinced he's guilty. They think he's responsible for all the shooting on Montelupo after the Rodolfi bankruptcy. It's possible that he was responsible for some of it."

"So what now?"

"He wasn't the only one firing off shots, I'm sure of that. There have always been poachers wandering about up there, and one of them was Palmiro."

"A poacher doesn't shoot a man in the stomach from close range, if what I've read about it in the newspapers is accurate."

"That's true, but the Woodsman would have shot at Palmiro. He went out on the higher ground every evening with his dogs," the commissario said, looking at Dolly. At that moment, a new suspicion, something more urgent than a doubt, came into his mind and required him immediately to put everything else aside until he had checked it out.

"What are you thinking?" Angela said, accustomed to his sudden silences.

"I'm thinking about the sort of person who would go for a walk with dogs at night time."

"At night time? Do you have a suspicion of who it might be?"

"No, but there's not a very wide choice."

"Remember you're supposed to be on holiday, and going into the woods where they're shooting on sight..."

"I've already run that risk, but at night it's harder for them to shoot."

"You want to go out at night?" she said in alarm.

"You're safer in a wood at night than you are in a well-lit street in a city."

"I'll phone you later to find out how it went," she said, but remained unconvinced.

Soneri left the *Rivara* and crossed the piazza, where the light was now sepia-coloured, as though filtered through a dark shade. He walked through the streets up to the Rodolfi factory, where a crowd of workers, some still in their white overalls, were milling about at the gates. He asked for Signorina Gualerzi and being told she was still inside, he decided to wait for her. She was one of the last to leave, on her own. The commissario watched her come towards him with the graceless, heavy gait of the mountain folk, dressed as she had been when he had first met her: flat shoes, thick stockings and long coat, perhaps adapted by an unskilled seamstress. He imagined that her imposing bulk intimidated men.

"Finished for the evening?" he said.

She looked at him distrustfully. "For all we get, we could've left earlier."

"It might have been better for you to have left earlier, but it would've been better still if you'd stayed at home. You might have been able to convince your father not to do all these crazy things."

The woman stopped in her tracks when she heard these words. "What's happened?" she said anxiously. "He only wanted them to leave us in peace."

"Today he killed one carabiniere and injured another two."

Lorenza Gualerzi bowed her head and said nothing. She must have been used to her father's acts of folly, but this was of a different dimension. "I can't do a thing about it. No-one can give him orders. All you can do is try and convince him as well as you can. When my mother was well…"

"Your father is sick too."

She nodded. "What kind of future do I have? Without money, without work and without my parents."

The commissario found it hard to fight back feelings of pity for that unfortunate woman who was out of place, out of time and so ill-equipped for a life alone. She faced a lonely life, derided behind her back by her peers because of her ugliness. She was perhaps the perfect image of the village falling back into poverty and isolated in the harshness of mountains where no-one would any longer wish to live.

"Why did he run away? With his condition, nobody could have done anything to him. At least, they would have given him some treatment," Soneri said.

"You can't force him to do anything he doesn't want to. It's never been possible. He's got no respect for authority. He grew up without parents, and now he feels these people are doing him a wrong. He says he knows nothing about Paride's death. If anything, his quarrel was with Palmiro, because he felt betrayed."

"Because of the money…"

"He left us ruined. We haven't even enough money to pay for my mother's treatment."

"Do you really believe he's got nothing to do with it?"

Lorenza summoned up all her courage. "I don't know. I believe him, but…"

The commissario used the pause in the conversation to light his cigar, then he looked at her once more, signalling to her to go on.

"I know he fired some shots on Montelupo, and at strange hours. My father was never one for the subtle approach. How am I supposed to know if he was hunting a boar, or something else?"

"He went looking for Palmiro, isn't that right?"

Once again she trembled and seemed overcome by awkwardness. "As I said, he ruined us. What my father really couldn't bear was the fact that he'd cheated him, of all people, putting him on the same level as all the others. They had grown up together and in spite of all that had happened between them, they carried on seeing each other. Sometimes, when old Rodolfi came up to the Madoni hills, I would watch them talk and I got the impression that the years had rolled away. At times my father would laugh uproariously in a way I never saw him do with anyone else."

"Palmiro never went out without his gun either," Soneri said, deep in thought.

"And he used it. He knew Montelupo well. When it came to getting things done, my father and Palmiro were equally single-minded. Sometimes they acted like savages, but when I thought of their childhood and the poverty they'd suffered, I was able to understand."

"How long do the doctors give your father?"

"Six months, perhaps a bit more. He's already lost a few kilos. But he won't live that long, because he's said from the start that at the first spasms of real pain..."

Lorenza burst into tears very suddenly. She covered her face with her hands and bent forward until the commissario reached out to support her. He had the impression she was looking for a shoulder to lean on, but Soneri, who was shorter than her, did not feel able to draw her close to him. "I'd like to prevent that happening," he said, in an attempt to console her, "but your father will never be captured. No-one will get near him."

"He wouldn't listen to anyone in the village and he's always hated the carabinieri on account of their support for the Fascists. He'll not change his mind now. It would take a man like your father. He had a lot of time for him, ever since they were together in the partisans."

"Do you think I should try?"

"Probably you're the only one who could."

"I'll go to Badignana and if he's still there, I'll try and persuade him to come down."

"At the very least, I'd get to see him during his last days," Lorenza sobbed.

IO

It was dark when Soneri returned to the piazza. The crescent moon, its outline blurry in the mist, was rising over Montelupo. The commissario's stomach was protesting, demanding nourishment. Delrio was standing outside the *Rivara*, smoking a cigarette. "What was it like when the Woodsman shot the carabiniere? They told me you were there," he said.

"I was too far away. Volpi had a better view through his binoculars."

"He's dead. The bullet shattered his ribs and tore away half his lungs. There's a hole the size of a water pipe in his back."

"Large calibre bullets, for boar hunting. You must know the sort of thing," Soneri said.

Delrio nodded. "The Woodsman doesn't fool about. If you ask me, he won't stop at one carabiniere."

Rivara came over and Soneri ordered dinner. "Have you anything with mushrooms?"

"It's been a bad year. All you can find are 'trumpets of death'," Rivara said, touching himself between the legs in a superstitious gesture which annoyed the commissario. He opted for *tortelli di patate* and while he was waiting, Rivara brought him a plate of cooked pears and chestnuts. He remembered that autumnal dish, when the two fruits were put in the one pot and left to boil together.

"How are the other two?" Rivara asked Delrio.

"They'll be O.K., but if I were them I would go and light a candle to San Martino."

"They obviously didn't expect to find him lying in wait for them, otherwise they'd never have gone strolling like day-trippers over the stony ground where there was no cover," Rivara said from behind the bar, but it was clear he had overheard someone else make that comment, because Delrio gave him a look of indifference before replying, "Ah well."

Soneri thought of the Woodsman in Badignana, hiding in one of those summer cabins reopened off-season, or sheltering for the night in some paddock, reflecting on life as it slipped away from him. Perhaps he was focusing on the last days in which he would really feel alive, up there, fighting them off, gun in hand. The commissario made every effort to get under the Woodsman's skin, but concluded that perhaps he neither reflected deeply nor tormented himself enough. Perhaps he was a man who simply took destiny and its judgments as they come.

As his main course, he had some very ordinary roast beef and began to feel nostalgic for Ida's cooking, but that was now a thing of the past. He got up and decided to go and keep the moon company. Rivara and Delrio watched him go out, but neither addressed him.

Dolly welcomed him, jumping up and putting her paws all over his duffel coat. He stroked her head and brought his face close to hers. They had an important matter to attend to. He wandered through the village with no fixed destination in mind. His route took him past the carcass of the burned-out car, and his nostrils were once more filled with the stench of melted plastic. He stopped to look down at the new town in the lower valley and at the headlights on the road leading to the Pass. As he walked back, he bumped into the man in the wheelchair, pushed as ever by his imperturbably zealous wife. Soneri was tempted to turn away, but the man had spotted him and even from some way off began talking. As he had done before, he babbled on about his adventures with Palmiro, until his wife made a sharp turn and took him in another direction. The commissario watched him vanish into the uncertain light under the lamp-posts, and thought wryly of yet another life descending into dementia.

He left the village and walked in the direction of Villa del Greppo, but turned off the road at a point where he knew he could pick up the path. As soon as they were near it, Dolly began wagging her tail and raced off in the direction of Croce so rapidly that the commissario had scarcely time to call her back. She seemed to be falling into a well-established routine. He made her sit, stroking her gently and speaking to her quietly in an effort to calm her. Dolly eventually settled, even if she was provoked by the many scents surrounding her. They did not move for some time. Soneri watched the moon move slowly across the sky, while the freezing cold embalmed the woods and fields in hoar frost. To keep Dolly calm, he placed his hand inside her collar. Every so often, the dog would give a shudder, and sit bolt upright, causing Soneri some alarm. An animal passed a very short distance from them, making the lower branches sway, but Dolly had already smelled it from a distance before it came within range of her hearing.

More time went by before Dolly began once again to show signs of agitation, but on this occasion she appeared unworried. Her tail began to beat against the commissario like a whip, and he had to hold her to prevent her making any noise. After a few seconds, a terrier appeared before them. The dog, attracted by Dolly, sniffed her from a distance and began to bark. Dolly did the same and Soneri withdrew behind a bush just in time to make out a hooded figure walking smartly towards Croce. He allowed him to draw close, but not before checking he had his pistol with him.

When he stepped out of the trees, he noted to his surprise that he was completely calm, perhaps because at that point he knew who he was dealing with. It was the other man who became alarmed and let out a shriek which caused the two dogs to bark in chorus. He made as if to run off, but Soneri stood blocking his way on the valley side, and flight through the Croce woods was obviously not an inviting prospect. Judging by his actions, he was already in a state of terror.

"It's an unusual time to be out for a stroll," Soneri said. "And you don't appear much at your ease in the dark."

The Philippino from the Rodolfi house mumbled something which the commissario did not pick up. He was wearing a heavy, corduroy overcoat with a hood which came down over his forehead, partially hiding his face.

"I walk dog," he managed to say.

Soneri laughed and the Philippino appeared disconcerted.

"I've never met anyone who walks his dogs at night."

"Signor Palmiro, yes. He come back late."

"Of course he did. He was out poaching. So where is your gun?"

The Philippino ingenuously turned out his pockets, and Soneri almost felt sorry for him, a poor soul sent out into the woods at night and perhaps not even paid as well as the other Rodolfi employees

"Why does she send you here?" Soneri asked peremptorily.

The Philippino bowed his head and did not speak for a few moments, then, having no answer to give, turned and made to run off. Soneri grabbed hold of him. He was so light he had no difficulty in pulling him back. He seemed to have got one sleeve caught in a tree.

"There's no point in running away," he said calmly. "I know where to find you. If you run home and tell your employer everything, you know what'll happen? She'll tell you to disappear, and you're out with no bonus and no salary."

The man was plainly terrified at that prospect but something still prevented him from speaking. Dolly and the terrier were sitting facing each other, giving the impression of being keen to help along a conversation which had not quite taken off.

"Me time only for dogs," he whined, his head bowed. "Search always Dolly who run away."

Soneri shook his head at these implausible excuses. He could feel his temper rising and had to make an effort not to let it get the better of him. However, in that silence and in the faint light of the new moon, various thoughts milled about in his head before gelling into one insight which linked Dolly's loud barking in the gorge before the meeting with Baldi and her familiarity with the path. Perhaps he should have allowed her to lead him on, for he now believed it would not have been a waste of time. And then there was the Philippino: he knew he was not there by chance.

As he mulled these matters over, he dropped his guard and relaxed. For a single second he looked up at the sky at the lights of an aeroplane flying low overhead, and in that second he lost control of the situation. With his clenched fist, the Philippino landed him a blow in the solar plexus and pushed him aside. The commissario stumbled off the path and slipped backwards, grabbing at branches to keep his balance and arousing the dogs who began barking wildly at this brawl. The Philippino took full advantage of the turmoil to free himself and run off down the road to Greppo. By the time Soneri struggled to his feet, the Philippino had a full twenty metres start on him, making it impossible to catch him. Soneri decided to let him go. The terrier went after him, while Dolly repressed her wish to do the same and watched them into the distance.

On another occasion, Soneri would in all probability have been furious with himself, but this time he remained calm. Putting pressure on that pathetic creature was not unduly important. His presence on this road at night time was more eloquent than any information he might have been willing to give, and his evident discomfort was confirmation enough of a hypothesis that was forming in Soneri's mind. He walked back towards the village and when he bent to pass under a barrier of branches, he felt a stab of pain at the place where the Philippino had struck him. A quarter of an hour later, he came out on the main road, and became aware of the nails in Dolly's paws clicking on the hard surface. It was only then he realised that she had been at his side all the time. He stopped and gave her a hug, thinking as he did so that a bond of affection had now been formed between him and the dog.

There was a great deal of to-ing and fro-ing outside the police station, while in the piazza itself the blue cars of the carabinieri were parked with their front wheels on the pavement. It looked like a meeting that had been called by the prefect, and reminded him of interminable, tedious afternoons in the questura. He ducked round the corner into the side streets with Dolly, who every so often raised her head and sniffed the air. Soneri had placed his hopes on such scents and on faint traces left by those who had recently been on Montelupo.

When he reached the *Scoiattolo,* all the lights had been switched off, even the sign outside. The place seemed dead, but he noticed a reddish light shining under a shutter on the ground floor. He put the key in the lock and went in, but the moment he switched on the light in the hall, a door opened and an elderly man made a timid appearance at the doorway.

"You must be the commissario?"

"Yes, Soneri," he replied

"Ida sends her apologies, but she won't be able to make your meals at this time," he said, stretching out his hand. "I'm her brother, Fulvio." The commissario shook his hand. "Anyway, you have your own keys, don't you? You're the only guest."

There was something disobliging in his tone, as though he had been hoping that Soneri too would have left, allowing him to close everything down and have no further responsibility for the place. The commissario looked around at the greying walls, the unfashionable furniture, the curtains fading through over-washing, and it occurred to him that he would indeed be the last guest, the last to stay there and the last to pay a bill.

"I'll not be staying long," he said, without looking at Fulvio, who made no reply.

"And the dog?"

"She'll be staying with me tonight."

On hearing these words, the man turned away, shrugged and as he went back into his room, could be heard muttering, "Well, at this point…"

The commissario slept fitfully. Dolly too was aroused every now and again at something that she alone could hear. Around 5.00, Soneri awoke, thinking he had heard a loud noise outside. Dolly was extremely restless and this seemed confirmation that there was someone moving about. The commissario threw open the shutters and peered into the darkness of the yard, but there was nothing to be seen. In spite of that, shortly afterwards he heard the sound of a car engine being revved up, and wondered if someone had come to look for something in the environs of the hotel. Since Dolly was so troubled, he supposed it might have been her they had come looking for. After all, his own suspicions had made him bring her up to his room in the first place.

As he thought the matter over, the alarm clock told him it was almost six o'clock. He opened the shutters again and was greeted by a gust of brutally cold air. He got ready and made his way out past closed doors behind which he imagined unmade beds, empty cupboards and curtains colonised by bugs. In the dining room, the tablecloths had been removed and the seats turned upside down. What he had previously seen as a sign of familiarity now seemed to him an omen of decay. He closed the door behind him and moved off.

He breakfasted in the *Rivara*. The village seen through the window overlooking the piazza seemed as calm as on a Sunday morning. "They were working late," the barman advised him, indicating the police station.

"Any idea if they came to any conclusions?"

Rivara shook his head. "None at all. Nobody knows anything. Crisafulli and the local lot haven't been seen."

It was at that moment that he heard the ignition being turned in the first truck as it set off for Montelupo. A line of vehicles, their headlights reflected on the thick layer of ground frost, drove past. The half-asleep carabinieri inside them were jolted at every bump in the road.

"They're not giving up, are they? They haven't had enough yet," Rivara said.

The commissario looked attentively at all the trucks as they went by, but he did not see Bovolenta. "Have they fired him?" he thought aloud.

"It wouldn't be a surprise. With all that's been going on, they could well have accused him of sending them out to be picked off."

Soneri drank his *caffelatte* while Dolly, sitting outside the window, looked on. Dawn was breaking, but light was struggling to break through the damp mist of the valley. He ordered bread, some slivers of parmesan and a hundred grams

-206-

of *culaccia*. He fed the fat of the ham to Dolly, and set off for Greppo where the night before he had met the Philippino. As soon as he was away from the shelter of the piazza, he felt the full force of the freezing wind like a slap in the face. The cold had grown yet more intense, and was coming, like the sun, from the east. When he reached the plain, he stopped to get his breath back. The dry air gave him a parched throat. He saw the carabinieri line up above Boldara to advance through the woods, and he wondered about the criteria they were using for deployment in the God-forsaken donkey's back that was Montelupo. They were being divided into two groups, perhaps with the plan of encircling the Woodsman. He heard the sound of other trucks on the mountainside and realised that reinforcements were arriving already.

He set off once more for Croce, with Dolly running ahead, darting in and out of the undergrowth. The commissario walked behind with a more measured pace, but as he proceeded he felt a growing sense of anxiety. When he heard shouts from lower down the valley, he understood the risks he was running. All it needed was one carabiniere to get him in his gun sights. He knew only too well that in those circumstances, they would not be required to take precautions. Montelupo was now a free-fire zone for the police forces, and there were simply no codes in place.

As he climbed higher, the sun lit up the mountain, increasing the chances that he would end up in some sniper's sights. There was a new danger at every corner, so he kept in the shadows or took shelter in gulleys or thickets where it was still freezing and where the wild boar ran. He left the path, walking parallel to it through the trees. The morning was silent and the light strong, but there was tension in the air. He still had some way to go along a route which took him past the bright trunks of the beech trees before he finally arrived at an almost sheer wall of crumbling sandstone. Looking up, he could see the path twist and turn as it ran alongside a crag where no plants grew. There was a crevice in the cliff which narrowed into a chimney leading over the summit and down the opposite side. Only at that point did he realise he was next to the gorge where Dolly had attempted to entice him down to the bottom the previous day.

He looked for the dog as he crossed over the muddy surface solidified by the freezing frost. He was familiar with that type of swampy terrain where it was possible to walk only in winter. He remembered an occasion when a hunter had sunk in it up to his waist, and when he was pulled out, he left behind his boots and trousers. The freezing conditions had made everything hard. Small pieces of rock broke away from the cliff higher up, causing the sandstone below to crumble like dry bread. Dolly was seated at the foot of the slope in the last of the undergrowth which closed off the gorge. In front of her there were signs of something having been dragged through the mud before the freeze. Soneri bent over, and it was then he noticed the butt of a rifle sticking a few centimetres out of the ground.

It had been driven in, barrels down, like a biscuit ready to sink to the bottom in a glass of milk. The commissario looked up. About twenty metres up the slope from where he was standing, the path ran along the cliffside. He then understood: the rifle must have fallen from there and the barrels had sunk in the mud, but all this had taken place before the freeze, in the soft dampness of the season of mists.

He pulled at the gun, but it was impossible to move. It was as if it had been set in cement. He attempted to dig it out with stones, branches and with his bare hands, knowing that if he managed to crack the frozen surface, the weapon would come away easily. He worked at it for some time, heedless of everything else around him. Montelupo continued to be enveloped in a silence undisturbed by the cawing of crows, the tap-tap of woodpeckers or the strident screech of vultures. The woods and the skies were shrouded in lethargic stillness.

Finally with one energy-sapping tug, he pulled the rifle free. It was encased in a sleeve of grey mud, like a cocoon, and patiently he began to scrape the mud away with a piece of wood, cutting from the top down as though he were slicing ham. After a time, he was successful and this made it possible to make out the shape of the barrels and handle, but the time it had spent under the mud had probably compromised the trigger and firing mechanisms. He retraced his steps, trying to get out of that morass of solid mud, but only when he felt the springy crackle of beech leaves under his feet did he allow himself to think of what was to be done next. But at that moment the battle broke out with renewed violence, not far above the path.

The carabinieri opened fire first, followed immediately by the more sonorous sound of the Woodsman's rifle as he returned fire from somewhere on the mountainside. Other weapons were discharged across a wide range, bullets whistled through the woods, criss-crossing each other and ending their flight with a bang as they exploded into wood or with a dull thud as they hit the ground. The commissario crouched down behind a beech tree whose roots had pushed through the soil to create a kind of rampart. The air carried the smell of gunshot towards him, while broken branches fell like rain onto the rotting wood beneath the trees. Soneri felt real fear when he heard the carabinieri running towards the pathway, but once they approached the foot of the gorge, a shot from the Woodsman exploded before them, throwing earth and leaves from the undergrowth up into the air. He was firing in the hope of bouncing his shot off a stone, knowing that if he struck a rock, the ricochet was certain to bring someone down. The carabinieri halted and then doubled back into the thick woods. Soneri took advantage of the pause to drag himself and Dolly along the gulley, and to dive behind the cement columns under a little bridge over a path in the woods. Dolly was reluctant to follow him but Soneri grabbed her by the collar and hauled her in.

They stayed in there, huddled against each other. Every so often Dolly would turn to him, giving the idea that she was obeying although she did not understand. The commissario for his part was besieged by images from long ago. He felt again like a boy in a cabin, as he recalled the resentful solitude of his teenage years as well as various stories told to him by his father. He seemed to hear his voice as he recounted the events of July '44, the S.S. round-ups, the three days spent hiding in a hole in the ground and the return to the light of day to find a landscape of death and fire. It was a miracle they had not killed him, and it was a miracle for Soneri that he had been born and was there.

He shook his head at that thought and Dolly, who took the gesture as an invitation, licked his hand. He was surprised at these mysterious associations which carried him back to relive episodes from the past, but these were all swept aside a few moments later by the heavy marching steps of the carabinieri. They were moving at a steady pace towards the spot from which the Woodsman had been firing. He heard the radios crackling and one voice communicating the direction they were to take. He assumed they were trying to surround the Woodsman, forcing him to higher ground where there was less shelter and less space for manoeuvre. From the sound of their footsteps, he calculated that there must be about fifteen of them. He had been hiding to avoid being shot by mistake, but even if he was now at liberty to come out and give himself up, he put his hand into Dolly's collar to keep her calm, and stayed where he was. He had no wish to expose himself to the carabinieri as he crawled out of his hole like a beetle. In there, he felt like a real man of the mountains, or like an animal in its den. He was different from those untrained, frightened and shivering policemen.

He waited until the marching, the shouts and the confusion had passed. When he came out into the sunlight, he thought once more of his father and of how he must have felt himself a survivor. There were so many things he did not know about him, but there was at least one memory which could be rescued from the oblivion into which his life had almost completely fallen, provided, of course, that Soneri could reach the Woodsman in time.

This thought drove him on. He called to Dolly and started down the valley. Time had flown, as he understood from the sun which seemed even brighter in the freezing wind from the north-east. He stopped at a sheltered spot near some rocks and since his stomach had been rumbling for about half an hour, he decided to have something to eat. He was certain they would not be able to capture the Woodsman as long as his cancer left him even a little strength, but he was equally certain that he himself would have little chance of meeting up with him in that rocky landscape, unless he chose to let himself be found.

With these thoughts in his mind, he set off again. He walked along the final stretch of the path until he felt himself out of danger. He heard one isolated shot fired by the Woodsman further up the Macchiaferro valley, but it wasn't at a great distance. Perhaps the gun had gone off by accident. When he reached Greppo, he took out his mobile, dialled the number of the police station and asked the officer on duty if Crisafulli was there.

"I'll put you through," was the reply. "Can I say who's calling?"

"Just put me through to Crisafulli."

As Soneri was wondering how Crisafulli had managed to dodge heavy duty yet again, he heard his voice. "What's the matter, Commissario?"

"Come up to Greppo. I've something interesting to show you."

"What've you found? A dozen huge ceps?"

"A really superior type of mushroom. Get up here and see for yourself."

He switched off his mobile, convinced he had done the right thing in calling the maresciallo rather than bringing the rifle down to the police station, since everybody in the village would have seen him. The case now seemed to him closed. There was only one further check to be made, but he could not do it himself, which was why he had called in Crisafulli.

He finished his meagre meal while Dolly chewed at the rind which she gripped between her paws. He lit his cigar and looked contentedly at the old village with its houses covered by slates of Montelupo stone darkened by moss. About ten minutes later he saw the carabiniere cap with the tongues of fire on the front, as Crisafulli himself walked towards him with his trademark, springy step. Soneri got to his feet as he drew near, and gave him time to get his breath back before he spoke.

"I wanted to give you this myself," he said, handing over the mud-encrusted rifle.

The maresciallo started back as though he was afraid of soiling his uniform. He took a good look at the weapon without touching it, until the commissario handed it firmly to him, leaving Crisafulli with no choice but to get his hands dirty.

"Where did you find this?"

"Along the Croce path."

The maresciallo's eyes lit up briefly. "You believe that…" he tried to say, before losing himself in a tangle of thoughts.

"I think the whole lot of you have made a mess of the entire business."

"Bovolenta is in charge of the enquiry," Crisafulli said, too emphatically for Soneri's taste.

"Palmiro didn't get lost that night," the commissario said.

"Obviously not. Now that we have this rifle, things which at first appeared absurd fall into place."

"Oh, there's still no shortage of absurd things. Life is full of them," Soneri said, with a bitter laugh.

The maresciallo looked hard at him without appreciating his meaning, while the commissario, turning serious, put a hand on his shoulder. "Listen, Crisafulli, you go back to the police station and hand this rifle over to the forensic people. Then go up to the Rodolfi villa and do a house search. Before you do that, have a look at the weapons licensed to Palmiro. If even one is missing in the villa…all the rest will come out in the report, won't it?"

The maresciallo looked at him like a schoolboy gazing at his teacher. "I will report that it was you who found the rifle."

Soneri shook his head energetically. "I don't give a damn about the case. I'm here on holiday. There are other matters which do interest me."

"I'll have to give some explanation of how I found it."

"Say that you had an anonymous tip-off, or that you followed your own line of enquiry. I didn't tell the officer on duty who I was."

The maresciallo's face lit up. "You are a saint and a bearer of grace."

Soneri shrugged.

"I'll let you know when I have the report. And I'll go to the villa as soon as I have put this weapon in safe custody."

"Thanks, even if I'm already sure how the whole thing went. I don't need to deal with magistrates. It's you who needs incontrovertible proof. I have the luxury of being able to follow my instincts."

"A terrible business," Crisafulli murmured.

"The world *is* terrible. Don't you find it disgusts you?" Soneri felt anger swelling inside him, or perhaps it was the pain of living which he had attempted in vain to dispel by coming to the one place where he should have been able to feel at home. "And there is no escape," he said, as though talking to himself.

The maresciallo listened with an expression of appropriate gravity, but it was clear he had not grasped the meaning of what Soneri was saying. "So what's going to happen when they realise the Woodsman had nothing to do with it?"

"They'll have to keep on searching for him. He has, after all, killed one of your colleagues."

"And he died for nothing," the maresciallo said. "I told Bovolenta to proceed cautiously. It wasn't certain it was the Woodsman, but the captain's not one for subtleties. He's a dangerous man."

"Have you got a towel?" Soneri said. "You'd better not let anyone see you with a muddy hunting rifle."

"You're right. I've got a blanket in the car." He stood there for a moment, looking quite sheepish, until he saw the commissario giving him a curious look. He stirred himself into action. "You're right. It does disgust me."

Soneri waited a moment or two, then whistled for Dolly and moved off.

Along the valley, in the shadow of the mountains, the light was fading rapidly, while on higher ground the sunlight was still falling on the copper-coloured leaves of the beech trees.

A freezing wind blew onto the piazza from the narrow streets where it met no obstacle. Delrio, Maini and Volpi turned up their collars to give themselves some protection.

Volpi had his binoculars trained on the near slope of Montelupo, now only half in sunlight. "They're still climbing up from both sides."

"Have they got him surrounded?" Delrio said.

"They'll have a hard time of it surrounding the Woodsman."

At that moment, a shot rang out along the valley.

"That's him," Volpi said.

Almost simultaneously the rifles, with their sharper report, returned fire. Rivara stepped out of the bar, slipping his coat over his apron. People in the houses opened their shutters and stood behind the windows listening. From the outset, the Montelupo war was one that could only be listened to. It had been so from the first shot fired days previously in the mist, followed by the other mysterious shots in the twilight or in the depths of the woods.

"They've definitely intercepted him, but they'll never take him," Volpi said.

There was no let-up in the heavy fire from the rifles, but the Woodsman's hunting rifle boomed out again, three shots discharged one after the other, then a pause, then another three shots, all clearly heard above the police weapons.

"They'd nearly trapped him in a pincer movement, but he slipped away before the circle closed," Volpi said, peering through his binoculars without turning round.

"Not one of them has one hundredth of the Woodsman's guts. I wouldn't be surprised if he gets another one," Delrio said.

"Now they're firing upwards, and that means he's escaped from the trap. When he's in danger, Gualerzi always makes for the high ground, like a hare."

A volley of shots rang out, the sound carried across the valley by the freezing east wind, the shots coming so closely one after the other as to seem like machine-gun fire. The Woodsman replied with three single shots, fired at regular intervals, followed by another two.

Something caused Volpi to grimace in seeming disappointment. "He'd got off the hook but now they're back on top of him," he mumbled, as though there was some flaw in the narrative. The Woodsman must have done something unexpected.

"Gualerzi's an old man. He's been on the run for days with no rest," Rivara said.

As though in reply, the Woodsman's rifle thundered out, the bullets skimming across the tops of the trees like a scythe. The sun was almost set and only the peak of Montelupo, bathed in a dark grey, aluminium colour, was still in light. The darkness was rising gradually up the mountainside, like water in a tub. In the semi-darkness, the battle continued, but the combatants were now firing at random, more out of fear than with any specific aim. The wind carried some stray yells down the valley, but there was no telling where they originated from.

"They're running up the slope. They look as though they'd been bitten by a tarantula," Volpi said, with some apprehension in his voice.

"They haven't wounded him, have they?" Maini asked.

Delrio shrugged as if to say that was not possible. "If anything, it'll be the other way about."

A new salvo was discharged, and it seemed to contain all the rage of the men who were pulling the triggers. The Woodsman, holed up in some inaccessible cave, seemed almost to be willing them to do their worst. He returned fire only when their shots were less frequent, but his rifle no longer had the same resonance.

"He's made a change. He's down to small bore fire," Volpi said.

"He won't scare them with that," Maini said.

"That means he's running out of ammunition," Delrio said.

Silence fell over the Montelupo woods.

"Yes," Volpi said. "Gualerzi must be low on bullets, but they'll not get him this evening, because it's already too dark to pursue him. He knows every last bush and tree."

The lights went on in the piazza, revealing the men's breath hanging in the air. Volpi replaced the binoculars, which he could no longer use, in their case. Shortly afterwards, they saw the first headlights shine out around the reservoir. The engines started up even before some squads were out the woods.

To get out of the cold, the group took refuge in the bar. The puddles were already covered by a layer of ice, and the wind blew the smoke from the chimneys this way and that. The commissario waited for the carabinieri to return. He followed the headlights as they bumped about in the darkness, slowly probing the compact mass of the trees. The procession reached a side road and stopped there. Two vehicles continued towards the main road, while the remainder turned in the direction of the village, arriving in the piazza a few minutes later. The carabinieri appeared exhausted. Some of their uniforms were filthy, and some were torn. They looked like an army in retreat.

Other trucks came slowly down the road towards Boldara. Soneri, who intended to leave Dolly at the *Scoiattolo* and then eat at Rivara's, moved off. The village had once more sunk into its shell of distrust and rancour. Shafts of light filtered from kitchens, while the sound of children crying or old men complaining could be heard through half-open shutters. Before Soneri got to the *pensione*, Dolly stopped in front of him and stood staring, barking into the darkness ahead of her.

The commissario saw a man emerge from the shadows, walking under the light of the lamps.

When they were only a few metres apart, Soneri recognised him as the shepherd he had met pasturing his flock up at Badignana. He had the usual roll-up cigarette between his fingers, one end wet with saliva and the lighted end with scarcely any ash. He smoked on the tip of his tongue, as though he were tasting the cigarette. Soneri stopped but said nothing. The other man stopped too, but seemed embarrassed, as though wishing to give the impression that he just happened to be there, or else was not at his ease away from the woods.

"Have you been here long?" the commissario said, to open the conversation.

The other man shrugged, but made no answer. Discussion must have seemed a superfluous luxury to someone accustomed to days of solitude following his flock from one field to another, or simply sitting on a rock waiting for evening.

"It's hell up there now," Soneri said.

Once again the man shrugged. "I came down a couple of days ago."

His voice and his attitude conveyed both a resignation which had been centuries in the making, and an acceptance of the reality, whatever that reality might be, to which it was necessary to adapt in order to survive in the mountains.

"You haven't set eyes on Gualerzi again, have you?"

The man made a clucking noise as if to say no, but after a few seconds he raised his eyes. "If you go up to the mountain bar very early, you might meet up with him."

"Did he tell you to tell me that?"

The man shook his head. "I met his daughter."

"He's being hunted down, and can't hold out much longer," the commissario said.

The man sniggered. "If it was just the carabinieri…" he

replied with a gesture of indifference. "He's got other things hunting him down."

Soneri assumed he was referring to the cancer.

"Is he starting to feel pain?"

"He's been in pain since San Martino."

"He would be better coming down and getting himself treated."

"He's not the sort of man who's prepared to go to a hospital to die. He couldn't stand being in closed spaces, hospitals, police stations, prisons, whatever. He sleeps with the windows open even in winter."

As he listened to the shepherd, the commissario became aware of how a sense of the arcane and primitive was gathering around the figure of the Woodsman, and of how his legend was growing day by day.

"He didn't wait for me the last time," the commissario said.

"He's got his own times. He's up before dawn, and these days he doesn't even sleep much."

Soneri nodded to let it be known he had understood, and watched the man move off slowly, disappearing into the night. The commissario took Dolly to the *Scoiattolo* and then, feeling the first pangs of hunger, turned back to where he had been. When he arrived at the *Olmo*, Crisafulli hurried out.

Soneri stopped to light a cigar before the maresciallo started talking. He invited him to walk with him along the street, since he preferred not to speak within earshot of the group of village elders. They walked some way without addressing each other. Crisafulli turned up the collar of his uniform and kept his hands in his pockets, but he seemed to be turning blue with the cold. He pulled up short, almost barring the commissario's path. "Commissario, I have to tell you all the rifles are in the right place." There was a shiver in his voice as he spoke.

"So you've been up at the villa?"

"I went there immediately after our conversation."

"Was the daughter-in-law there?"

"Yes, and the Philippino."

"And they let you see the weapons?"

"Yes, all three of them, as per the licence. Two double-barrelled guns and one sporting rifle for deer-hunting."

"Where were they?"

"In a locked cabinet."

The commissario inhaled his cigar as he reflected on this information. "You also went to the house in the woods, Paride's house?"

"Of course," the maresciallo said, slightly piqued. "But the two weapons for which a licence had been issued were there, and they didn't look to have been used recently."

The commissario stood in silence. The matter now seemed more complex than he had expected, but he was still of the view that the rifle explained everything. "Are we talking about recent models, or ones a couple of years old?"

Crisafulli was hopping from foot to foot in the cold. "The licences were issued some years ago."

"The forensic squad have examined the rifle we found?"

"They're still working on it, but they'll get back to me tomorrow."

"If I were you, I'd send someone along to do a check on the gun shops around here," Soneri said, choosing his words with care. "It's just possible somebody's made some purchases in the not too distant past."

Crisafulli looked at him quizzically, but his expression turned more defiant. "Commissario, do you really think that each and every one of us in the carabinieri is a complete idiot? I've already given orders to the men to carry out investigations. And I've started to put the screw on that Romanian we've got under arrest because of those fifty grams of some substance found in his house by our colleagues from the Santo Stefano division."

"And has he been any use to you?" Soneri said mildly, ignoring the maresciallo's petulance.

"If you ask me, he knows more than he's letting on, but I want to talk to him when I've got more information, that is, as soon as the forensic people pass on to me what they've found. These foreigners try to make a fool of you, unless you've got them with their backs to the wall," Crisafulli said, in a crescendo of anger.

The commissario looked him straight in the face, then waved the hand holding the cigar. "I was not doubting your ability. It's just that two heads are better than one, and I was only thinking aloud."

The maresciallo gave him a pat on the elbow as he turned to go. "Tomorrow, I'll share everything with you," he promised, moving off with those distinctive little steps of his, and letting it be understood he could no longer put up with the cold.

Before he reached the piazza, Dolly appeared at his side, leaping happily up at him. He wondered how she had managed to jump over the wall at the *Scoiattolo* and, especially, to leave a dish of offal. He stroked her to calm her down, while she gazed at him as though her entire world was contained within the confines of his duffel coat. He took out his mobile and phoned Angela. "I have to communicate to you that we have a new member of the family."

"It's usually women who make that kind of announcement," she said. "Or have you found a babe in the woods?"

"No, I've decided to keep Dolly."

"Really. It took me longer to convince you to keep me."

"So, you agree?"

"I've always believed that a dog is the ideal companion

for introverted, taciturn types like you. Faithful and reliable, something that can make itself understood with signs, who has no need of words, and who'll never interrupt your train of thought."

Soneri felt, not for the first time, that yet again Angela had got it exactly right. His mind filled with memories of those silent afternoons in the woods gathering chestnuts, firewood or mushrooms with his father, and of the perfect understanding achieved between them with glances or gestures. This was now an obsession with him.

"Dolly has solved the case," he said.

"She's certainly got a better nose than you."

"Well, it *was* a question of a nose."

"What did she sniff out?"

"A rifle which had ended up in the mud, and if it hadn't been for the freezing weather, not even Dolly would've found it."

"Are you talking about the weapon that killed Paride?"

"I think so, but the carabinieri are still investigating."

He was still speaking when he saw a carabiniere uniform march across the piazza in his direction. As it came closer, he recognised Bovolenta. He quickly said goodbye to Angela and put the mobile back in his pocket. When they came face to face, he saw how exhausted and dejected the captain looked. The cold made the wrinkles under his nose seem even deeper, and his eyes were bloodshot. Soneri held out his hand to shake Bovolenta's, but the captain awkwardly stretched out his left hand.

"What's happened to you?" the commissario said, only then noting a plaster cast protruding from the right sleeve.

"Nothing, just a bit of a shrapnel which got me side on."

"I told you. It was never going to be easy trying to bring Gualerzi in."

"He's nearly killed another four men. He's mad."

"Any more wounded?"

"Five. He's firing dum-dum bullets which become grenades the moment they hit a rock."

"There's no point in going after him any more. He's not got long to go. You should never have…"

Bovolenta glowered at him, struggling not to lose his temper. He calmed himself down and spoke in a deliberately measured tone. "Crisafulli spoke to me about the rifle. Was it you who found it?"

"Why do you ask me that question?"

"I know the maresciallo. He couldn't walk for more than twenty minutes at a stretch."

"There are other people who could do the walking."

"No-one in this village would lift a finger in this business. You've seen them, haven't you? They don't speak to each other, they look daggers at one another, they burn down barns, they set fire to cars and houses, they stab each other in the back."

"That rifle will tell you many things, above all that the Woodsman has nothing to do with it."

The captain looked down, considering this remark. "It has already started telling its tale. The registration number has been partially scored out."

"Has it been used to shoot recently?"

"It seems so, but we need to do further tests. The weapon is not in the best condition because of the mud."

"How long will it be before you get the full results?"

"Tomorrow." The captain's reply was hissed out, with an edge of impatience, but from the dark expression on his face, Soneri deduced that this was due to a stab of pain in his arm. "What I really wanted to ask you to do was to mediate with the Woodsman."

"Gualerzi is not the type who welcomes mediation, as you will have noticed."

"I know, but up there, on his own, running short of ammunition, hungry... and in addition, I understand he's seriously ill."

"He's on his way out."

"Exactly. There's no point in him carrying on with this resistance. He'd never surrender to us, but you're from here, and then there's your father..."

"Have you seen the documents?" the commissario asked anxiously.

"Yes, I have, but they don't say very much. At least they don't resolve the doubt that's been gnawing at you."

Soneri's expression darkened.

"I believe the Woodsman disposed of most of the papers," the captain continued. "Or perhaps he's hidden them somewhere."

The commissario imagined Gualerzi making off with all he could carry to prevent the past from being exhumed, but once again Bovolenta's words took him by surprise. "I'm asking you to go, as much because of your personal interest as anything else."

Soneri needed only a few seconds to think it over before replying, "I will go."

II

Since he wanted to be well on his way before the sun appeared behind the mountains, Soneri was out before daybreak. Bovolenta had promised him a truce until midday, after which, if the Woodsman had not given himself up, they would resume their pursuit of him. What worried him was not the carabinieri but that obsessive question to which he had found no reply. He was convinced Gualerzi would not accept any terms for surrender, and he feared he knew how the story would end. That was another reason why he was in a hurry.

He headed for Boldara then, with the first, faint morning light, turned onto the path to Malpasso. The ascent was gentle enough, but he was walking into a bitterly cold wind which whistled angrily around him and battered against the side of Montelupo which the sunlight had reached. Around the cabins, he saw figures making their way down, off the path, and he assumed these were the last of the herdsmen leaving before the snows blocked the passes, and taking advantage of the hours when the carabinieri were not likely to be patrolling the mountain. Twenty minutes further on, the dark, lonely outlines of the mountain bar appeared. Baldi had made a thorough job of closing the place down. The doors and windows were boarded up with wood covered by metal panels to prevent the snow knocking down the shutters, the roof was reinforced by wooden planks for protection against the north wind and the drainage channels had been dug deeper to prevent damage in the thaw.

He walked round the bar, which appeared impregnable. To the west, he saw a bank of thick clouds, and although they were still far off, he was sure they would soon arrive overhead to bury Montelupo and all its stories. He stood for a while gazing at the summit against the shifting landscape of late autumn. He felt he was engaged in a farewell ceremony which had nothing to do with the seasons, but had everything to do with himself. It was the feeling he had already had with Sante and the people in the village, but now the experience was more violent, like a time of mourning.

He was overwhelmed by a sense of deep foreboding, but recognised the need to make immediate contact with the Woodsman. He started calling out, yelling into the wind at the top of his voice. That too was an act of violence for a man accustomed to subdued tones or to the soundless words of his long debates with himself. He hoped the Woodsman would come out, to alleviate his solitude and hold back time a few seconds longer.

He heard Dolly bark at the hut where the logs were stored. The door opened outwards and Soneri saw a power-fully built man bend under the frame of the door and then straighten up again. The Woodsman was even bigger than he had imagined. No-one could fail to be intimidated by that giant with the long beard, heavy step and hands like shovels. He held a rifle which looked like a toy next to his enormous body. Plainly distrustful, he stopped a few metres from the commissario.

"I'm on my own," Soneri said, raising his hands slightly.

"I know," Gualerzi replied in his baritone voice. "I've been watching you for the last half an hour coming up Malpasso."

Soneri glanced at the ammunition belt which Gualerzi was

wearing round his waist and saw he had only a few cartridges left.

"If you've been sent by that carabiniere officer, you can tell him he's wasting his time," the Woodsman said, in a tone of terrifying calmness. At that moment, the sun rose over the heights to the east of Montelupo and lit up the peak where the bar was. Gualerzi glanced at the light, while the freezing wind blew around him without causing him to shiver.

"It wasn't him who sent me. I've wanted to meet you for some time. It's a personal matter."

For a second, the Woodsman showed some curiosity, but immediately repressed that feeling. "I never wait for anyone. Up here, nobody makes appointments. You might happen to bump into someone, that's all."

"You waited for me this time."

"Today is different. The time has come –" he stopped abruptly.

"The time for what?"

The Woodsman waved vaguely towards the west, indicating the white clouds on the horizon which were growing ever more menacing. "It's going to snow tonight, and that'll make everything more difficult. For a few days, you'll be able to walk about in the woods, and then not even there. The snow betrays you," he said, ambiguously.

It was clear he had lost the thread of his thought. The explanation had done nothing to calm him down.

"How are things?" the commissario said, to relieve the tension.

"There's no escape for me. There isn't for anyone. Sooner or later, it comes to us all. The doctor said it was the fault of the coal I've been breathing in ever since I was a child."

"Wouldn't it be better to get treatment?" the commissario suggested tentatively.

"That makes no sense now," the Woodsman said brusquely. "I've killed a carabiniere. I'd end up suffering in a police cell. It's better to put up with the pain where I've always been. We all have the right to die in the place we were born, don't we? My own earth on top of me and a chestnut tree where the sun rises in the morning as my gravestone."

"Palmiro Rodolfi too…" Soneri started to say, stopping in mid-sentence.

The Woodsman shrugged. "They put him in a little hole in a cemetery wall, and closed it off with cement. I don't want to end up like that. I want to draw my last breath in the fresh air and then give myself to the earth."

"We could come to an arrangement with the carabinieri," Soneri said, thinking aloud.

"I did not kill Palmiro's son," he growled, in a tone calculated to arouse fear. "He ruined me, but he did the same to lots of other people. If anything, I was bitter with Palmiro himself. He cheated and tricked me too often."

"Did you go looking for him recently? Did you want him to repay you?"

"I hadn't the money to get my wife looked after. She could have been saved, not me."

"So you shot at him."

The Woodsman glowered at the commissario, angered at what was turning into an interrogation, but he must have decided it did not matter any more. "Yes, I shot at him, and he shot at me. But it was misty, and Palmiro's cunning." There was a pause before he asked, "How did you know?"

"Once you came close to getting me. Above Boldara. I was looking for mushrooms."

"In the mist, nobody goes out in the woods above Boldara, except him and me. There was a game we used to play with our catapults as boys. One hid, trying not to make any noise, and the other one fired his sling at him if he heard him. It couldn't have been anyone else."

"You were both so sure of yourselves that you didn't stop to think someone else might be there?"

"There are some places nobody goes when it's misty. Nobody knows Montelupo well enough, not even Volpi, the gamekeeper."

"I was there."

The Woodsman turned away, looking at the mountain and at the reflection of the sun on the metal panels over the bar. "You used to go there with your father. You've obviously got a good memory," he said.

"You knew each other quite well. My father used to talk about you."

Gualerzi nodded. "A good man. A man of few words, but the right words."

Soneri was about to question him further, when the Woodsman turned the conversation back to the carabinieri. "If one of them got killed, the fault lies with the people who dispatched him. I tried to warn them off all day by firing in the air, but they kept coming forward, shooting like madmen. At Badignana, they came into the open on the stony ground, but they were still firing with their rifles. The bullet that got him was a ricochet. I didn't aim at him, the way they were doing. If I'd wanted, I could have picked off ten of them."

A sudden noise from somewhere below the bar alerted him. Dolly too jumped to her feet. The Woodsman relaxed. "A deer," he said.

The commissario observed him carefully, trying to work out what he really wanted to say, but only ugly thoughts suggested themselves to him.

"Tell the captain it was me that killed Palmiro's son," Gualerzi said, with wild, staring eyes but speaking with the authority of a man accustomed to giving orders. "And tell him too that the death of the carabiniere was his fault. Among these rocks, bullets have a will of their own. He should have respected me enough not to hunt me like a beast. When someone starts firing, he's got to expect people to fire back. And remember, I've never taken orders from anyone, not even from Mussolini," he declared, his voice rising in a menacing crescendo. Then, with a sinister inflection of his voice, he added, "And I'm not going to start now."

A grim silence fell. The clouds were gathering overhead more quickly than expected. The Woodsman turned to look at them, with the expression of someone recognising a face. He breathed a deep sigh and under his overcoat his chest seemed to swell. Unexpectedly, he started talking again, with the calm flow of words of a man resigned to his fate. "In the last couple of years, Palmiro and I had nothing to lose. If he'd shot me or I'd shot him, we'd have been doing each other a favour. Dying in our own woods while running away like a wild boar, playing a children's game … that would have been a good way to go. We were suffering from two different illnesses, both mortal. Mine was cancer and his was shame and ruination, and his was the worse disease. There was no escape and we both knew it."

"Palmiro could have run off with his daughter-in-law, as she wished."

"No. He wouldn't have been able to live away from this land, Montelupo, his hunting ground, his dogs. He'd have died of a broken heart."

"Do you think that woman had anything to do with it?"

"She hated her husband and went to bed with Palmiro, so you could say she had some interest in getting rid of Paride, but then Palmiro himself had no love for his son. He considered him a waster who would ruin the business. He used to say he'd built up everything by himself and he wasn't going to let anyone destroy it. If Paride had been like his father, they'd have been at each other's throats from the outset, but the son always went along with anything his father said, but then did what he liked. He moved money about as though it was a sack of beans, and Palmiro had no idea of what was going on. Paride always told him what he was doing, but latterly the old man realised his son had him by the balls."

"Did he speak about it when you met?"

"Sometimes, before our relationship broke down completely."

"Did Paride come up to Montelupo as well?"

"Occasionally, with that strange servant of his, but in the woods he was like a priest in a brothel."

"Was he afraid?"

"Maybe. Young people now don't know how to live in the woods. They spend too much time in their cars."

Soneri looked his watch: ten o'clock. The sun had heated the air and thawed the ice on the leaves a little. The summit dominated the whole valley that lay at the foot of Montelupo. The Woodsman scoured the area with expert, careful eyes.

"They won't come. The captain has given me his word."

The Woodsman gave him a surly look. "Even if they did…" he muttered.

The commissario realised he had chosen that spot because it was the best outlook point. Anyone trying to sneak up on them would have been sighted when they were at least half an hour away.

"What do you do when the mist comes down?" Soneri said, nodding in the direction of the valley.

"I move to an out-of-the-way place in some section of the mountains, where only a dog could find me."

The commissario thought of Dolly and of the rifle he had pulled out of the mud. "When did you find Paride's body?"

"I think it was the day after, if everything went the way I think it did."

"The mist was very dense."

"Exactly."

"What does that mean?"

"That whoever fired the shot was not seen by Paride."

"Does that matter?"

"Not at all," the Woodsman said, trying to minimise what he had said and to get off the subject.

Soneri realised he had made a false move. Gualerzi was keeping something back, something he preferred not to say. "Were you close by when the shots were fired?"

"Not very close. I was climbing up, using the Macchiaferro as a landmark. The shot was fired a bit lower down, but I couldn't make out precisely from where. The mist always makes it more difficult. I ran down to the Croce path, but the silence was as profound as inside a well. I did hear a dog whine down at the foot of a gorge, but I couldn't see anything. Next thing I heard was a round of shots discharged in the general direction of the mountain, pellets that fell like hail among the dry branches. I don't know if he was aiming at the dog or if he'd heard me coming down, but it seemed the dog was the target because I heard him pounding over the leaves. Another shot rang out from somewhere else in the woods. If he'd been on higher ground, further away from the path, I'd have had no doubts about who it was, but there it could have been a poacher. What's more, it was already dark and the mist was getting thicker and rising from below up towards the summit. Later I heard the trucks, and people and carabinieri bawling into that wall of mist which distorted their voices. There must have been a squad going over every track down to the valley. Then I heard them shouting for Palmiro and I guessed at what had occurred."

Soneri lowered his head, realising that his own guess had been correct. "The following day you found him and sent for me. You'd worked everything out in your mind."

"Two and two make four. Anyway, I expected it. Palmiro said he'd created the family fortune and it would go with him. He felt betrayed by his son, and when he watched his grandson growing up…" The Woodsman sighed deeply. "He'd nobody left. That woman, his daughter-in-law, she'd have dropped him the moment the money he'd accumulated had been squandered, which it would have been, as surely as the rock on these mountains crumbles in the frost. Years ago, I told him and Capelli they were deluding themselves with their passion for money. Even when they'd made themselves rich, they couldn't relax. Palmiro came to the woods to search for that serenity his business affairs took away from him. He wasn't happy, for the simple reason that wealth gives you too much to worry about. The stupidest thing of all is to imagine that it's going to bring you happiness. Look at this village. When they were all poor, they could laugh. Now they're stabbing each other in the back." He spat to one side, and immediately afterwards his body was wracked by a dry, violent coughing fit. "I at least," he went on when the coughing passed, "have been able to stay here and live the life I chose without taking orders from anyone. And that's how I will end my days," he declared.

"Living as you choose is not worth another man's life," Soneri said, thinking of the dead carabiniere.

"I didn't go looking for them. They knew what I'm made of. Was I supposed to let myself be dragged down the valley, bound hand and foot like a beast? I wasn't going to allow them to cage me up. I'd sooner be dead, and that's why I defended myself," he thundered. "I suppose you need a certain kind of courage to be untrue to yourself, and I lack that kind of courage.

I've got courage of another kind, and if they're going to take me, they'll need to have more of it than I have. So far it hasn't happened, and now…"

The light was now shining with its mid-morning brightness and the day promised to be one of brief, intense radiance. The commissario screwed up his eyes as he looked at the sky, and saw that it was growing greyer and heavier towards the western horizon where it came down to touch the plain. "Sometimes it is more painful to renounce than to resist," he said.

The Woodsman nodded. "Your father had the strength to renounce, or to sacrifice himself, if you prefer to put it that way. He knew how to master himself, unlike me. He was able to tell you why he did what he did and there were times when he convinced even me. Sometimes I admired him, but at others I'd have happily punched him."

Images of his father swirled about in Soneri's head. Contrary to what Gualerzi was now saying, he had always considered his father a resolute, strong-minded man, and found it difficult to cope with a description of him in different terms.

"He was a man of few words, and in any case there are things you don't tell your children." The commissario was trying to defend his father, but in words addressed more to himself than to the Woodsman.

"You don't tell them, no," the Woodsman agreed, as though talking to himself. "And he wasn't a man to go boasting about anything."

"What should he have boasted about?"

"Of having dedicated many years of his life to you," Gualerzi replied dryly, almost with contempt.

"Isn't that what a father is supposed to do?" Soneri said. He knew there was something more behind his words, and fear gave his voice an awkward tone.

"He wanted to get away from this village, to go to the city, but he had to take you into account. He preferred to stay with the Rodolfis, to hold on to a job he hated and to live in the family home where he didn't have to pay rent. He hung on until you'd finished school. That takes guts. He buried himself before his time so you wouldn't have to face the grim life he endured."

Soneri understood where his fear was coming from. From incomprehension and ingratitude. From taking everything for granted. Now he felt merely mean-minded, crushed by a sentence against which there was no appeal. He still regretted all the time he had not spent with his father. He knew it would have been hard to have discussed all the things the Woodsman was telling him, but he had not even made the effort. He cursed the profession which required him to investigate under orders the lives of people he did not even know, when he should have undertaken a more private enquiry, one in which he would have been simultaneously the investigator and the investigated, the policeman and the criminal, the victim and the killer. Only in that way could he have found relief from the sense of alienation he now felt.

The Woodsman had another coughing fit, which took the commissario's mind off these thoughts. "You'd better get on your way now. I want to be able to stare at the sun," he said, in a sinister tone.

Soneri stared at him and understood his intentions. His throat tightened, but the man was unshakeably determined his story would end the way the commissario most feared.

"Life must be spent, like money," the Woodsman said, with a mixture of ferocity and amusement. "Anyway, come what may, life always ends in bankruptcy."

Soneri understood that there was more than a little pride in those words. Gualerzi had sought only to spend his days without pursuing any particular objective. He had never left the Montelupo woods, a tiny kingdom from whose heights he had watched everything change while he himself remained unchanged, like the seasons or the snow. He had conducted himself with the carabinieri as he had with the Germans. His life was as it had always been.

"I've never let money go to my head," he shouted over his shoulder as he took his first steps on his journey. By now it was clear he was at the terminus, and, in the bright, eleven o'clock sunlight, he seemed to be preparing himself for some pagan rite. The commissario tried to approach him, but the Woodsman stopped him with a peremptory gesture. "Some things must be done alone."

"Stay here," Soneri tried to coax him.

"I must go. I've a long way ahead of me and I want to arrive before the light fails," he said, moving on. "I'm doing the same as an ageing animal who knows his time has come."

"Tell me one last thing about my father," the commissario said, fighting off his own fear. "Tell me if it's true that he went to ask the Rodolfis to give him a job when he was unemployed."

The Woodsman's expression betrayed his indifference. He shook his head and shrugged. As he continued on his way, the commissario heard him mutter that it was all nonsense, but he had not the courage to call him back. He watched him climb the path towards the Duca pass, and as he turned the first corner, their eyes met once again. He raised his arm in a final salute, another farewell destined to lie on the commissario's spirit as heavily as a spadeful of earth. He stood where he was, leaning on a boulder, while in the valley below, in the pitiless sun, life went on. Not far off, the Woodsman was setting out on his final journey, and soon would leave the woods and consign himself to a cave in the rocks.

Soneri thought again of his father, of the life he had lived, of the opportunities he had forgone to guarantee them for his son, who in his turn had wasted them pounding the pavements of a misty city, trailing along the corridors of police stations and criminal courts, or else hanging about at the corners of streets, hour after hour, waiting for someone to appear.

It was past midday and already the light was beginning to fade. The clouds to the west now filled half the sky, and the sun was making an attempt to take refuge behind the mountains. Soneri waited, without being aware of anything other than the light, the space and the immensity of the woods. A time he could not measure passed, and when he turned away, the rays struck him in the eyes with that subdued light which was a foretaste of winter twilight. It was then that he heard a shot ring out in the infinite prism of the mountains. The air retained the echo for some time, and when it died away, Soneri understood that the Woodsman had closed his account and said farewell to all that he had held most dear: the sun, the woods and the sky over Montelupo. He looked in the direction from which he believed the shot had been fired. An obscure trigonometry suggested to him that it came from the Pass of the Snows. That night the snow would fall and cover forever the master of those mountains.

12

In the morning, dirty, slushy snow lay on the fields and the roofs around the village. On the higher ground, the snow-flakes had finally closed the eyes which had remained open as the Woodsman savoured for the last time the enchantment of the peaks. Soneri tossed his clothes pell-mell into his suitcase and carried it out to the Alfa Romeo. The previous evening, Ida had come round to settle the bill. She told him that Sante would survive, but would be confined to a wheelchair. "He doesn't understand anything any more, but maybe it's better that way. I mean, better for him not to see how it's all ended."

There was never going to be a happy ending, the commis-sario thought to himself, leaning on his car and contemplating the *pensione* and restaurant of the *Scoiattolo*, whose doors were now locked and barred. He had previously come to the conclu-sion that people were made up of many things, including the things they loved and were familiar with, and so the closure of the *Scoiattolo* meant the death of that part of him which was tied up with it. Bit by bit, people became like Sante, who had no longer the use of his legs and whose mind was muddled.

He took out his phone and called Angela. "I'm leaving," he said. "There's nothing more for me to do here."

"It sounds as though you are keen to get out."

"If I hang about a couple of hours more, I'll not be able to move. It's snowing heavily."

"But you always liked the snow."

Soneri looked at the *pensione,* thinking he had been the last guest. This was something more than a goodbye. "Palmiro killed his son: the past cancelling the present," he said.

"The father?" Angela murmured.

"He couldn't see a future for himself. There was nothing but shame ahead of him. Men like Palmiro think that everything belongs to them, even their own sons. They carry inside themselves both success and failure. The very qualities which raise them up bring them down."

"They ought to find someone stronger than themselves," Angela said, "but they only produce sons who are inept."

"It can't be easy having a father like Palmiro."

"A man accustomed to hunger who devoured life, his own and other people's."

"Around here, you either had some desperate strength, or you went under. A whole generation was impelled to accumulate in order to exorcise the demons of hunger and need, and they cared not a whit for other people. They were all engaged in a solitary struggle to keep their heads above water. Once money began to circulate, some of them lost their heads thinking it would always be there, others did try to share it out, but you never have the same will to work if you've always had it easy in life. Paride had never experienced pain, and that was the root of everything."

"Don't start praising your own cross," Angela warned him.

"Cross or no cross, I've never really done anything."

"You're depressed. I recognise this talk. The mountain air has done you no good. Get out as fast as you can."

"I can't even say that my father didn't think of me," Soneri said, as though he had not heard Angela. "He sacrificed his life for me."

"Stop thinking about the past. All you find there are mistakes. And anyway, it's useless."

"The thing is that I don't recognise myself in my present, any more than Palmiro did. Nor in my future."

As he switched off the phone, a gust of wind blew some snow in his face. A flake flew into his mouth and for a second he savoured the fragile fragrance of the crystals. They had an unmistakable flavour, and it was curious that this was the result of the absence of any specific characteristic. The taste was the equivalent of the zero degrees recorded on the thermometer in the pharmacy on the piazza, where Soneri parked shortly afterwards. It matched his current state of mind.

Crisafulli had asked to see him at nine. He arrived in the small Fiat used by the carabinieri, and flashed his lights at him. "Come on in. You'll be warmer," he said through a tiny opening in the car window. He had the heating turned up to the maximum, and the fan was roaring like the north wind.

"Are you on your way?" the maresciallo said.

"Shortly," was the commissario's laconic reply.

"You're lucky. I'm totally fed up with this village, and now we're facing a long, cold winter. As soon as the first snow falls, I feel unwell."

"You prefer the mists? The snow will bury all that's taken place. If you play your cards right, you should get a posting to a sunny place, maybe even near to your home town."

"Who knows!" he sighed, but then his face lit up. "The Romanian has confessed to acting as intermediary between some Albanians and the Philippino who was looking for a hunting rifle. The weapon was handed over a week before the crime was committed, at a meeting on Montelupo. Even though the number was partly rubbed out, we've managed to find the owner, a man from La Spezia who'd been burgled months ago. He reported the theft at the time."

"Had the rifle been fired recently?"

"Yes, and the spent shell is compatible with the wound inflicted on Paride Rodolfi."

"So it's all tied up. The case is closed."

"If only! We don't yet have proof of who pulled the trigger."

"All you have to do is exert a bit of pressure on the Philippino. If he doesn't speak up, he's going to find himself in big trouble."

"Yes," the maresciallo said thoughtfully. "We got there just in time. He was running off."

"He's got nothing to do with it. He's a pathetic creature."

"Maybe I just can't bring myself to believe it. The whole affair is so massive. What's happened is not normal, a father killing his own son. I don't get it."

Soneri turned down the heater two notches to reduce the noise. The words spoken by the maresciallo echoed his own thoughts, which in spite of his efforts to impose some order on them were still confused. For that reason, he did his best to avoid getting into a detailed discussion, and threw in the catch-all term "self-interest" to bring the conversation to an end.

Crisafulli would not be put off. "Have you formed some idea of how the murder was committed?"

On the basis of that question, the commissario measured the enormous gulf that existed between the maresciallo and himself, as well as between his private world and the world of the investigator. It was the same gulf that separated his life as commissario from his life as human being.

"Do you remember the shots in the mist? Palmiro and the Woodsman were at war up there on Montelupo, and neither man cared any more about dying, because they both knew they were at the end of the line, especially Palmiro. Apart from being ruined, he feared the prospect of shame. It was then he decided to cancel out everything, including the son who had started to play at high finance, which he believed was to blame for his bankruptcy."

"So when do you think he did it?"

"The day you went searching for him on Montelupo. He went out with the rifle he'd told his Philippino servant to acquire for him. He knew that Paride would not go too far up the mountain, so he waited for him at the edge of the gorge where we found him. He hid in the undergrowth, and of course the mist was very thick. That's where he shot him. Paride's body rolled down, but someone higher up heard everything, including the subsequent shots when Palmiro tried to shoot his son's dog. He chased Dolly, thereby wasting a lot of time. The mist grew thicker and thicker, so when darkness fell he was lost. The daughter-in-law saw the old dog return on its own and raised the alarm. She had no idea of what Palmiro had done."

"He certainly couldn't have told her," Crisafulli said.

"This way, suspicion was bound to fall on other people, above all on the Woodsman. Palmiro knew he was sick and hadn't long to live. What could it matter to him? He was sure he'd never talk. Besides, didn't Gualerzi have every good reason for murdering Paride? He's been ruined, and so…Everybody in the village would've approved, but a father killing his own son, no, no. Palmiro was a man who held to ideas of honour. He couldn't bear being remembered only for that terrible crime, so he arranged things in such a way that no-one would be too badly damaged by them, and that they would seem perfectly plausible. He would be seen to have hanged himself in the name of outraged honour, Gualerzi was dying anyway and Paride had been shot, perhaps by some creditor or other. A dreadful story, but perfectly logical in its own way. The stolen rifle he used for the killing was essential for this plot. Obviously he couldn't use one of his own weapons, and that's why when Palmiro heard them looking for him in the woods, he had to get rid the rifle earlier than he had planned. He went up to the swamp and threw it in, believing that the mud would swallow it up, but he hadn't allowed for the freezing conditions.

"He then turned up at home as though nothing had happened. That same evening he killed his own dog, not because he felt he'd been let down by him but because he was the only creature who had remained faithful to him and he couldn't bear leaving him alone. When he shot his son, he knew what the final outcome would be, and the following day they found him dangling on a rope." With these words, Soneri laid his hands flat on his thighs to indicate that he had nothing more to relate.

"I believe that's all true," the maresciallo said slowly, "but how are we going to prove events that happened in the mists of Montelupo?"

"There were the shots fired that day. Did you not tell me that you had taken a note of the chronology? And then there was a witness, but you'll not be able to call on him."

"So you're telling me he's..."

"Yes, he's dead and you won't find him till the spring. He'll be buried in the snow by now."

"But you took his evidence, didn't you?"

"Leave me out of it. This is your case, Maresciallo. I'm handing it all over to you. There's nothing more I can do for you," he said gruffly.

Crisafulli looked at him in disbelief, but the commissario headed off his objection. "I think I can claim to have been a good informer."

Crisafulli smiled and relaxed.

"Where is Bovolenta now?" Soneri said.

"He left this morning for the provincial H.Q. The future's not too bright for him either."

"A pity. He's one more victim of this affair."

"He was in too big a rush. They'd told him Gualerzi was a savage, and, you know, after spending seven years on Aspromonte hunting bandits, you develop certain habits. All he did was follow procedures."

Soneri's mind went back to that absurd manhunt, to those shots fired off senselessly and to the needless death of the carabiniere officer. He was more than ever convinced that the one essential talent of an investigator is knowing when to ignore procedures. It is crucial to recognise reality, to adapt to it and even to breathe it in, but Bovolenta lacked that quality. He wished to bend reality, to forge it, even if, as Soneri admitted to himself now, at the end the worries and the questions were more numerous than they had been at the outset. An enquiry was a procedure which only superficially aimed at re-establishing order. In fact, the opposite happened. Searching meant creating disorder.

"Commissario." Crisafulli brought him back to himself.

He turned back to him. "I was thinking of Bovolenta. They'll pack him off to some police academy to teach procedures," he said bitterly.

"Early retirement, out of harm's way. The carabinieri never leave you on your knees. They always guarantee your salary," Crisafulli said.

"And yet he's a decent man. If only that bullet hadn't ricocheted."

"Which bullet?"

"The one that killed your colleague. Gualerzi told me he didn't want to kill him, but with those rocks it's like playing billiards with grenades."

"And you believed him?" Crisafulli asked incredulously.

"Why not? What reason could he possibly have had for lying to me? He had made up his mind to die and at that moment what could it have mattered to him?" Crisafulli had a sceptical expression on his face, and Soneri realised again that he was a small-minded man. "It was a matter of chance," he said. The commissario was keen to leave and start recuperating from a long period of unhappiness. "It nearly always is," he added, opening the door.

"Just a minute. Before he left, Bovolenta asked me to give you this envelope." The maresciallo handed him a sealed package bearing his name and the instruction that it be delivered by hand.

"Thanks," Soneri said. "I hope they send you to a place by the sea."

"Goodbye, Commissario," Crisafulli said.

It was snowing when Soneri reached his car. Dolly in the back seat licked his cheek and battered the window in her eagerness to get out. Soneri could not wait any longer, and tore the envelope open. Inside, there was a hand-written note, in a formal style.

Dear Commissario,

I made it my personal responsibility to execute a thorough search through the material removed from the Gualerzi residence in the Madoni locality, and I uncovered some documents which may be of interest to you. They were contained in a folder concealed in a cavity (I quote from the report) in the cellar. On the frontispiece, there was written the word "Collaborators" and I have reason to believe that the whole consisted of a dossier prepared by the Partisan Command on those residents of the village who had entered into a relationship with the Fascists, either as spies or as sympathisers. Your knowledge of local history is superior to mine, so you will be aware of what befell such persons in the aftermath of the Liberation. Since Palmiro Rodolfi survived, I also have reason to believe that circulation of the attached document was counteracted.

Perhaps this is the response you were expecting.

Il comandante Bovolenta

Soneri stared at the yellowing document, now almost coming apart along the folds. It was the authorisation issued by the then mayor, complete with the official Fascist stamp, guaranteeing the activities of the salame-producer Palmiro Rodolfi, and setting out the details of the commercial contract for the supply of pork products to schools, canteens and markets in the area. That page would have been the equivalent of a death sentence on Palmiro, but the Woodsman and Soneri's father had in some way prevented it. All that had subsequently occurred was born of that act. There was no way of knowing if it was dictated by courage, pity or whatever. What the partisans had failed to do, Palmiro had himself carried out many years later.

It was time to leave the whole story behind him. What remained was a late-flowering affection for his father, even if it was a feeling that could not find any expression. Dolly licked his ear while he concentrated on the now completely white road. The falling snow was covering everything, Montelupo, the Woodsman, the Rodolfis, the dull, dishonest village now inhabited only by an ageing population, the woods and even the mushrooms he had come to collect. It was also covering a part of his own past, one he was now leaving for good.

VALERIO VARESI is a journalist with *La Repubblica*. *The Dark Valley* is the second in a series of thrillers featuring Commissario Soneri, now the protagonist of one of Italy's most popular television dramas. The first, *River of Shadows*, was shortlisted for the Crime Writers' Association International Dagger.

JOSEPH FARRELL is professor of Italian at the University of Strathclyde. He is the distinguished translator of novels by Leonardo Sciascia and Vincenzo Consolo, and plays by the Nobel Laureate Dario Fo.